THE NEW COUNTESS

1905: King Edward VII has invited himself and his mistress to a shooting weekend with the Dilbernes. Now Isobel, the Countess, must turn a run-down mansion into a palace fit for a king, but money can't resolve everything ... not even a kidnapping. The servants refuse to condone the King's morals; Isobel's daughter, Lady Rosina, insists on publishing a scandalous book, and the mis-spent pasts of Viscount Arthur and his Irish-American wife Minnie rear up to blacken the family name. When fate deals a hand in the middle of the shooting party, Isobel must consider not only her leading position in Society, but her entire future.

THE NEW COUNTESS

THE NEW COUNTESS

by

Fay Weldon

Magna Large Print Books
Long Preston, North Yorkshire,
BD23 4ND, England.

British Library Cataloguing in Publication Data.

Weldon, Fay
The new countess.

A catalogue record of this book is available from the British Library

ISBN 978-0-7505-4038-4

First published in Great Britain in 2013 by Head of Zeus Ltd.

Cover illustration by arrangement with Head of Zeus Ltd.

Published in Large Print 2014 by arrangement with Head of Zeus

Magna Large Print is an imprint of Library Magna Books Ltd.

Printed and bound in Great Britain by
T.J. (International) Ltd., Cornwall, PL28 8RW

This is a work of fiction. All characters, organizations, and events portrayed in this novel are either products of the author's imagination or are used fictitiously.

PART ONE

A Visit to Stonehenge

Midsummer's Day, 22nd June 1905

'Right on time,' said Anthony.

'One should hope so,' said his sister.

They took it as a good omen, though no more than they deserved. At ten to five the rising sun's first rays caught the Friar's Heel monolith: just as they were meant to. The famous stone glowed like a beacon while all around was still undefined, and misty grey. Then all of a sudden there was glorious light, you could see everything bright and clear, and the longest day of the year was upon them.

Then it was time to take the train back to an overcast London. They'd travelled down the night before, snatched a few hours' sleep at the Rose and Crown in Salisbury, travelled the nine miles by cab to Stonehenge, and each paid a shilling's entry. Anthony was not particularly superstitious, but he was now Editor of *The Modern Idler*, a literary magazine, and needed to keep up with contemporary trends. He had observed an increasing preoccupation with all things occult and semi-occult in both readers and writers. Golden Dawns, the sacred fires of the Druids, the leaping and dancing of the cloven-hoofed Great God Pan and so forth now seemed to interest the progressive world almost as much as the wilder shores of experimental sex. If a man was obliged to earn a living, and Anthony now had no other option, he should at least enter into the spirit of things and do it thoroughly. A chilly Stonehenge dawn and a cavorting assembly of chanting white-gowned Druids – male and female and no telling which was which – would make a good editorial and was no real hardship.

Anthony didn't particularly like going anywhere alone without an audience, so he'd asked his sister to come with him. It happened to be Diana's birthday – she was twenty-eight, surely a rather terrible milestone for an unmarried woman – and no one else he knew was prepared to get up so early. More importantly, he had a proposition to make to her. He put it off until they were on the train back to Waterloo, during the course of a late Pullman-car breakfast. He had porridge and cream, kippers, and eggs, bacon, and sausages; she had grapefruit segments and scrambled egg on toast. Even the coffee was good.

'Diana,' he said, 'I must talk to you seriously.'

'I feared that was the case,' she said. She was a lively, clever, cheerful girl of the kind men made best friends of rather than wives – or so her brother feared. She was bold, direct, noisy, had too pronounced a chin for beauty, and seemed to him to be without any of the erotic principle that men looked for in a woman. Worse, she was penniless, as he was. Their father, Eric, Lord Ashenwold, had died three months earlier having made only the most meagre provisions for

Anthony and Diana – the peerage, the estates and the money going to his eldest son and heir Bevis. Yet Diana's unmarried state did not seem to disconcert her at all.

'The fact must be faced,' said Anthony, after the customary clearing of the throat that went before one of his serious announcements (such as *'We have decided after much deliberation, Mr Kipling* – or Haggard, or Benson, or Wells, or Hardy, or whichever wildly successful writer it was *'that we will publish your next story'*). 'You are twenty-eight today, Diana, and as an older woman have reduced marital prospects.'

'Don't be such an old crotchet, Redbreast,' said Diana. 'I daresay someone will come along. Not someone from the peerage, to suit Bevis, not some famous writer, to suit you, but somebody who suits me. Besides, I never want to marry. I don't like children any more than you do.'

'A man is not required to like children,' he said, 'only to do what he can for them. But a woman most properly is.'

'Then perhaps I am not a proper woman,' she said.

'What can you mean?' he said. 'What a pair we are!'

His voice was somehow strangulated, but then many men of his social background spoke in the same manner – as though all statements had to go through some kind of filter before they were released. The Honourable Anthony Robin, a second son, was a tall man with an overhung brow and startlingly blue eyes. He had the commanding and kindly stoop of an old Etonian of the non-sporting kind, but was not, Diana had concluded long ago, necessarily kindly. She suspected he had invited her on this excursion – much as she was enjoying it – not out of altruism, but to forward some devious scheme of his own. She was right.

'Your prospects being as they are,' he went on, 'you have no choice but to earn a living. You can work for me as my housekeeper.'

He waxed lyrical. He had just leased new premises from which to run *The Modern Idler*. From now on it was to be published monthly. He had found a charming little house in Fleet Street, looking straight into the Law Courts with Chancery Lane beyond. It was an area where journalists came and went and writers had their clubs. It had crooked walls and leaning floors and at night you could hear the death-watch beetle tapping away, though the old oak beams had such hard heartwood he'd been assured all their gnashings were in vain. An eccentric place for a dwelling, perhaps, but a fine one for the editor of a political and literary magazine.

'Oh Anthony, I see,' she said. 'You want me to move in and do all the work? Distemper walls, sand floors, fix lights, buy furniture, I daresay even create a garden where you can drink your coffee while you read your manuscripts and turn down aspiring hopefuls?'

'It sounds divine,' he said.

When the building work was done, he said, she could be his secretary.

'You can type, you can do the layouts, and the pasting up, and you can help with the editing, the subscription lists and so on.'

'Oh thank you, Redbreast,' she said. 'What if you got married and she hated me and threw me out?'

'I am not the marrying sort,' he said. 'You know that. I am a man of letters. I am the philandering kind. I believe in the Life Force and the odd whiff of opium, draught of cocaine. But you know that too. All is legal, all will come from the Fleet Street pharmacy down the road. But I do have my little ways. You will have to put up with them.'

'I might overlook them,' she said, 'if I have half a page of my own in your *Modern Idler* once a month. Not about fashion, or recipes, or how to polish a kettle, but about politics.'

'Not under your own name,' he said. 'I don't want to be a figure of fun.'

'Mrs Humphrey Ward publishes under her own name,' Diana protested.

'But she is married. You would be a Miss with no brain or experience. Perhaps you should make a marriage of convenience.'

Diana raised her eyebrows and Anthony Robin said she had until Waterloo Station to think about the advantages of living under his wing. Otherwise he would make alternative plans. They were at Basingstoke, so she had about an hour.

They fell silent. She took honey with her toast. Anthony took marmalade. He opened *The Times* while she stared out the window at green fields and growing wheat. There was a sudden bark of annoyance from Anthony which quite made her jump.

'Engineering genius, my foot,' he said. 'Bumbling young puppy. Used to be my fag at Eton. How he yelped if I beat him, the crawling little ninny. Couldn't find his way round a tin of boot polish.'

Arthur Hedleigh had entered his new touring model, the Jehu III, for the Isle of Man race in September, and according to *The Times,* was considered the new white hope of the British automobile industry. The piece seemed to have quite upset Anthony. Asked why, he said that Dilberne was a sleazy rotter, a jumped-up bounder, a silver spooner, a mother's darling, an effete cissy, a rogue, and no gentleman – who with his father the Earl's connivance had once cheated him, Anthony, out of fifty pounds and tried to get him into trouble with the law. A swinish family.

'Oh Anthony, I know his sister Rosina rather well,' said Diana, mildly. 'She went to Australia and I really miss her still.'

'You can keep the sister,' said Anthony. 'At least, having a brain in her head, she took off for the other side of the world. But the brother – I execrate. He married a thin little Roman Papist heiress from Chicago: no virgin she. I say let him tumble into a vat of his own engine oil and choke to death, and drag her with him.'

'Oh Anthony,' she protested, 'people can love each other.' His vehemence took her aback. She poured him another cup from the tall silver coffee pot, without using a napkin, forgetting how hot E.P.N.S. handles could get. Something to do with the specific heat of nickel, she imagined, rather than that of the copper of silver plate. Real silver, of course, the proper stuff, was slow to heat. Diana had studied chemistry at Oxford, along with ethnography. She had not been able to take her degree, women couldn't. It didn't worry her; when was the world anything other than unfair? Anthony, on the other hand, chafed against injustice. Arthur Hedleigh rankled him because he had his picture in the paper, was going to end up an Earl and he, Anthony, would never inherit a title, let alone catch an heiress.

'I speak metaphorically,' said Anthony, 'but it won't last. She's not his type.'

'Oh?' asked Diana, interested. 'What type's that?'

'Round, blonde, fair and stupid.'

Diana was wise enough not to ask how he knew – the sooner he calmed down the better.

They were pulling out of Woking in a great cloud of steam and melancholy hooting. Before long they would be at Waterloo. He was right – her choices were limited. She could live as a spinster sister with her rich boring brother Bevis, or as a housekeeper with her less boring brother Anthony. She was not good at making up her mind.

'Though of course the wife might be the one to stray,' Anthony said, speculatively. 'She has quite a past.'

'Oh Anthony,' said Diana. 'Don't be like that.'

'I hope she's unfaithful and gives him hell,' he said, but she thought he said it as much to punish her, Diana, for not supporting him in his wrath as because he really meant it. Or so she hoped.

'Oh for Heaven's sake, Redbreast,' said his sister.

He wished she would not call him Redbreast: it was a name attached to him in his schooldays when he was young and silly and had edited the *Eton Chronicle*. And the 'Ohs' with which she peppered her conversation annoyed him, she seemed to be always reproaching him. But then, he supposed, that's what women did. And he was fond of her, and she needed him.

'Will you?' asked Anthony.

'Oh Anthony, of course I will,' she replied.

Minnie Gives a Birthday Party

25th June 1905, Belgrave Square

'My life is perfect,' murmured Melinda, otherwise Minnie, the Viscountess, Lady Hedleigh. But even as she spoke, if to no one in particular, she looked down from the wide windows of No. 17 Belgrave Square and saw a lad, distinctive in the peaked cap and gaiters of the new-style telegraph boy, leaping up the front steps. He had the jaunty air – or so Minnie thought – of someone delivering good, not bad news.

Minnie listened but couldn't hear the bell over the noise of infant revelry. No doubt bells jangled appropriately in the servants' quarters. The party had turned noisy, in spite of the subduing presence of nannies and nursemaids. Little children swarmed recklessly from table to floor, shrieked and threw jelly and cake. Isobel, Countess of Dilberne, who had invited her daughter-in-law Minnie plus her two small children to London for the week, winced slightly as greasy hands endangered the pale-yellow chintz of the new upholstery of the morning room, but said nothing. Today was to do with celebration.

'Ah,' said Isobel generously, 'let them have fun. Birthdays are only once a year.' So the nannies held back and the six little guests and Edgar and his little brother Connor rolled about on the floor and laughed and giggled and kicked one another.

Minnie's eldest son Edgar was three years old today, and could do no wrong. Connor Hedleigh, born a year to the day after Edgar, could do quite a lot of wrong, at least in the eyes of his English grandparents, not having the saving grace of being the first-born. Minnie had tried to explain to her parents, the O'Briens of Chicago, the necessary complexity of names and titles in the English aristocracy but without success.

'Mother of God!' Tessa had protested, when her daughter brought the children over to the stockyards of God's Own Country for inspection. 'Why is Edgar a Dilberne and Connor only a Hedleigh? They're full brothers, aren't they?'

'You have to be English to understand,' Minnie had replied.

'At least neither one of them's a bloody Turlock,' their grandfather Billy O'Brien, the pork baron, had said – fortunately not in Arthur's hearing. The last thing Minnie wanted was her past raked up; and least of all her doubtful liaison with the deranged American artist Stanton Turlock. Her father liked to speak plainly, but it could be an embarrassment.

Both her sons were fine, brawny, straight-backed lads, of whom their father Arthur was pleasingly proud. Minnie loved them both equally, but perhaps Connor a little bit more, since he was always in trouble and second in line. Edgar the heir would inherit the title. Connor was the 'spare'. Even Arthur sometimes called him that – 'the spare' – as in 'Tell the spare to stop that noise and be a man' – although she wished he wouldn't. She was sensible enough not to say so. Life with her father had taught her that if you asked a man not to do something he was the more likely to do it again.

Now, as the noise level rose, Arthur spoke. He had been sitting at a distance and silent, though smiling indulgently, if perhaps a little fixedly, in his effort not to mind the mayhem. He had a deep voice: it was very male, cutting through the squeaks and squeals of women and children. Minnie loved him.

'Risus abundat in ore puerorum,' Arthur said.

'Oh, Arthur,' said her mother-in-law, 'another Latin tag. Just like your father. You are so clever. What does it mean?'

'Laughter is plentiful in the mouths of small boys,' said Arthur. 'But enough is surely enough. The nursery world can be very noisy and annoying. No wonder Father's found a pressing engagement.'

'Very well,' said Isobel. 'Let there be an end to misrule,' and she nodded to the bank of nannies who swooped into action as they had been longing to do, and quick as a flash the little ones were back on their chairs again, too startled to object, hands and mouths wiped clean, neat and sweet like the little lambs they were on a good day, little lions no more.

Arthur smiled and caught Minnie's hand. He had his father's long straight nose, square jaw and thick blond hair and seemed to gain in gravitas by the year – no longer the boy but very much the man. He had come up to London with Minnie and the boys to spend the day with their grandparents, for once delegating the care of his motor-car workshops to others. Four years and more into the marriage and she found she still thrilled to the sound of his voice, the touch of his hand. She was very lucky.

A pity that the Earl, Grandfather Robert, couldn't be with them after all. He had been called away as ever by affairs of State – the occasion was genuine enough – some kind of insurrection in Russia that demanded the Privy Council's attention even though it was a Sunday. With the modern world proceeding at the pace it did, politics was becoming a full-time job, not the diversion of a wealthy and patriotic man. Robert was not one to shirk his duties.

Minnie still found her father-in-law intimidating; but she liked the feeling of being at the centre of things, and sometimes he would regale the assembled company with what was going on abroad or at the Colonial Office, which was one of the reasons she so enjoyed coming up to Belgrave Square. Arthur's interests were increasingly confined, she was beginning to find, to the insides of automobiles, the beauty of the Arnold Jehu III, the virtues of air-cooled engines as compared to water-cooled. She did her best to stay enthusiastic, but sometimes late at night she would fall asleep on the pillow while Arthur talked.

She'd said something of the sort to Tessa when her parents were over. 'Better that he's besotted by an automobile,' Tessa had retorted briskly, 'than by some chorus girl.' And Minnie could see that it was true.

Tomorrow Minnie would go with Isobel to Heal's to inspect their newly arrived range of bamboo furniture to see if any was suitable for the Belgrave Square back bedrooms – out of the question of course for Dilberne Court, with its massive four-posters, settles and cedar linen chests: the staff would just have to go on heaving and straining and polishing ancient oak – and then perhaps the ladies would go on to Bond Street to look at the new circular skirts from Paris, tiered and braided but two inches shorter than of late, so they cleared the ground and did not require the endless brushing that took up so much of the parlourmaids' time. There was a great deal in modern life to be thankful for. The form and shape of furniture interested her. Once, she vaguely remembered, she had had dreams of becoming a sculptress. Stanton Turlock had even spoken of her as being a Camille Claudel to his Rodin – not that he had ever got beyond paint on canvas. She liked the touch, feel and colour of fabric, but Isobel's obsession with fashion eluded her. All the same, for Isobel's sake she would pretend a deep interest. You opened your eyes wide, looked intent and thought of other things.

Minnie had forgotten all about the telegram, when Reginald the head footman arrived with it on a silver tray. He had taken his time, having no doubt steamed open the thin brown envelope, read its contents, then hastily resealed it. He was a villain, if an amiable one. Isobel opened the telegram, read it, and nodded to Reginald to leave the room. She had the same stunned and unbelieving expression on her face as little Edgar had when suddenly snatched up from the floor and sat in his chair.

Reginald backed but did not leave the room. He would not be reprimanded, Minnie knew. He never was.

'A good-looking feller, quite the swank,' Billy had said of him the previous year when the in-laws were over for Wimbledon. 'Gets away with anything. You bet he knows more than he should.' Which Minnie thought was probably the case. It was one of the problems with living with servants. Not that the others seemed to notice, let alone worry about that.

Isobel let the envelope drop from her hand as if it was of little account.

'It's your sister Rosina,' she said to Arthur, in what was almost a tone of accusation. 'The steam ship *Ortona* docks at Tilbury tomorrow afternoon. Rosina will be on it. No explanation, no information, nothing. She just announces her arrival. How very rude, how very Rosina.'

'Rosina! But how wonderful!' cried Minnie into a silence which fell on the whole party. Even the little children stopped their clatter. Minnie hesitated. Rosina was disapproved of. But why? Rosina was difficult, and moody, true, and had left peremptorily for Australia, married suddenly under some kind of cloud, but she was family, only daughter of the house. Some show of enthusiasm was surely allowed? Back home in Chicago there'd have been shrieks of joy and everyone embracing, and tears shed, and a rushing out to tell everybody the good news. The prodigal sister returned. But this was Belgrave Square and spontaneity was not the way of things.

'Dear Rosina,' said Arthur, casually and calmly. 'The mischief maker!' And then, with a glance at Minnie, 'Though naturally one's jolly glad to hear from her after so long. How long, eh? Three years?'

'Your sister embraces silence,' said Isobel. 'Only ever the briefest of letters and there's been nothing for a good six months.'

'No news of the husband or a child?'

'Nothing. Not even that courtesy.'

'How about her parrot?'

His mother ignored him and turned to Reginald.

'The *Ortona* docks at Tilbury. Is it the Orient Pacific line?'

'I'm afraid it is, my lady. An immigrant ship, returning half empty.' He seemed rather amused.

'How very uncomfortable for her,' said her Ladyship. 'Why always this perverse *nostalgie de la boue* – this desire to play the bedraggled?'

'Even so, it's our Rosina!' protested Minnie. 'It's such good news! Someone to talk to!' This sounded a little ungracious. Isobel looked at her rather strangely. So did Arthur. Minnie always tried very hard not to blurt things out and for the most part she succeeded, but today she had failed.

'I have you to talk to, my dear, of course I do,' she said to Arthur, to make amends, 'at least I do when you are at home but you are so often in your workshop.' She had made matters worse. Why did life have to be so difficult?

'And I am sure you are busy enough with our children,' he said, sensing an accusation. 'You hardly have time these days to give me a second look.'

'Well, well,' said Isobel, fearing there was the making of a squabble in the air. 'We will send Reginald to meet the *Ortona* tomorrow. Rest assured, Minnie, Rosina shall have a prodigal daughter's welcome home. Though she could at least have given one proper notice.'

'You could hardly expect that. A parrot doesn't change its feathers, eh?' said Arthur.

Minnie giggled, as she should not have.

Rosina had departed to Western Australia, with almost no warning, some three years before, in the company of a new husband, a Mr Frank Overshaw, theosophist and landowner. He was no catch for an Earl's daughter, but Rosina was unmarried, past thirty, tall and ungainly, too clever for her own good and hardly in a position to be particular. Even so, the speed of the engagement and her departure had been unseemly, even scandalous, especially since Rosina had sailed on a ticket reserved for her own cousin Adela, Frank's first choice of bride. It had been assumed there'd been the normal reason for haste but it had proved not to be the case. At any rate there had been no mention of a baby in the few brief letters Rosina had sent home: just descriptions of a land hot and dangerous beyond belief where the mail was bad and servants non-existent, and some requests for reference books: Emile Durkheim's *Rules of the Sociological Method,* his treatise on suicide in aboriginal culture, and any of Max Weber's early publications.

'But Mama,' said Minnie now – it was at Isobel's request that Minnie called her 'Mama' – 'someone from the family must be there to meet her. She has been away for three whole years – for all we know she may be ill.'

'But the *Ortona!*' said Isobel. 'Tilbury, not even Liverpool,' as if that settled the matter. But she put no difficulty in Minnie's way, and even said their shopping trip to Heal's could be delayed until Tuesday well enough: Minnie must certainly go and meet Rosina if she'd like to. One could only hope the boat got in reasonably on time, and poor Minnie didn't have to wait around all day. Meeting boats was better left to the servants – but if it was what Minnie wanted... Isobel for one would spend the day with Robert at the House.

Then Arthur said that alas, he couldn't go with Minnie; the Jehu III was at a critical stage: he had decided air cooling was a mistake, he must get back by the morning but Minnie was to wish Rosina very well and he would see her before long. He assumed she would be staying at least for a while at Belgrave Square.

So all was well, but Minnie wished she hadn't thought, 'My life is perfect,' so loud and clear in her head. She had a niggling feeling the Gods had overheard and the ring of the front door bell, so close upon the thought, had been a sign of their displeasure. But how could Rosina coming home be bad?

An Alarming Proposition

26th June 1905, Newmarket

Robert took Isobel to Newmarket for the last of the flat racing. His wife did not care for horses but at least in an enclosure she was far enough from the animals to be safe. He had been insistent.

'Westminster's far too dull at the moment,' he said, when Isobel suggested she meet him for lunch at the House of Lords, having spent the morning in the Visitors' Gallery. He would take her instead to Newmarket, and show her off. 'Cherry Lass is tipped to win the 1,000 Guineas and you shall wear a straw hat with flowers, a white mink stole, a skirt with a train and any amount of lace and frills.'

'But I so like listening to a good Lords debate,' she said, 'and then lunching with you. The Thames sparkles and the river boats go by: it is a great treat.'

'It will be a grand day at Newmarket,' he said. She could see he was determined to go. 'There's nothing on in the House but the military stores reports, which means yet another post-mortem on the war in South Africa, and more nonsense from the Liberals about the poor enslaved Chinamen working in our mines there.' He added that in case rumours had unsettled her, so far as their own Modder Kloof was concerned, all their particular miners, whether white or Chinese, enjoyed excellent conditions, had freedom of movement, very reasonable wages and lived as well as his own estate workers in Sussex. 'Not a rock fall or a death has been reported for months,' he said.

'As any mine owner says before the rocks fall,' said Isobel. Her father had started life as a miner and ended up as a coal magnate, and she knew well enough how the view from the worker's end differed from that of the owner.

'Oh my dear,' said his Lordship. 'Leave all that to Rosina when she returns. She was born to be the conscience of the family.'

Isobel was happy enough to do so, resigning herself to a day at the races, while murmuring that she hoped three years in the Antipodes had taught their daughter a few of the realities of life.

'At least she is alive and presumably well,' said his Lordship. 'And there is no objection, I suppose, to her having her old rooms back at the house in Sussex now Adela is gone.'

Adela was Rosina's cousin, who had lately married and gone to live in Switzerland where the progressive Ascona movement had its headquarters and naked sun worship was earnestly practised.

'She will be company for Minnie,' said Isobel. 'I have no doubt Rosina will say she must stay in Belgrave Square, not be stuck away at Dilberne Court, but for once she must do as she's told. It would be plainly foolish to have her living round the corner from the House. The last thing we want is her turning up in the middle of a debate waving flags and complaining that Chinese coolies are oppressed. She is quite capable of it.'

Robert agreed that would be unfortunate but added rather sadly, 'Most people can be relied upon to tailor their beliefs to suit their interests, just not Rosina. Funnily enough, I rather admire her for it. Now, shall we just go off to the races and leave Minnie to meet the *Ortona*.'

Isobel felt suddenly cheerful: whatever had taken place before, her only daughter was coming home from over the seas after a three-year absence and she was glad. If a divorce had to be faced, so be it. An unfortunate marriage was better than no marriage at all: it could be seen as the way of the world rather than the fault of a neglectful mother. Now Adela had gone Rosina's arrival was even something of a blessing. Arthur was so very much caught up with his business and his automobiles that Minnie must often feel alone. Perhaps Isobel should have gone with Minnie to Tilbury – but Robert needed her and one's duty was surely more to one's husband than one's children. There were lots of children but only one spouse. And a day at the races was not so dreadful a fate.

Isobel chose a nautical theme for her day in Newmarket – a jaunty sailor-suit skirt and blouse in matching navy *moiré,* with a square white lace bib that fell over the head back and front – a wide white leather belt with an anchor buckle, and a cheerful little straw boater with an ostrich feather which one wore on the side of one's head – Lily her lady's maid fixed the hat with an extra-long turquoise and diamond hat pin which quite lifted the severity of the outfit. One did not want to look like some business woman on her way to an office, which was always the danger these days. She and Lily toyed with the idea of adding a bunch of velvet cherries to the brim, in honour of Cherry Lass, the season's favourite, but decided against it. It would have amused Robert, but seemed dishonourable – she really could not tell one racehorse from another, nor did she care.

Newmarket scarcely offered the sartorial splendour one found at Ascot, but then they came across His Majesty walking amongst the crowds. Isobel thought Bertie was looking remarkably jovial and very much the man of the people, if not quite so flamboyant as once he had been – rather thinner, and his chest less gleaming with medals than it had been in the past. Indeed, he and Lord Rosebery, who walked beside him, could have been just another couple of portly gentlemen of means and status strolling by. As for Rosebery, he was looking decidedly less dissolute than usual, some remnant of his former good looks firming his jaw and brightening his eye.

'It's because his Cicero won the Derby at Ascot,' said Robert. Isobel refrained from remarking that racing men seemed to be as invigorated by 'winning a race' as if they themselves had run the course and not left it to the horse.

A mixed group of familiar faces, hats gleaming and beards wagging, followed close behind: Isobel recognized young Ponsonby the King's private secretary, and his pretty wife Victoria Lily, walking next to Sidney Greville, the Queen's secretary, his notebook as ever clasped to his bosom. But no Queen. Instead Mrs Keppel the King's mistress walked with the little cluster of grandees. Alice Keppel was on Rosebery's arm rather than the King's: so much presumably being owed to tact. Rather unnecessarily, Isobel thought, since a few years earlier Alice Keppel had been on show at the Coronation with all the other royal mistresses – in what the Queen had referred to a little bitterly as 'The Loose Box'.

Keppel was looking most attractive, light and bright and cool in a pale-blue and white fine cotton plaid, its leg-of-mutton sleeves in voile, and a flat straw skimmer which might have been a man's hat, other than for its broad satin ribbon and bow. Isobel at once felt far too hot and stuffy in her navy *moiré*, and that she was wearing quite the wrong outfit. But as Robert and she moved closer, Isobel could see what looked like goose bumps on the arms beneath the voile sleeves – there was quite a chilly easterly wind for such a bright summer's day – and a small bunch of velvet cherries on the bow of her skimmer, and felt no, if anyone had chosen unwisely it was Alice. Alice was over thirty and only young girls could get away with cotton plaid, voile sleeves, and cheap red velvet cherries.

When His Majesty greeted Robert and Isobel it was with enthusiasm, but requiring of their sympathy. Had he not had remarkably little luck at the races lately? Was not Rosebery the man of the moment, what with his third Derby winner at Ascot, and everyone so admiring the Party of the Decade, the great staff celebration at Durbans down the road – five thousand people and beer and cakes for everyone?

'It is my great misfortune,' lamented the King, 'that no one these days allows me to be lavish. What is permitted to Archibald Rosebery, a mere former leader of the House, is not allowed to a monarch. My partying is sadly restrained. If I served beer the Temperance League would be at my throat. If I served cake they'd remember Marie Antoinette. There'd be questions in the House. Keir Hardie would thunder at my extravagance. It seems we must all be socialists now. More, Dilberne, you find me a prisoner. I must not go about alone any more. I am protected. There are policemen everywhere.'

It was true that a discreet scattering of tall young men, none of whom Isobel recognized, surrounded and mixed with the royal party. They were well set up, but though they dressed like gentlemen they did not carry themselves like gentlemen. They were too watchful, too quick and easy in their movements: Bertie's security party, of course – Robert had talked of them.

'The King doesn't want them,' he'd said. 'Bertie is blind to danger, quite unlike the Kaiser, who jumps at the squeak of a mouse and has protectors everywhere. But then the Kaiser isn't loved by all, and Bertie is – or so he profoundly imagines. When Balfour suggests that perhaps he is not, the King takes offence. But Balfour's insisted and won.'

Isobel now saw at first hand how this victory seemed to have rankled the King.

'Balfour instructs Akers-Douglas, who instructs the Metropolitan Police,' the King thundered to all and sundry, and Mrs Keppel stroked his arm to calm him, 'who instruct Inspector Strachan here, who tells me where I can and cannot go for fear of anarchists and communards. Isn't that so, Strachan?' He addressed the most senior of his protectors.

'Indeed, Your Majesty,' said Inspector Strachan who looked rather like a bright-eyed eagle, spoke in educated tones but had very big boots and a paper collar, and whose social origins were hard to determine. Certainly not gentry, Isobel thought, nor professional, but not quite working-man either. But well enough versed in the ways of the courtier, it seemed. There was certainly something sensible and reassuring about him.

'Danger tends to come from foreigners, Sir, from anarchists and nihilists, not from your own people – who would gladly die to keep you safe,' he was saying. 'But since ease of travel now fills our prisons with aliens, a threefold burgeoning in the last five years, it is only reasonable to take precautions.'

'Against foreigners and madmen,' said the King, 'may the Good Lord, and brave Strachan, protect us,' and for a moment the little group was sombre.

But then someone in the crowd recognized the King and a shout went up, *'Bertie! Bertie!'* At a slight nod from the Inspector, the tall young men moved to form a defensive circle around the royal party, but when there was the sound of applause and someone even struck up with 'God Save the King', a slight move of Strachan's head and they melted away again. It was tactfully, and quite elegantly, done, thought Isobel, and she would have liked to have complimented Inspector Strachan, but circumstances did not allow it. Mrs Keppel was complaining to her of a chilly wind.

'You are so wise to be wearing that charming *moiré*, I am hopelessly exposed in cotton. The weather is not what it was: one cannot expect to be warm any more just because it is high Summer.'

Alice Keppel spoke casually and easily as one equal to another and Isobel, while making some normal response or other about the sudden inclemency of the day, was somewhat taken aback. They had been introduced once or twice before, it was true: Alice Keppel was charm itself, known to be an accomplished hostess and accepted in Society – if at its more rackety end; known to be the King's official mistress, and though both her own husband and Queen Alexandra accepted the situation, Isobel thought – well, what *did* she think? That there should be some extra deference paid to her own virtue, to her position as a proper wife, a respectable woman, one superior in rank? No, not quite that, but perhaps one did expect some hesitancy, some deference, in Mrs Keppel's approach? Well, there was not. The world changed as the weather changed and one must accept it.

At the remark upon the weather Robert had started to take off his own black cashmere coat to place it round Mrs Keppel's elegant shoulders, but Frederick Ponsonby got in first with his camel jacket. It was the turn of Ponsonby's wife, Victoria Lily, to look put out. Without female influence, Isobel decided, the world would simply descend into a swamp of untrammelled male passion in all respects – war without honour, rank without duty, and passion without love.

Mrs Keppel was now rich beyond belief, according to Robert, the King having given her some rubber shares which under Eric Baum's financial management had done inordinately well. Isobel was in no position to think ill of her for that, for the Dilberne family had themselves profited well enough under Baum's guidance; now Baum and his wife had gone to live in Palestine; Robert still wrote to him, Isobel knew, when he needed guidance on financial matters.

Now the King's grievances reverted to an earlier

tack, as His Majesty again deplored his current lack of success when it came to racing. He had, he claimed, got the Navy and even his nephew the Kaiser under control, but his stable was suffering. He had not had a winner for years, though he hoped that Cyllene, son of Bona Vista out of Arcadia, the stallion he had just hired from Rosebery, would in time produce a foal worth bringing on. Cyllene had, after all, sired the winning Cicero, much to everyone's surprise.

'It may have surprised others,' said Rosebery. 'It didn't surprise me. Blood will out.'

'I certainly like to think I am very much my father's son,' said Bertie, 'though the Good Prince was never one for the nags. But he was almost daily in pursuit of game. I too look forward to the closing in of the summer days and a gleam of a winter sun on a raised gun barrel. Nothing like the whir of startled wings to stir the spirits.'

The King could become quite poetic when it came to killing birds. Isobel could not help but remember something her friend the Countess d'Asti had once said. 'When an English gentleman grows too old for sex, his romantic impulses find their outlet in the mud and cold of the shooting party.' These days the remark came to her mind more and more often. She tried not to think of His Majesty in mid-congress with Alice Keppel. It was hard not to: he was so old and fat, Alice so elegant. The embarrassment about mistresses was that one always imagined them at it: when it came to wives the imagination veered discreetly away. Love-making within marriage was confined to the procreation of children, or was meant to be.

The King turned to Robert, and to Isobel's alarm asked him if the shooting at Dilberne looked promising for the Autumn. She assumed Robert would make some prudent excuse, but he was rash enough to say the shooting would be marvellous: he anticipated a really good season. The weather had been mild through the Spring and the pheasant chicks were plentiful. One of the gamekeepers had reported thirty eggs in one nest now they'd started clipping wings. The keepers were forsaking their old traditional ways and taking a scientific approach to breeding, and it was, Robert assured him, really paying off. Only the grey partridge had had a bad year, he told the King: too many predators around in the early Spring when the chicks were small: the sparrowhawks had been a particular bugbear.

'Then I'd like to visit you in mid-December,' the King said, 'the weekend after the big birthday shoot at Sandringham.' Greville took out his notebook; Ponsonby searched for his. The King turned to Isobel. 'Would we be welcome, Lady Dilberne?'

'But of course,' said Isobel, faintly, 'we will be honoured.'

'Not too big a party,' said the King. 'Just de Grey and possibly the Oliff-Coopers, Leicester perhaps – a really fine shot but I usually end up with a better bag – and a few other friends. How does the idea suit you, Alice? Bring George with you if necessary.'

Alice murmured that she too looked forward to it. Isobel did not. *George?* – thought Isobel.

'George' could only be George Keppel, Alice's husband. It was a nightmare. Less than six months to make Dilberne Court fit for a king. And worse, fit to survive the eagle eye of the King's mistress. The place had been left to itself for years. Lighting and plumbing were antiquated and primitive; the domestic staff were mostly untrained in London ways, and accustomed to taking advantage. She could just about cope with the annual day-long meet of the hunt at Dilberne, but the prospect of a royal shooting weekend, probably dragging on for a week, was worrying.

The more she thought about it the more terrifying it became. The London house was more modern, and set up for entertaining, but Dilberne Court like so many ancient houses was a warren of back staircases and rooms that led one out of the other without corridors, so offering no proper privacy. It needed an imaginative architect to bring it up to rationality – unnecessary staircases could be turned into water closets: some rooms split into two, others turned into one. A lot of people these days were heating their nurseries, though Nanny of course objected: 'Fumes and vapours bring the agues, not God's good fresh air.' Attics and basements were prone to damp. The old yellowed bed linen needed throwing out and replacing: the camphorwood and cedar chests which had done so well for blankets needed to be replaced with proper storage cupboards. The place was oppressive. Family portraits looked down upon the present and disapproved. But once you began to rectify that sort of thing there was no end to it: one needed help.

Alice Keppel would despise them and carry tales of rural dereliction back to her friends. The kitchens needed to be equipped with gas stoves to make them fit for proper entertaining. The kitchens were one thing, but what about the staff? The Nevilles, butler and housekeeper, were getting old, were sometimes the worse for drink: it was high time they were put out to grass. Nanny Margaret too; she was over-indulgent with the children, employed too many laxatives and was sometimes forgetful, though at least she stood out against Minnie's rather extreme ideas on nutrition. Minnie was sweet with the little ones but had no idea of discipline. Cook was an excellent country cook, but the King had foreign tastes; a French chef would have to be brought in and where could one find such a one at short notice? Even ten guests meant finding rooms for at least thirty staff – the royal couple were famous for having turned up once with a retinue of sixty – though that was mostly Alexandra and her jewels – the King travelled comparatively lightly. Even so, existing staff would have to move up and share beds, which always made them sulky and resentful just when they should not be.

And then the marquees – the midwinter days were short and valuable – daylight must not be wasted walking back to the house. Lunch must come to the guests, not they to the lunch. Pathways must be constructed so the ladies would not get their feet muddy as they joined the men, and field kitchens erected so that dishes could be served hot and claret warmed. At least the King's champagne – he had to have champagne when shooting, though frugal enough with alcohol otherwise – would be cold enough. The Dilberne icehouse had collapsed years ago.

Five months to prepare for one weekend – it was a monstrous task. And was she, Isobel, to see to the sleeping arrangements – was Alice Keppel meant to be nearer her husband or the King? Isobel found her heart beating hard and her breath coming short. She was dizzy. She swayed and would have fallen but the Inspector was at her elbow steadying her.

'Breathe slowly and deeply, your Ladyship,' he said quietly. She did, and stood straight and firm again. No one else had noticed. Robert was in the meanwhile bowing and scraping before the King, boasting of a bag of three thousand pheasants or more last December, which whetted the royal appetite for yet more slaughter.

Alice Keppel alone seemed to understand, 'Oh my poor dear,' she said. 'So much bother. Shall I try to put Bertie off?'

But Isobel felt haughty and said, 'Of course not, Mrs Keppel. I shall be more than delighted to entertain both you and the King.'

And God did not strike her with lightning as she almost expected, so great was the lie.

Waiting for Rosina

26th June 1905, Tilbury

Minnie was accustomed to the splendid granite docks of Liverpool, where the big transatlantic liners arrived and there was organized and spacious stabling for both horses and automobiles; well-serviced, comfortable waiting rooms with refreshments; and frequent announcements about anticipated docking times. But at Tilbury, a shambles of docks where grain ships were unloaded and emigrants came and went, things were an altogether different matter, and quite startling to anyone accustomed to comfort and convenience. Here a cold east wind drove over a marshy estuary landscape to stir up choppy water where river and tides met and clashed: it was a busy working world of shabby warehouses, rusty cranes and inadequately clad workmen swearing, heaving crates and pulling ropes. No one seemed to know anything or care less. Only by constant enquiry and the exchange of the odd coin could Reginald even find out where the *Ortona* would dock.

Reginald was driving the prototype Jehu III Thunderer, one of Arthur's latest and most progressive designs: chain drive, air cooled, two cylinders and four passenger seats, the chauffeur sitting outside as in a motor bus; a little draughty for the passengers but a well-sprung and comfortable enough vehicle of which Minnie's husband was very proud. He had planned to put the Thunderer into production early in the New Year – batches of ten at a time – but was now considering the merits of a design review: water cooling was more reliable than air, especially in Summer, but any extra weight meant wider tyres and a stronger chassis – all putting up costs. Every solution meant another problem. Comfort had to be balanced against running costs; the price of petrol and oil was rising. It was already a significant part of the cost of running a car, at three farthings per mile.

More, the pharmacist at Dilberne village, who currently obliged Arthur by providing him with the paraffin and oil, and latterly petrol, he had made do with so far, was beginning to complain about fire hazard. Arthur now looked forward to a world in which there would be safe stabling and fuel supplies for cars on every highway in the land, provided by the Jehu Automobile Company. There was so very much on Arthur's mind, Minnie once lamented in a letter to her mother, that so long as she and the children were safe and well, and she was in the double-poster bed when he got back from the workshops, there was little room left in his mind for his wife.

'Then don't be in his bed from time to time, girl,' her mother had written back. 'That should soon bring him to his senses.'

Such scheming was not in Minnie's nature. She

felt bad for writing of these matters in the first place. Arthur was eager enough to be with her, she knew, just so tired when he got into the bed he fell asleep when his head touched the pillow. And then he'd wake early and have to be up and out, for there was so much to be attended to. Well, better this than being married to some man who had too little to do but hunt and fish and shoot, or own racehorses, as had happened to so many of her friends who had married Englishmen, and had nothing to do but change their clothes all day or, like Isobel, keep herself so busy entertaining she scarcely had time to read a book. And better than living with a man like Stanton Turlock, an artist so charismatically insane he tried to murder you. But she would not let her mind wander off in that direction. The past was the past.

It transpired that the *Ortona* was docked off shore waiting for the tide, and Minnie settled down in the back of the Jehu to wait. Rosina would come, as she had gone, in her own good time. She felt a sudden desire for proper tea, of the kind her mother would make her – *'Nothing like a nice cup of tay, my darling girl, black and strong'* – and none being available, accepted a drop of brandy from Reginald's flask, and half of a rather crude ham sandwich he offered her, the ham hacked, no doubt illegitimately, from one of Cook's best joints when Cook wasn't looking.

She was disturbed by a tap on the window. A girl's face smiled in at her. Minnie wiped her mouth hurriedly of crumbs and tried to remember who it was. The face was familiar but who, where? Of course. Diana Robin, the bright, cheerful, energetic girl who had been to Oxford and would often sometimes accompany Rosina and herself to what Rosina's mother referred to as 'blue-stocking lectures'. But then Rosina had run off with the Australian Frank Overshaw, and that was the end of that. Minnie should feel really glad to see Diana but she was not. Why? Of course. Diana was Anthony Robin's sister. And Anthony Robin was the schoolmate Arthur had had dealings with over the matter of the flat Anthony maintained in Shepherds Bush for a kept woman. Flora. Arthur had been tempted and had fallen, briefly, into that temptation, after the manner of many a young man before marriage. It had been troubling at the time but Minnie had forgiven him. She had been in love. Was in love, still, surely. Why the 'had been' in her head?

'It's me, Diana, remember! It is you, Minnie, isn't it?'

Minnie, well trained by Isobel in the arts of prudent social discourse, took time to wind down the window further to cover any trace of discomposure – it juddered and squeaked a little – Arthur would have to attend to it: forget water cooling, these details made a great difference in a competitive market and men were slow to spot them. She must mention it when she saw him. She arranged her mouth into an agreeable if slightly cool smile and said that she was indeed Minnie. Of course, she remembered: Diana had been the one who brought news of Arthur's misbehaviour back to his family. But that had been some years back: a significant episode in her own life, small in everyone else's, no doubt, and quickly forgotten.

Minnie had no doubt now of Arthur's fidelity and uxorious attention, if only – the thought drifted through her mind – because he was so dedicated to the engineering of automobiles he had no time to stray in thought, word or deed. And here was clever, friendly Diana and Diana was smiling, young and cheerful, and all that was long ago and past, thank Heaven, and there was no need for embarrassment. Diana's face was altogether welcome and reassuring in this desolate place. She felt herself relaxing, and her smile broadened and became genuine.

'Oh Minnie, how thrilling to see you!' said Diana. Her voice was husky and soft. 'And that you've come to meet Rosina too! Brother Redbreast and I came by train; doesn't road just take for ever? He's at the newsagent, spending money. They've built such a splendid new station here. Please let me jump in, Minnie, there's such a horrid cold wind! The *Ortona's* just out in the estuary somewhere, they say, waiting for tides or tugs or something.'

Reginald had leapt down from his seat and was already opening the door for Diana. She was looking most presentable in a lingerie dress of a white cotton with black puffed lower sleeves, a black bib, a white starched collar and a green and mauve tie, rather mannish, and very much *à la mode*. Arthur would have died if she, Minnie, had worn such a thing – the female aping the male in the form of collar and tie! But it looked splendid on Diana, who was very much the new woman, moving with the kind of freedom of limb and confidence which Minnie recollected herself enjoying when a girl. Not now; she was a Viscount's wife and had adapted herself to her position in the world, moving slowly, with dignity and precision. Collar and tie! Diana would have joined the W.S.P.U., Minnie supposed: the Women's Social and Political Union, she was just the kind. She collapsed on the seat opposite Minnie and was gazing at her, admiringly.

'Oh, such centuries since I've seen you, Minnie. You're looking so English and ladylike I might hardly have recognized you.'

Minnie decided to take that as a compliment. They talked about Rosina, and Diana confessed to knowing little more than Minnie about Rosina's circumstances other than having received a letter of condolence from her when Lord Ashenwold had died, so at least she'd known Rosina was alive and kicking – and then suddenly the telegram saying she was on the *Ortona*.

Minnie looked for a ring on Diana's finger and was surprised to see none. Diana must be well into her thirties. Even Rosina, so independent of mind, had succumbed and married rather than live out her life as a spinster. A girl so good-looking and of such a good family as Diana's could hardly have been short of suitors. So why? It was a mystery. Minnie vaguely remembered Robert and Isobel going to Lord Ashenwold's funeral – hadn't there been some talk of the brother, Anthony – a broken engagement – something? She could not remember. Having small children seemed to wipe one's memory clean: Isobel kept saying she was too much in their company, and that she should leave it to the nursemaids.

Would the Robins want a lift back to London? If Rosina turned up with too many trunks there wouldn't be room for extra passengers the trouble with cars was that if they carried people they couldn't carry much else.

'Redbreast!' Diana had her head out of the window and was practically yelling, so much so that people turned their heads and stared. Diana, Minnie decided, was very much the new woman. 'Oh Tony! Oh Redbreast! Come out of the wind.'

Anthony came.

'It's little Minnie O'Brien from Chicago,' she was saying. 'Now Lady Melinda Hedleigh, lucky thing!'

Little Minnie? Was that how she struck people? She was at least as tall as Diana. So why this diminutive? But now Anthony Robin was inside the Thunderer and had plumped himself down not opposite her, next to his sister, as would have seemed better mannered, but next to Minnie herself, and so firmly and decidedly that he was quite squashed up against her side and she could feel the warmth of his leg against hers. There was such a lot of him; he was taller and bigger than Arthur.

'This one of young Arthur's horseless carriages?' enquired Anthony Robin. 'Tell him he really mustn't design cars for midgets. The future is to the large and well fed.'

'Not necessarily,' said Minnie. She did not like the way this man spoke of Arthur in so belittling a way. He was a mere younger son, a scion of the Robin family, only recently ennobled at that. Arthur was heir to an ancient earldom and father of her son the future Earl. Anthony was a mere *flâneur* in Fleet Street, editing some ineffectual literary magazine of which her father-in-law spoke dismissively; Arthur was a manufacturer and a landowner. Miraculously, her brain seemed to be working again, and time had returned to its proper speed.

'On the contrary, many scientists say we are evolving into rather little creatures with very big heads, the better to make room for our brains.'

'Oh, quite contrary, little Minnie,' he said, and oddly, she didn't mind being 'little Minnie' to him at all. 'Arthur told me you weren't so meek and mild as you looked.'

'Oh Anthony! My brother's in a grumpy mood, Minnie,' said Diana. 'Take no notice. I had to drag him along to this godforsaken spot and he's cold and hungry and doesn't want to be here at all. Rosina's my friend, not his, or he would be behaving so differently. Men are always happy to volunteer, I find, but really hate being asked to oblige.'

'Don't speak on my behalf, Diana,' said Anthony. 'I am more than happy to be here with the Viscountess; just truly sorry she is married to another.' His thigh was still warm against Minnie's; she shifted herself in the seat so as to lessen the contact, but he simply collapsed more into the seat so she gave up. When it came to it the warmth was welcome. What he had said was of course outrageous: he was assuming an intimacy and friendship which did not exist, but she found she rather wished it did. She felt quite light-headed, young and irresponsible again: as if anything could happen and just had.

'Oh Redbreast! And very happily married, to all accounts, and what's more a mother of two,' said Diana – quite sharply, Minnie thought – 'so leave her alone and bloody well behave.'

Then Diana turned to Minnie and said, 'Redbreast and your husband had quite a falling-out, Minnie, once upon a time, over some girl. That was long ago, when Arthur was a single man, of course. But it's all forgiven and forgotten now, isn't it, Anthony.'

So Diana did remember. But remembering hadn't stopped her knocking on the Thunderer's window: if Diana was not embarrassed to renew the acquaintance, why should she, Minnie, be?

'Any difference I may have had with the young Viscount is long over and forgotten,' said Anthony. He had a drawling voice, which seemed to savour words. 'He was my fag at Eton. One must be slow to wrath, they taught us, so one does one's best.' He looked into Minnie's eyes with his dark-lashed ones and held them until she was the one to look away: he took her gloved hand in his.

'And of course one is a writer. One understands the frailties of the human disposition.' So Stanton Turlock had looked into her eyes, while talking about the artist as the only purveyor of truth and beauty to the world. She took away her hand. She was no fool.

'Your husband is a very lucky man,' he said in a way she could only take as soulful, and then, in a businesslike tone, 'Do give him my regards and tell him I plan to give him an order for a Jehu III as soon as he has sorted out the problem of the mushroom valves. I have read all about them in the press.'

'Oh, do place an order, Mr Robin,' Minnie said, smiling sweetly. She had learned so much from Isobel – never admit ignorance, never apologize, never explain. To do so was both weak and unwise. To smile sweetly when one played for time was always safe. What did he mean by lucky? To share a bed with her? Surely not. No one could be so coarse. Mushroom valves? What on Earth were they?

'I am sure he will be very grateful for your support,' she added, to be on the safe side.

Anthony Robin was not unattractive. He had an undoubted air of authority. Her father would have given him house room – Stanton the artist he had beaten half to death. If Arthur seemed sometimes a romping puppy, sometimes a grand young lion, Anthony Robin seemed a gazelle, forever about to leave for better pastures, ones he knew about and no one else did. Both had the same formal, straight nose typical of the old Etonian, but where Arthur's face was sturdily jawed, and then a complex of well-rounded curves, Anthony's was dominated by a prominent brow, and then all lean planes and angles. And Anthony was fashionably-dressed in a light well-cut tweed suit, and was even clean-shaven, not even a moustache like Arthur. Arthur was careless of his appearance, black oil under his nails as often as not, and his hair always needing the attention of a barber. Sometimes, Minnie thought, those who didn't know him better might take him for a labourer. But who was she, daughter of a pork butcher out of Chicago, an ex-art school student, a *bohémienne* at heart, to think such thoughts, to care in the least for appearance? She despised herself: she loved her husband. Anthony had long, delicate fingers, manicured nails – so unlike Arthur's stubby, black-lined ones: she averted her eyes. She was a married woman. These feelings were better not thought.

But Anthony Robin seemed to have lost interest in her. He was handing his sister a magazine.

'Carry this for me, Diana,' he said. 'I found it at W. H. Smith's. This is a truly splendid railway station for somewhere out in the sticks. Today is all such pleasant surprises!'

The magazine was the *Atlantic Monthly*. Minnie had not seen one since her student days, recognizing it at once by its pale yellow cover. 'There's a piece by Torrey on Thoreau,' Anthony was saying. 'Are you interested in such obscure matters, Lady Hedleigh?'

'I used to be,' she said.

'Ah,' said Robin. 'But not now. I can see that Dilberne Court and Belgrave Square are not places where a genius of a writer and thinker such as Mr Thoreau – a poverty-proud genius, as his disciple Mr Torrey describes him in this article – would raise much enthusiasm. But then nor, I imagine, would Mr Torrey, being so keen an ornithologist.'

'No indeed,' said Minnie. She was moderately acquainted with the works of Henry Thoreau the anarchist, from whose books Stanton used to read aloud to her, and indeed with Mr Torrey, whose book *The Footpath Way* sat unread on the shelves of the little Chicago house Stanton and she had lived in. 'It would not. I'm afraid you are right, Mr Robin. The English interest in birds is confined to counting how many they have killed.'

She was disloyal in saying it, she knew, but a nice turn of phrase was a lure it was sometimes hard to resist, and she did not want this tall, attractive, dangerous man to think her dull. What was the matter with her? She was conscious of Diana as a witness. But to what? Nothing observable, certainly.

She was saved from further indiscretion as the dark shape of the *Ortona* loomed up and slid alongside. Its rails were crowded with passengers whose clapping and cheers were swept away by the wind to mingle with the mournful hooting of river craft and the screams of seagulls flurrying in to swoop upon the effluence that belched from the outlets of the *Ortona's* kitchens and piled up between the ship's side and the dock. You didn't see such a thing at Liverpool.

At first there was no sign of Rosina, and then suddenly there she was, a lone distinctive figure coming down the gangway, first passenger out. Straight and handsome, dressed in a kind of explorer's suit in khaki linen, a divided skirt, ankles visible above sensible shoes, a sturdy leather belt with canvas pockets hanging from it, cropped hair beneath a sort of bushman's hat, a sunburned face, a bulging leather valise, a bag slung over her shoulder, and her parrot Pappagallo on her shoulder. She was so familiar and yet so strange: she was a being from the future.

The words formed themselves silently in Minnie's head: 'It has been a long day and I feel very tired.'

In the Servants' Hall

27th June 1905, Dilberne Court

'Do I have something to tell you lot!' said Reginald, to the assembled servants. There were twelve of them already taking their tea – ham and mustard sauce, potatoes, cabbage, raspberry and Cardinal pudding with sago – when he and Lily joined them, having been sent back from Belgrave Square in some haste. The Countess, it seemed, had come back from Newmarket in a right old fluster.

The journey in the Jehu Thunderer – fifty-odd miles and a modicum of petrol – had taken more than three hours. Lady Minnie and the children had returned earlier in the day, along with old Margaret their nanny and the two nursemaids Molly and Maureen, taking much the same time.

The servants marvelled that Minnie liked to travel with the children, something many a lady would rather not do. Master Connor, as was the way with younger children, could be quite a handful, albeit, all agreed, a cheerful one, much like Master Arthur in his childhood days.

Nanny Margaret was cutting thin slices of bread for the nursery tea and was not really listening to Reginald, if indeed she listened to anyone. The nursery was her world; nothing outside it interested her. She spread the loaf with softened butter first, pressing it on so that the bread sliced really thinly, creating the lace-like effect which made the two little boys crow with delight. They would have scrambled eggs. She had already squeezed the oranges. Lady Minnie insisted on two a day for each child: oranges were rich in anti-scorbutic properties and would ward off scurvy. She also insisted that the little ones were fed unpasteurized milk. Nanny Margaret tried to tell her that untreated milk was a breeding ground for the consumption germs, just as orange juice was too acid for little tummies, but Lady Minnie overruled her. When it came to matters of nutrition Americans always thought they knew best.

'Lady Rosina got off that boat looking more like a tiger hunter than a lady,' Reginald was saying. 'When she left for Australia she was wearing a ring; when she came back she wasn't. She said she was a widow. But doesn't a widow keep her ring?'

'Perhaps she threw it away,' said Lily. 'What is a ring but a mark of servitude? An owner's brand. Like a farmer marks a cow or a sheep, so a husband marks his wife.'

The others shook their heads in disapproval. She was so smart she'd cut herself. But once a Londoner always a Londoner. Lily had started selling flowers outside Big Ben, a gutter waif, and what could be more Cockney than that?

'A woman without a wedding ring isn't a proper woman at all,' said Cook, never one to be outdone in aphorisms. That upset Elsie, the head parlourmaid, who had been pining for her promised ring for years. She had been saving up with her betrothed, Alan Barker the head gamekeeper, since 1898 but the more she saved the more he spent. Elsie gulped and snivelled, as perhaps Cook knew she would. Cook could be spiteful. Years spent slaving over a hot stove improved no one's temper.

'That's enough gossip,' said Mr Neville the butler but not before asking, 'What did she say he died of?'

'I had the impression he died of a snakebite and left her a fortune,' said Reginald. 'But they were talking outside the car, and the boat was letting off steam and whistling. I didn't hear it all. Lady Rosina did say now she could do as she liked. Lady Minnie was expecting her to come back home to Belgrave Square, but she went off on the train with Mr Anthony Robin and that sister of his, parrot and all. I think Lady Minnie was rather put out. We'd had a long wait in the cold.'

'Mr Anthony Robin!' exclaimed Mr Neville. 'That's a memory we can do without. But wasn't he the one who, well – whatever it was went on, went on?'

'He was indeed,' said Reginald. 'And went on it

did. Many's the time I watched him and Master Arthur go in that door in Half Moon Street, with that dolly mop waiting for them to go in one side, and me waiting on the other side of it for them to come out. They'd stay a couple of hours, Mr Robin sometimes longer; he had the bigger appetite, I'd say.'

'Enough, Reginald, enough,' said Mrs Neville. 'There are respectable women present. Wasn't her name Flora? A pretty name, I always thought.'

'Pretty name, pretty girl,' said Reginald. 'Best dairies in all London. But least said soonest mended, I daresay.'

'That's rich coming from you, Reginald,' said Mrs Neville. 'Miss Rosina, widowed and wealthy! Well, well! Good luck to her, say I. So long as that parrot doesn't end up in this house, all foul mouth and mites.'

'I never cared for the husband,' said Elsie. 'A Mr Overshaw and not even a title. He slurped his soup and spat out the bits in his marmalade while he talked about strange gods. I don't know why she married him.'

'She married him for the normal reason, because she was in the family way,' said Lily.

'Fine kind of lady's maid you are,' said Cook. 'You should pay more attention to her Ladyship's laundry and less to idle gossip. Miss Rosina was pure as the driven snow.'

'I know what I know,' said Lily calmly. 'And what would you know, Cook, stuck away down here in the kitchens. I'm the one who makes the beds.'

'I see her Ladyship whenever she's here in the country,' said Cook. 'I see her in person as much as you do. Don't I, Mrs Neville?'

'You certainly do, Cook,' said Mrs Neville. 'And a very fine dinner you've made for us today, and you'd do well to remember it, Lily.'

'Sorry, Cook,' said Lily, apparently contrite. But then she added, 'Her Ladyship told me she's thinking of employing a French chef, not an English cook.'

'More fibs, Lily, more fibs. Untrue things. As well as, perhaps, Lily. Never instead of,' said Cook. 'All very well up in London, French cooking, but not down here in the country. You can't get the ingredients. You can't worry me, my girl.'

'But you don't know what I do,' said Lily. 'When her Ladyship came back from the races she was all of a shiver, and not just because the wind was cold. You think you've got news, Reginald, but it's not one half of what I've got. His Lordship invited the King and Mrs Keppel down for a shooting weekend in December. Cross my heart and hope to die. Her Ladyship's going to turn things upside down here, you wait and see. Not just a French cook, I expect, but pastrycooks too. Dozens of them.'

There was a sudden silence as it dawned on the assembled company that for once Lily was not making up stories. Someone said:

'Royalty? At Dilberne? We can't. We're still fetching slops.' And someone else said:

'Mrs Keppel? That brazen hussy? Here?'

And Matthew the groom said: 'I used to clean Mrs Keppel's shoes at Moulton Paddocks. Very fine leather; came up a treat. She was ever so nice.'

Molly the nursemaid spoke up for the first

time, saying, 'It's all right. They're just friends. The King's too old.'

'And too fat,' someone added unkindly.

Mr Neville said: 'That's enough, everyone. We'll hear what we hear in good time, and from the proper sources. Any more of the sago pudding, Cook? It is most delicious.'

'The King admired my Yorkshire puddings,' Cook said, 'when he was only the Prince of Wales. You remind her Ladyship of that, Lily, when next you see her. There's just a scrape of the sago left, Lily. Would you care for it?'

'I'll always do what I can to help, Cook,' said Lily, as Cook scraped the remains of the sago pudding – browned, indeed slightly caramelized and totally delicious where the hot oven had burned it round its edges – into her bowl. Mr Neville sighed, and went without.

'It's the Queen I'm sorry for,' said Elsie, 'waiting for a husband who never comes home,' and she dissolved into tears and ran from the room. Mrs Neville went after her.

'Just as well for Lady Rosina that God took the husband,' Reginald said into the tumult. 'If he did, she fell on her feet, if you ask me. I wonder how he died. That is the question.'

But it was no good; Lily's news had trumped his. All had lost interest in Miss Rosina's homecoming. Reginald applied himself to his yet uneaten plate of ham and mustard sauce. He was disappointed by Lily; she showed him no gratitude. Had it not been him who'd picked her out of the gutter when she was a child, a coughing, starving bundle of skin and bones selling flowers outside the House of Lords? Brought her back out of the kindness of his heart to Belgrave Square, where she'd taken root and flourished like the green bay tree? Now he regretted it. She thought herself above the rest of them. Where would it end? Lily had her eye on higher things – more especially, Reginald was coming to suspect, the master. Why else did her Ladyship keep banishing her from his presence?

His Lordship, like so many of the great and famous, was not above temptation – the brave deserved the fair – though Lily, in Reginald's opinion, was not sufficiently fair to attract other than the very temporary attention of the brave. She was wasting her time. She should stick to the man she knew, himself, and show more loyalty.

Lady Dilberne Confronts her Daughter

28th June 1905, Belgrave Square

'I really don't understand you, Rosina,' said Isobel. She paced up and down the morning room. The sun was bright and high and the day was warm. She herself was dressed in a kimono, finding herself at a loss as to what she should wear for the morning. It was such a temptation to do without stays and corsets – and even the new elastic suspender belts could grip one uncomfortably – that she had succumbed, it being midsummer and Lily not being there to insist on a proper formality, Rosina having turned up unannounced, two days late, parrot on her shoulder, at scarcely nine o'clock in the morning. Lily had been sent down to Dilberne Court to warn Mr Neville of Rosina's arrival and make sure the girl had a respectable wardrobe. Rosina, Isobel had decided, was to have her old rooms in the East Wing, but they'd been unoccupied for a good six months since Adela left, so drawers and wardrobes would have to be brushed out, aired and dusted, polish applied, spider webs got rid of – they lived in procreative bliss in four-hundred-year-old buildings – and the place made generally cheerful. Better that Rosina had not turned up at all just now, with the King's visit to prepare for, and so much to be done, but better to have her safely ensconced in Dilberne Court than causing embarrassment in London.

And here was her daughter Rosina in person, strangely attired in split skirts, bare ankles showing, with one small string bag hung over her shoulders which apparently contained all her worldly possessions.

'I don't understand you either, Mama,' said Rosina. 'But that doesn't mean we can't get on together. I am sorry if I didn't come straight back home to meet you as I expected, and it was sweet of Minnie to come all the way to meet me, but Anthony had set up a meeting with my publisher in Paternoster Row on Friday, and he and Diana are just round the corner from there in Fleet Street, and really all I wanted to do was go to bed and sleep. You know what these sea voyages are. I plead exhaustion.'

'Publisher?' asked Isobel faintly. 'And who are Anthony and Diana? Do I know them?'

'Anthony and Diana Robin. They are perfectly well bred. You even know their father,' said Rosina. 'You went to his funeral. Lord Ashenwold. Diana is my friend; Anthony is her brother.'

The name Anthony Robin rang some kind of bell but Isobel could not place it. She put in many obligatory appearances at the funerals of grandees she scarcely knew, looking suitably grave and solemn.

'At least they sound respectable,' said Isobel. 'But Fleet Street? What a strange place to live.'

'It's very suitable,' explained Rosina. 'Anthony is the editor of a literary magazine called *The Modern Idler*.'

'I've not heard of it,' said Isobel, thus dismissing it as being of no consequence. 'But I don't understand. Do you see yourself as a writer now? From what Minnie tells me, you have returned to us a widow but quite a large landowner.'

'I married a man whom everyone spoke ill of but whom I loved,' said Rosina, briskly. 'He was bitten by a brown snake and died of the bite, rather quickly and horribly, which was most distressing to me and everyone on the station. But that was eighteen months ago, and as for being a widow, I do not define myself in terms of my marital status. No sensible woman does. I inherited the station, all forty thousand acres of it, and with the advent of a passable road from Geraldton to Perth land prices have soared, as has that of the wheat which we produce. If I wanted to sell I could, and even as it is I shall never need a penny from you and Pater, Mama, for the rest of my life.'

'And do you then plan to sell?' asked Isobel. 'A pity you didn't see fit to give us more information or more warning as to your return. Let alone your departure from these shores.' Isobel spoke a little acidly. She could not help herself. Her daughter's sudden marriage had given rise to a good deal of gossip. Rosina was known to have spent a night with her suitor in the Savoy before even announcing her engagement. Word had got round. Society turned out not as forward thinking as many had supposed. Isobel had been cut dead once or twice. These things got forgotten but Isobel had spent a disagreeable year. Since the Prince of Wales had become King, free love had become unfashionable. Mrs Keppel was still seen out and about with His Majesty, but no longer took his arm in public. And now she, Isobel, was expected to receive Mrs Keppel, and Rosina wore no wedding ring. Scandal could be so easily revived.

Pappagallo the parrot, seeming to feel tension in the air, stirred on Rosina's shoulder, cleared its throat rather horribly, and then spoke. 'Too right, mate. Too right,' it squawked, fluttered to adjust its position, and left a grey splash on the white Aubusson rug Isobel had recently chosen with Minnie at Maples. Isobel kept her composure, though she rang at once for Mary the parlourmaid. If it was quickly removed it would do less damage.

'I am in two minds about selling,' said Rosina,

when order was restored. Mother and daughter waited in vain for Robert to return for lunch, as he had sent a message to say he would. Rosina rather remarkably asked the kitchen to send up steak and a fried egg for lunch 'to remind her of home'. Isobel picked at a cheese omelette when finally they gave up waiting for Robert and lunch was served.

'I find outback life quite appealing, if rather hot and full of quite dangerous creepy-crawlies,' she told her mother, 'but it is quite fun telling other people what to do, sending them here and there to do as one decides. It is almost like being a man.'

'I thought Australia was all desert,' said Isobel, who was trying to absorb what she felt was too much information, too unambiguously passed on, and still keep her equanimity. It was evidently Rosina, but a Rosina who had become quite the foreigner in her absence; even her vowels had a drawling quality, no longer clipped and authoritative, and her sentences, though well-constructed, rose in pitch at their end as though to cheer rather than command the listener. But yet she was speaking with Robert's eloquence.

If only Rosina had been born a boy how much better off everyone would have been. Rosina as, say, Roland Earl of Dilberne would have quite enjoyed managing the estate. As it was, it was becoming clear that Arthur's heart was not in the land. All his energy and emotion was spent on the development of smelly, noisy, expensive engines for the road, when it would have been better spent on new ways of farming, the breeding of dairy cattle, or even the development of an automobile plough, which was now much talked of. She had been very glad when he married Minnie and ceased being an idle young man and 'found his interest', but the interest now seemed to dominate his life. He had none of his father's knack of easy approach. Which Rosina seemed to have developed in good measure, seeming to have no reticence at all. Steak and fried egg! One had these children, and one was never free of concern, both for them, and about them. It was too bad.

Rosina explained that though most of Australia was desert-like, hot, dry and for the most part unpopulated, it was so vast anything could happen. There were pockets of great fertility wherever there was water. She herself farmed wheat and lupins, very productively, on a farm called Wandanooka in the Nyoobgah tribal areas.

Oh yes. My daughter in Nyoobgah. Where, your Ladyship? Oh, you must know. Her Wandanooka estate! Everyone knows the delights of Wandanooka! My little grandchildren Nyoob and Gah simply love it there.

Isobel felt she was on the brink of hysteria. Rosina sat with her legs plonked apart as if she were Long John Silver, a man with a parrot perched on his shoulder, digesting steak and fried egg. Her daughter, quite unchaperoned, a widow, said she was developing a dairy farm and a 'training school for the black fellas', where she was 'teaching basic literacy and good farming practice'. The aboriginals were apparently nomadic within their tribal areas, but when there was a purpose to it they would settle in one place.

'If it's so very pleasant, why have you left?' Isobel asked.

'I've finished the book. Seebohm Rowntree has read it and thought well of it and wrote to Longman's the publishers to recommend it. I took it round to them yesterday. If the book's a success I daresay I will stay in London and be a literary person: if I find I am wasting my time I will go back to Wandanooka.'

'How nice, dear,' she said. 'Is what you're writing a novel? I hope it is nothing to embarrass your father.'

'It is about the marital customs of the aboriginals. Well, hardly marital; let's say sexual. We in Europe have a lot to learn. A man can have up to ten wives and treat his child as his wife but must never speak to his mother-in-law. I compare it with the equally irrational practices of Sussex villagers. Do you know about bundling, Mama? It is very commonplace in Sussex.'

'I do not,' said Isobel grimly. 'Write what you will, but please, not under the family name Hedleigh. Have some mercy on your father, please.'

'Father doesn't notice anything I do,' said Rosina, 'I hadn't seen him for over three years and he couldn't be bothered to welcome me home. It was nice of Minnie to come.'

'He would have come if he could,' said Isobel, 'and so would I. The Russian business has flared up again. Odessa is in revolt: the Foreign Office has to give an opinion and your father is needed to help form it. He has become quite a force in politics in your absence. You should be very proud of him.'

'Father was always extremely good at being elsewhere when required,' said Rosina. 'The gambling den or the bookmaker or the company of some Duchess always tempted him away. How you put up with it for so long I cannot imagine. At least my aboriginals can see what's going on under their funny flat noses.'

Isobel wished her daughter well, but just not in this room now. Enough was enough. She suffered a spasm of rage. She felt it rise in her loins, tauten her stomach, tighten her chest, constrict her throat and heard it burst from her mouth in a low, hard pitch, as if she was spitting out a lump of coal.

'Go back where you came from!' Once it was out Isobel felt better. There had been some blockage, she realized, now released, caused by decades of never saying what she wanted to say.

'But of course, my dear,' she added quickly, moderating what had been so intemperately said, and even managing a little light laugh, 'this is exactly where you do come from. This is your home.'

In turn Rosina's hostility seemed to ebb away, like molten iron cooling as it drained from a cauldron. Her legs closed, her shoulders drooped, her chin dropped, her mouth worked; she sobbed – great gulping sobs – and tears ran down her poor sunburned cheeks. 'I'm sorry, I'm sorry, I'm sorry.'

She wept loudly and unreservedly, like a servant,

and Mary quickly packed up her brush and basin of soapy water and disappeared from the room. At least, thought Isobel, my servants, unlike my children, know how to behave.

'I'm sorry, Mama, I am,' Rosina wailed. 'I don't mean to be horrid. I've had such a terrible time, Frank dying so awfully and only me and him for hundreds of miles. You've no idea. He was a really good man but he had very strange habits. He'd have never left me up the duff the way he did it, for all he tried. He just wouldn't listen. Do you understand?' Isobel, gently reared, didn't. 'And it was a terrible voyage back; I travelled steerage. I don't see just because I'm so rich I should be more comfortable than anyone else, but people kept vomiting all over me and when finally I got off the bloody boat I took one look at Reginald and Minnie and couldn't face coming back here. I knew you'd be cross. I try so hard to be brave and not to care about anything but then I just go to pieces like this. Mama, I'm just so tired and upset.'

Isobel allowed herself to be embraced but remained stiff.

'Oh please, I've said I'm sorry. Please.'

Isobel allowed herself to soften a little. Rosina hugged her tighter and snivelled and gulped and quietened.

'But this book of yours simply won't do, Rosina. You know that.'

It was Rosina's turn to stiffen.

'I *am* the book, Mama. I can hardly not publish it. It's the truth, that's all. We have to be able to face the truth.'

'I don't see the virtue of rubbing people's noses

in what is distasteful. And truth is no good at all for the populace, as your father well knows. They don't have the wit to make sense of it. The whole art of government lies in the distortion of facts in the interests of the nation as a whole. You're simply overtired and need a good rest in the country, some food other than steak and eggs, and to keep out of the sun. You must go down to Dilberne.'

'Very well, Mama.'

'And now you must go to your old room – I have had it opened up for you, and you must lie down and have a little sleep and recover your composure. And then you can go home and be with Minnie.'

Rosina went, meekly, and Isobel was much relieved.

Ah, Minnie, thought Rosina, as she composed herself to sleep in the room where she had spent so much of her childhood. (Pappagallo flew without questioning to his old perch. Parrots had very good memories.) Of all her family she was perhaps fondest of Minnie; it had been good to see her, even if briefly, on the dockside at Tilbury. It was just the crushing weight of what lay behind her, the complexity, the formality, the implicit reproaches, that had made her take to her heels and flee. But the previous evening, when they had been well into the absinthe, there had been a rather strange scene, which made her wonder if she had fled from a frying pan into a fire. Anthony had remarked that Minnie seemed to be a very sweet and pretty girl, and no doubt a kind mother, but unawakened. She was the kind of girl to whom you would be doing a kindness by teaching her a thing or two before sending her back to her husband.

'Oh Redbreast!' Diana had exclaimed, seeming to take unwarranted offence, and had hit Anthony on the arm and told him not to be so ghastly. He'd got her in an armlock and made her cry. Rosina had then got Anthony in a headlock but he'd hooked her leg and brought her down on the carpet and stood over her with his foot planted in her stomach. She'd wondered what was going to happen next, and no doubt would have happened in some native encampment back home in Western Australia. But this was Fleet Street round the corner from Paternoster Row and nothing happened, at least then.

Anthony just laughed as Rosina squirmed beneath him – she had landed on her hip – and said blue-stockings were not his style, being 'too judge-mental': he only liked silly girls, and then not much, and helped her up. They had all drunk too much, of course. She, Rosina, had become accustomed to the alcohol of the Nyoobgah, fermented gum tree sap and wild honey, which rendered those who drank it friendly, not mad. The episode had all been so sudden, oddly disturbing and upsetting.

Lunch with a Publisher

30th June 1905, Fleet Street

At around twelve noon, as Rosina slept in Belgrave Square, the doorbell jangled at No. 3 Fleet Street and Anthony Robin opened the door to William Brown from Longman's the publishers. Brown had had a brisk walk down the hill from No. 39 Paternoster Row and had the alert and cheerful air of a man who was not afraid of exercise; his knock on the door was convincing and brooked no argument, as befitted a partner in a prestigious publishing business that had brought the works of the greatest and best writers to the attention of the public for two centuries. Even Anthony was slightly awed: for the publisher of *The Modern Idler,* a small imprint which dealt in large part with the stories, poems and essays of the young and untried, a personal visit from a publisher of Longman's status was full of promise. Someone, something, in the magazine had caught their attention.

It had been at Diana's insistence that he had taken Rosina and her manuscript round to Longman's in the shadow of St Paul's the previous day. Finding Mr William Brown out – what had Diana expected? – they had left the manuscript with a young man at the reception desk and departed.

Anthony had assumed it was an improbable mission: he had glanced through the manuscript of *The Sexual Manners and Traditions of Australian Aboriginals* and assumed it was unpublishable – too long, too untidy, badly-typed, written by a woman, and with almost more numbers on the page than words. A publisher such as Longman's was hardly going to be interested in the louche habits of savages. But Diana had persisted, and he liked Rosina: she was quite the opposite of her brother, a natural socialist with a lively mind – though people had stared slightly as they walked up the hill to St Paul's. Gentlewomen – and she obviously was one – did not go about the streets wearing neither hat nor gloves; let alone with bare ankles showing, no matter how hot the day.

But here was Mr Brown on Anthony's turf asking if he could speak to Miss Rosina Hedleigh. Anthony told him she had been staying overnight but had now gone home to her parents in Belgrave Square.

'The Earl and Countess of Dilberne,' Anthony added. People might as well know where they stood.

'Sister to the Motoring Viscount then?' asked Mr Brown. 'An interesting family. It obviously has talent. Perhaps he could be induced to write a guide to motoring.'

'It would hardly be literature,' said Anthony. He was conscious of still being in his dressing gown, albeit one bought at some expense from Henry Poole, in rather elegant grey and black stripes.

'Perhaps not,' said Mr Brown. 'But today's

readers want nothing more than to read about the motor car which is transforming all our lives. Anyhow, I read Miss Hedleigh's manuscript overnight. I find it admirably written, and excellently researched.'

'Indeed,' said Anthony. 'So you mean to make her an offer?'

'I do,' said Mr Brown, 'and I thought it would be preferable to do so in person. Readers these days are fascinated by other lands and other customs, especially if they are of an intimate nature. I understand Miss Hedleigh prefers not to be known by her married name. Since she gives this address am I to understand that she is perhaps under your guardianship?'

Mr Brown stood hesitating on the step. An admirable figure, Anthony thought, in spite of wanting the upstart Viscount to write him a book on motoring. He was wearing an American-style, single-breasted, cutaway frock-coat in grey tweed, fetchingly tailored to allow an agreeable amount of bleached linen shirt to show, its creaminess smartly punctuated with a narrow red tie with a very small knot. His trousers were of the new loose style. The lot was topped by a shiny light-brown bowler with a curly brim. Anthony's impulse was to ask him where he had acquired the suit – Savile Row normally provided only the most conservative of suiting – but since he himself, after a hard night's carousing, was still in his dressing gown and rather the worse for wear, he desisted. But he asked Mr Brown in.

'Yes,' he said, 'I think you can safely infer that.'

To his credit William Brown did not blench at

the full sight of Anthony's *déshabille* and bare feet, nor at the sight of Diana, who, though at least up and dressed, had a broom in her hand and was surrounded by packing cases and furniture. Anthony quickly introduced Diana as his sister, aware that appearances might be misleading.

'I am glad Miss Hedleigh finds herself amongst literary friends. And so these are the new premises of the *The Modern Idler*,' Brown said, rifling amongst the confusion of papers on various surfaces with such assurance Anthony could not object. 'You have taken over from Jerome, I understand.'

'Not quite,' said Anthony. '*The Modern* is a mere offshoot while the *Idler* itself lies fallow.'

'I had heard,' said Brown. 'Jerome Jerome has left the gentle slopes of humour and taken to religion. It's rather ill-advised of him, but don't cite me as saying so. He is writing some play, I believe, about the presence of Jesus amongst us.'

'The interest now is less in the Christian God and more in the esoteric,' observed Anthony. 'We seem to crave a return to the reign of many gods rather than just the one.'

'Ward Lock is certainly doing tremendously well with Haggard's *Ayesha*,' said Brown. 'We at Longman take that rather badly – we've published so many of the Haggard stories from the *Idler*. And the Kipling. Of course he's in a different league.'

'I nearly took Rosina round to Ward Lock at Salisbury Square,' said Anthony, 'but you were nearer.'

'Oh Anthony!' came a little wail of protest from

Diana, quickly curbed by a look from her brother.

'Well,' said William Brown, 'if anything else interesting turns up in your post, do remember us at Longman. Minor talents can blossom into major with a little help from a good publisher.'

'Or indeed a good editor,' said Anthony, and Mr Brown suggested that they all go down and lunch peacefully at the recently renovated Simpson's in the Strand and continue this most stimulating conversation. He would pay.

'Ooh yes!' said Diana. The last few days of life without servants had been tolerable, except for the way food did not automatically appear at set intervals, but had to be bought and cooked before it could be served – where was the time for an educated woman to think about art, literature and politics, let alone be involved, even if you weren't your brother's dogsbody. The socialist principle of doing away with the servant class was all very well for the men who espoused it, but, she agreed with Rosina, women who looked forward to a servantless world were out of their minds.

Last night everyone had only unmade beds to get into. So no one could be bothered to do so, and had settled down after a night of absinthe drinking – and for Anthony and Rosina some nameless white powder – to sleep in their clothes on armchairs and sofas. Diana hoped Rosina was getting on well with her parents, fearing that after such a night she might be at her contentious worst. But it was wonderful news about the book, though dreadful the way Anthony had told lies – Ward Lock had not yet been even considered let alone approached – and she supposed Anthony might now try and get the work himself to serialize in *The Modern Idler;* she would have to caution Rosina against it. In the meanwhile she was hungry. Lunch at Simpson's with its rich red beef, starched white tablecloths and attentive waiters sounded very inviting indeed.

And William Brown was most agreeable, thought Diana, if something of a dandy and given to waving his hands about, and was currently re-publishing Oscar Wilde's response to Henry James' essay on the *Art of Fiction.* One could possibly marry such a man and not share a bed with him by mutual consent but no doubt there were other ways in which he would be trying. There would be no room in the wardrobes, for one thing.

It took her five minutes to comb her hair, find a fresh blouse – she had found a Chinese laundry round the corner – put on gloves and a hat, and make herself respectable enough just – for Simpson's in the Strand. Anthony took longer but looked agreeably artistic when he finally emerged, with almost as much white shirt as Mr Brown on display, the new baggy trousers and some very fetching two-tone shoes in cream and beige with brown ribbon laces.

She was hungry and since it was Friday chose a lemon sole after her mushroom soup, while Anthony and William had the roast beef after oysters on crushed ice. The beef was spit-roasted by the waiters in front of a roaring open fire. Diana hoped the waiters got paid more for the heat, the fumes, the burns and the flying cinders entailed but didn't suppose so. The honour of working at Simpson's would be considered reward enough. The beef looked so moist and tender she rather regretted her virtuous and simple sole.

'Miss Hedleigh will have to be prepared for a lot of public attention when we publish,' said William. 'I hope she is prepared for that. When a man enquires into society's sexual practices it is one thing – Havelock Ellis has got into trouble with the law over *Sexual Inversion* but still has some friends – it may be different for a woman.'

'I think she is sufficiently brave,' said Anthony. 'She presents the truth, after all. By the way, Diana here tells me she has already written a great deal about the life of the rural peasant in this country.'

'Oh Anthony,' said Diana. 'Don't mention that. Mostly about their wages: only a little about how they avoid pregnancy.'

She thought William's eyes lit up. So did Anthony's. She should not have spoken. Rosina had taken that section out before she had let Anthony see it. It was too near to home and her family – and she still cared about them – would not like it. They could just about put up with the courtship customs of Australian aboriginals – and the mating habits of horse and hound were of great interest to them, as was the fecundity of the birds they loved to rear the better to shoot – but the less they knew about those of their employees the better. Mr Brown said he would call on Miss

Rosina at Belgrave Square in the afternoon – or was it Lady Rosina? – to talk about it.

Diana said Rosina abhorred titles and preferred to be called Miss. Titles were nonsensical. She and Anthony would be 'Honourables' but their father, although a Lord, was only a baron. So only the older brother got to inherit and end up a Lord. But she had annoyed Anthony again. He said sharply that such matters were hardly of interest to Mr Brown, and when Mr Brown said on the contrary, a titled author could be guaranteed to sell, Anthony looked positively sulky.

Mr Brown left promptly at three and Diana lingered on with Anthony in the bar while he had a glass of brandy. A corner was reserved for chess players, and one of them, unusually, was a girl, and a young and pretty girl at that; at any rate she attracted Anthony's attention. She was very much Anthony's 'type' – fair, bright blue-eyed, animated, rounded to the point of fatness but with a little waist: she was the kind one of her male fellow-students at Cambridge had graphically described as 'round-heeled' – that was to say 'one push and she falls flat on her back.' Many students resented the presence of women around them, and would take pleasure in shocking young girls – 'if they want to be men, let them live like men' – and made no effort to moderate their language, rather the contrary. The trouble with being educated with men was that you grew up knowing only too well what they were like – why would one want to marry one if there was any way of managing not to?

The girl finished her game – she lost – and came over to Anthony, whom it seemed she already knew. Anthony introduced her.

'Eve Braintree, on the Woman's Page of the *Daily Mirror;* we published a story of hers last Christmas. It was very well received.'

'That's a year back,' she said, and her voice was light and sweet. 'I'm promoted to the motoring column. I write under Evelyn Braintree.'

Anthony expressed surprise.

'I can write about motors,' she said, 'as well as any man. They are not so difficult to understand. Bits go round which link with other bits which make the wheels turn, that's all. Fletcher Robinson promoted me just before he died.'

'A tragedy,' said Anthony. 'He was only thirty-seven. Completely sudden. Struck down in his prime. I spoke to him just before he died: he was convinced the Egyptian "Unlucky Mummy" was responsible for his illness. She certainly looks a malevolent creature, only just containable by all the pillars and stones of the British Museum.'

'Fletcher put me onto that story,' Evelyn said, 'but then he said it wasn't safe, and took me off the Woman's Page and put me on Motoring. He wrote it up himself and now he's dead.'

'Perhaps you'd write for us on the subject?' he suggested. She said she'd think about it, but would need danger money. He said his proprietors didn't have any danger money, so she shrugged. Perhaps *Longman's Review* would take it. They liked other-worldly stuff and were well funded. So what had he been talking to William Brown about?

'I'm Rosina Hedleigh's agent,' he said.

'Oh Anthony,' protested Diana, but he was looking so hard into Evelyn Braintree's eyes he scarcely heard her.

'Longman are thinking of publishing her book,' Anthony went on, 'but she might do better with me – I can run it as a serial.'

'Rosina Hedleigh? Isn't she the Motoring Viscount's sister, who ran off to Australia? The brother's all over the news. So good-looking and they say he's – well, never mind what they say. I'm going down to Dilberne to interview him. He's entering his Jehu for the Isle of Man race in September.'

'I might pay danger money for a piece on Arthur Hedleigh,' said Anthony, 'if it wasn't too flattering a piece, that is. Idle young upstart.'

'I can read you like a book,' said Evelyn, and, having ascertained that Anthony would actually commission a piece, said she'd think about it and went off out of the dark, smoky recesses of Simpson's into the hot summer glare of the Strand.

'What do they say about Arthur Hedleigh that Eve wouldn't say?' Anthony Robin asked his sister when she had gone. 'There's very little Eve won't say. A very new woman indeed.'

'Oh, never mind,' said his sister.

'Tell me,' said her brother.

'You know how on Boat Race day there's always a competition between Oxford and Cambridge to see who can field the biggest, well, you know what, I shan't be indelicate. Hedleigh was always in the team.'

Anthony seemed a little taken aback but then laughed lightly.

'I rather doubt the truth of that,' he said. 'I daresay he spread the tale himself. Lucky little Miss Minnie O'Brien from Chicago.'

Diana shuddered.

Never Darken My Doors Again

29th July 1905, Belgrave Square

While Rosina composed herself for an afternoon rest, Isobel took action. She sent Reginald to buy a ticket for an evening train back to Dilberne Halt, and arranged for Mr Courtney the family's solicitor to go down within the week to talk to Rosina and set about selling the Wandanooka property in Western Australia and transferring the proceeds to her father's estate. It was perhaps unfortunate that Rosina couldn't settle and came down in time to overhear some of the conversation. Isobel put the phone down.

'But Mother–'

'Rosina. Leave financial matters to Mr Courtney and your father. You are not in a fit state to decide anything for yourself.'

'But Mama–'

'I heard you say that because one is rich, that is no reason to travel comfortably. It hardly makes sense, Rosina. You are distraught. This book of yours – it comes from the same stable as Havelock Ellis, I imagine, and propagates vile ideas. Mr Ellis' name is hardly mentioned in polite society. Do you want this for yourself? It will affect your father's reputation.'

'Father hasn't written the book, I have. What has he got to do with it?'

'Don't be so naïve, child. You know perfectly well. He will be mocked because he can't control his family. If he can't control his family, how can he control a nation? And your poor brother Arthur; people will giggle and point after him because his sister writes these appalling books and no one will buy the Jehu. They will feel besmirched just sitting on its cushions.'

Rosina, unfortunately, took it into her head to giggle.

'Not much sitting goes on, I can tell you, in the outback. People walk, or run, or stand, or dance, or chant, or crawl, or occasionally stoop, but you don't often see them just sitting.'

Isobel ignored her but inwardly she seethed.

'And poor little Minnie! Her parents will ask her not to let their grandchildren associate with you. Give me the manuscript and I'll burn it.'

'But it's with a publisher, Mama.'

'Then our solicitor Mr Courtney will write to them and forbid them to publish it.'

'I can do as I like. I have enough money and to spare, thanks to my marrying someone you did not want me to marry. And now I have no husband to stop me doing whatever I want.'

'You're a silly little girl who has no idea how to

look after herself.'

Her mother's words cut into Rosina. She felt she was eleven again. She remembered climbing trees in the park with Arthur: she'd worn a pair of his trousers, taken from his wardrobe when Nanny wasn't looking, because skirts got in the way. They'd been discovered. Her mother's rage had been great. There had been talk at the time of sending her to Roedean on the coast, a school set up for girls who had the misfortune to be 'clever', but after the tree-climbing incident the talk had abruptly ceased. Rosina remembered the rare hard edge of her mother's voice. 'You're nothing but a silly little girl.' Thus for life, she had been defined.

You could escape and marry, she realized, in order to come to terms with those absurdities; you could go to the ends of the Earth and suffer freezing cold and burning heat, to a place where a letter home cost you two weeks of your life getting to a post box – but come home and nothing had changed. You were still nothing but a silly little girl, and so you would always be. This was the reality of it. She had failed. Her whole side still ached, black and blue from where a bad sea in the Bay of Biscay had thrown her to the deck. She should have stayed in her cabin as the passengers had been ordered to do. She had thought she was immune from disaster but she was not. Every movement of her hip still reminded her. Mother was right. Mother had won.

'Yes, Mama,' she said. 'It's only a book. I don't suppose they'll publish it anyway.'

Her mother lifted her eyes to Heaven in thankfulness and smiled upon her daughter once again. She told Rosina she was booked on the five-thirty from Waterloo Station to Dilberne Halt. There was a late debate in the House so there was no point in Rosina waiting up for Robert. Her father would be down to see her as soon as affairs of State allowed, no doubt. Minnie would be so happy to have her about.

Rosina was to have back her old rooms in the East Wing. Isobel had had the place renovated, plumbed and wired for Adela when she had moved in.

'But Mummy,' cried Rosina. 'They were my rooms. You shouldn't have given them away like that. How could you have altered them without asking me! And all my books and papers? Seebohm's letters!'

'I burned them. You shouldn't have gone without warning, and without proper discussion. What was I meant to do? Close the East Wing and use it as a shrine to your memory?'

All the chairs and sofas, Isobel said, had been re-upholstered with a nice new chestnut and cream-coloured print from Liberty's and the walls papered with a pretty floral pattern which quite enhanced its tranquility. Minnie had helped her choose. Of course, Rosina had not had the privilege of meeting her cousin Adela – such a spiritual girl – now married to the charming young Hungarian Count, Michael Nàdasdy, and had moved with him to Ascona in Switzerland.

'She writes to say she plays a lively part in a religious community,' said Isobel proudly. 'Hardly a week passes, Rosina, in which she doesn't write to me.'

'She must be very bored, then,' observed Rosina. 'And an Austrian Princess marrying a Hungarian Count? Rather a come-down, surely. Though not as bad, I can see, as me marrying a colonial theosophist whose only claim to family was an aunt related to a bishop by marriage. But at least Frank was rich. Continental nobility are usually poor as anything.'

'I'm sorry, Rosina,' said her mother, 'Adela was as much a member of this family as you are. And more of a daughter to me, come to that. All you've done all your life is upset everyone, forever chasing after false gods.'

Rosina held her tongue, though it was difficult. It was not prudent to make too much trouble. Her head was in turmoil. Mention of Adela did not help. Adela had nearly married Frank; that was water under the bridge, of course, but it was still difficult to feel generous. Frank had come across an old copy of the London *Times* in the Geraldton store and read the news of her betrothal to the Count of Nàdasdy.

'To think I nearly married her,' Frank had said. 'How pretty and ethereal she looks! Princess by name and princess by nature! But we're nature's lords and ladies at Wandanooka, aren't we, sweetheart. I don't regret choosing you one bit.'

Had he chosen her, or just wanted not to waste a fare to Fremantle? She had to acknowledge that his 'love' seemed to be more practical than ethereal. On the way back from Geraldton, a mile or so inland, they'd dismounted, and Frank had thrown down a horse blanket and proved his love for her then and there, the better to make his point. But it was, she felt, as much Frank's way of making the most of what he had as anything more romantic.

It was on just such an occasion that the brown snake had bitten Frank on his naked buttock; she and he had rolled up against a rocky crag when it attacked him. The ludicrous nature of the world outside all established order struck Rosina so powerfully these days. Tears were now running down her cheeks. Mother was right. She, Rosina, was very tired. Was it grief for Frank that made her cry? She'd never liked being the girl Frank had run off with when his real fiancée had disappeared: the younger sister without an education because she was only a female: the kind of person who went to the lecture but never the one who gave it; the one who was seen as good company for Minnie the Viscountess, never the other way round.

And her book, her book? It had been in another country, long ago. Her mother was probably right; it was rash to publish. But when in her younger days had she ever been prudent? All she reported was what actually happened in other cultures: she wasn't recommending them, although it did relieve women of the burden of procreation in a land where food was short. She felt a sudden stirring of hope.

It occurred to her that perhaps she could publish the book under Anthony's name? *Sexual Manners and Traditions in Pagan Australia and Rural England: A Comparison* by Anthony Robin rather than Rosina Hedleigh. It was certainly a solution. But would he mind?

'And I will be down at Dilberne Court quite a lot in the near future,' her mother was saying. 'We can take some nice walks, though I am going to be really busy.'

'Too right, mate. Too right,' Pappagallo squawked and plopped a chunk of greyish-white liquid from under his tail feathers onto the table. Isobel rang for Mary.

'Busy?' Rosina asked.

'I'm having enough trouble getting the place seen to before Mrs Keppel visits,' said Isobel, forgetting her smile. 'And that bird can't possibly go with you. It's just mess, mess, mess. You have no idea how much needs to be done and what a trouble it all is.'

'You have Minnie,' said Rosina.

'Minnie is very sweet and being a great help, but her taste in furniture is a little, shall we say, colonial. She likes all the dark, old-fashioned, mahogany stuff. Heavy to look at, heavy to carry. To my mind it just needs burning, and she keeps arguing.'

'Mrs Keppel the King's harlot?' asked Rosina. 'You have invited Mrs Keppel to stay at Dilberne Court? Is that respectable?'

'The King is coming down for a shooting weekend in December. You know how he hates to be dull. He is bringing Mrs Keppel with him.'

'But where will you sleep her? A lady of Mrs Keppel's discrimination can't be expected to put up with the cracked chamber pots of Dilberne Court. And how can she entertain the King properly without an electric lamp to guide him to her bed? Though they do say candles are much kinder to the complexion. One does rather fear for her when the King dies and Princess May becomes Queen. There will be no King's favourites then.'

'Mrs Keppel is bringing her husband with her,' said Isobel, feebly. Rosina was outraged.

'Worse and worse,' said Rosina. Perhaps I should add a new chapter to my book – "Sexual Traditions of the English Aristocracy".'

And now Isobel was asking Mary to bring down Pappagallo's old cage from the attic and set it up in the servants' hall.

'But what for?' asked Rosina. 'Where I go Pappagallo goes. I'm not leaving for Dilberne Court without him. He'd pine and die.'

'Nonsense,' said Isobel. 'He's a bird. Birds don't love people; birds don't suffer. Birds just stay around with whoever feeds them. You go, the parrot stays.'

'Where I go Pappagallo goes,' Rosina repeated, stirred at last to protest. Let her father take her money, let her mother take her chance of recognition, let them exile her in disgrace to the depths of the country – but they would not take her parrot and friend, let alone relegate it to the servants' quarters.

'That scrofulous bird stays here,' Isobel was saying, almost screeching, 'and be grateful I don't strangle it. I am my father's daughter. I will not have it spreading its little visitors in my nice new East Wing. Fleas! See how the mangy thing scratches!'

‘I mean to publish, Mother. I’m sorry, but I do.’

And with Pappagallo on her shoulder and her spirits quite restored, Rosina stalked out of the room, out of the house, and took one of the new motor taxicabs back to Fleet Street and her friends Diana and Anthony Robin. As she left there shot out from beneath Pappagallo’s tail feathers another dismissive spurt of greyish sludge which splat on the wide front steps of No. 17 Belgrave Square. Mary was sent to clean up the mess.

What the Butler Knew

7th August 1905, The Servants’ Hall

The Countess seemed unable to decide which her main residence was. The old rules – Belgrave Square for the Season: balls, dancing, dinner parties, charity events, soirées and shopping – and Dilberne Court in the Winter for shooting: the gentlemen vying as to the size of their bags and the ladies their jewels, costumes and conquests – were being ignored. The Earl spent most of his time in London to be near the House, Her Ladyship kept turning up in Sussex with architects, master builders and designers. Mr Neville was feeling his age and was in a constant state of confusion as to who qualified for the dining room and who should be content with the servants’ hall. Old Tommy was exhausted from opening and shutting the gates for tradesmen in their coughing and spluttering but gleaming new auto vans, Royal Warrants on the side panels. 'Bloody royalty, they's no different from us under their fine clothes,' he was heard to mutter.

The staff were tired of shuttling between Dilberne Court and Belgrave Square as her Ladyship changed her mind about which staff she needed this end or that. They seemed to be forever packing and unpacking. It was now more peaceful at Belgrave Square than at Dilberne Court. Who could have imagined it? Even the staff bedrooms were being 'seen to' and central heating put in, which made the servants complain about feeling stuffy and unhealthy. The sound of hammering and the smell of paint offended everyone. Lady Minnie worried that there was lead in the paint, which of course there was, but it had never been shown to do any child any harm. Lady Minnie was full of worries. Lily said it was because Lord Arthur didn't pay her enough attention.

'Those who change the sheets know the truth: old country saying,' said Lily over a cup of tea and a Huntley and Palmer ginger-nut. Chocolate biscuits were for upstairs.

'You made that up,' said Mary. 'I've never heard it.' She came from London too, and was still talking of the way she'd had to clear up Pappagallo's mess from the steps, which was surely an outdoor man's job. She was a plain girl with a double chin and pimples, who flourished on resentment, and whose sulky look had somehow taken root in her appearance, and who, as Reginald remarked, was not likely to attract his Lordship's attention – Lordship the father or Lordship the son, come to that, if what Lily said was true.

'I don't tell lies,' said Lily.

'Ho, ho, ho,' said Reginald. He was fed up with Lily. She was saucy but never came through.

This evening Cook was serving a supper for the staff of boiled salmon, very cheap in August, neck of mutton stew with dumplings and bread and butter pudding. Nanny had got in her way sieving green beans for the children and blanching cucumbers for salad, according to Lady Minnie's instructions, so Cook was running late and not in a good mood. The Earl was at the House as usual – there was so much trouble in the world he spent more and more of his time in London – so the Countess could have her way with the menus while at Dilberne.

Today her Ladyship had demanded *côtelettes d'agneau à la Constance* for dinner, trying out a menu which came from Mrs Keppel's cook. It was little better, Cook thought, than lamb in a white sauce but flavoured with sliced cocks-combs, which in Cook's opinion meant no proper flavour at all, like the truffles Lady Isobel was so suddenly keen on. The Earl would have turned up his nose at it, he being a roast beef and Yorkshire pudding kind of man, but in his absence her Ladyship liked to experiment.

The recipe came via Lily, whose habit it was to meet Mrs Keppel's lady's maid Agnes in St

James's Park on her day off every second Sunday. Agnes (or so she claimed) could wind Mrs Keppel's chef, the famous Monsieur Delachaume, round her little finger, and so was able to pass on to Lily – in exchange for a small fee, paid for by her Ladyship, and in an extra half-day off when Lily was in London – recipes for exotic dishes served in the Keppel household at No. 30 Portman Square.

'Tell you what, Lily,' Cook said, 'do me a favour and taste those foreign recipes before you pass them on. Don't give me any more cockscombs. Nasty flabby things, you have to soak them in hot water and then rub the red skin between finger and thumb.'

'In other words,' said Reginald, 'you're a decent Englishwoman, not a dirty French trollop.'

Cook was taken aback but all others round the table laughed, except Mary, who took offence and made no attempt to hide it.

'That's enough of that, Reginald,' said Mr Neville, the butler.

'There'll be no lewd talk around this table,' said Mrs Neville, the housekeeper.

'Surprised you know what I'm talking about,' said Reginald.

'You're getting too big for your boots, Reginald,' said Mr Neville. 'One day you'll go too far.'

'Oh, I don't think so,' said Reginald, 'I know where too many bodies are buried. Isn't that so, Lily? And you just be thankful, Mary,' said Reginald, 'that Lady Rosina didn't turn up here with her parrot. Forget inside outside, you'd have been scrubbing off its shit all day and night too. She'd work all night, in the East Wing, in the gazebo, in the library, wherever and whenever the fancy took her.'

'All places were alike to her, oh-my-best-beloved,' said Lily, 'as Rudyard Kipling says.'

'And no showing off knowledge others don't have, Lily,' said Mrs Neville, 'no matter however many half-days off you now have. It causes embarrassment and distress.'

'Strange how Lady Rosina vanished off into the blue like that,' said Mr Neville the butler, 'and never even been down to see her own brother. Let alone Lady Minnie, with whom she used to be so thick. But that was before your time, Mary.'

'She didn't "vanish into the blue like that",' said Reginald. 'She went to stay at No. 3 Fleet Street. I know that from the cab driver she hired in the street. I caught up with him in a cabbie shelter the other day. And guess who lives at No. 3 Fleet Street?'

'You never told me that,' complained Lily. 'Well, who?'

'Mr Anthony Robin, that's who.'

'Who's he when he's at home?' asked Mr Neville.

'Oh no!' said Mrs Neville. 'Anthony Robin? Isn't he the one–'

'Lord Ashenwold's younger son,' said Reginald. 'What a memory you have, Mrs W! That's right, the one who owned the flat in Half Moon Street. The flat where I'd take Master Arthur to see his fancy girl Flora, just before he got wed. Flora being the one her Ladyship got so upset about. Not that I suppose Lady Rosina knows about that, or cares for that matter – she and her Ladyship not being on the best of terms. Lady Rosina would have done better to stay in the land of the cannibals.'

'Science tells us, Reginald,' said Mr Neville, 'that there is no culture on Earth which practises cannibalism. It is against God and nature.'

'So's a lot of things I could mention,' said Reginald darkly, 'that go against both and still happen. Mr Anthony Robin and Master Arthur for instance.'

'That's enough,' said Mr Neville sharply. 'There are ladies present.'

'Some of them are more ladies than others,' said Reginald, or less.' But he shut up. Lily too knew where bodies were buried. He couldn't go too far.

'The macadamia nuts I used to have to get in for that bird,' said Mrs Neville. 'Husks everywhere and clouds of little flies.'

'Mrs Beeton has a recipe for parrot pie,' said Cook, meditatively. 'A dozen parakeets, a few slices of beef and lemon peel. Hard-boiled eggs too, as I remember. I'd take comfort from it, just planning the plucking.'

Cook asked if the table preferred egg custard to Bird's custard on the bread and butter pudding, but everyone said no, they liked the bright yellow of the Bird's; while some suggested that Cook could make it a little more thinly so it soaked into the bread better. Cook's good humour was restored.

'So are we to take it,' asked Mrs Neville, returning to the subject in point, 'that within days of getting back from the land of the kangaroos, our Lady Rosina is living with a single man in Fleet Street?'

'Not necessarily,' said Reginald cautiously. 'We should not jump to conclusions. Mr Robin lives with his sister Diana as chaperone.'

'Nevertheless,' said Mrs Neville, 'our Miss Rosina was always a one for a quick decision. Within a couple of weeks of meeting her cousin's fiancé she'd married him by special licence and was honeymooning on a ship to Fremantle. And then quick as a wink she lost him to a snake in Australia. More people go into that land than ever come out of it. Not a year later she was back with a book about the nasty habits of the natives of the land of the kangaroo. She had no shame the way she talked, Mary said. Oh yes, quick, very quick.'

'Mary only heard part of the conversation,' said Mr Neville judiciously. He scraped the pudding bowl around the edges where the crust had caramelized in the oven. Such was a butler's privilege.

'I heard what I heard. If Lily said it you wouldn't doubt her,' complained Mary.

'Because I only speak the truth,' said Lily, with a little smile and a lick of pretty pink tongue around delicate curved lips, making it clear that she was lying.

'You have a hard heart and a wicked tongue, Lily,' Mary burst out. 'Poor Miss Rosina began to cry so I left the room. I felt quite sorry for her.'

'More fool you,' said Lily. She and Mary did not get on.

'Don't waste your pity,' said Elsie the head

parlourmaid. 'Always complaining her bath water wasn't hot and making me fetch more, though the East Wing was miles from the kitchens. Of course when she ran off and Princess Adela moved in, the running hot water came soon enough. Her Ladyship soon saw to it.'

'Always asking impertinent questions, that Lady Rosina,' said Peter, one of the outside men, who lived in one of the cottages, had bad arthritis and had recently been widowed. Mr Neville was sorry for him so he sometimes came in for supper with the servants. 'How much we got paid and what we got up to in bed. No end to it.'

'Did you tell her?' asked Lily.

'I told her a load of old apple sauce,' said Peter, 'we all did so. But she wrote it down just the same.'

'It was Lady Rosina told Lady Minnie what Master Arthur was up to,' said Lily. 'I was there when it happened. She was the bringer of bad news, but Lady Minnie forgave her, more fool her, and Master Arthur too, come to that. And now all Master Arthur has eyes for is his beloved Jehu. But why should Lady Minnie care? She has the two boys; she can do what she wants.'

'Miss this and Master that,' said Mr Neville. 'All very well for the older staff who brought them up from when they were little, and not a title to their name, but a young thing like you, Lily, should show them proper respect. Lady Rosina, Lady Minnie and his Lordship if you please.'

'Respect is owed when respect is due,' said Lily. 'Old country saying. I'll say no more than that.'

Minnie Goes to Church, but Arthur Does Not Come with Her

20th August 1905, Dilberne

'Today,' said Mr Stacey the vicar, 'I want you to think about the words of John Newton's wonderful hymn:

Approach, my soul, the mercy seat
Where Jesus answers prayer,
There humbly fall before his feet,
For none can perish there.

'John Newton, once a trader in slaves, had himself plumbed the depths of sin, and had known the dark cloud of sorrow which accompanies sin. In Leviticus Chapter 16, we learn of the scapegoat upon whom the lot falls to go into the wilderness, carrying the sins of mankind with him...'

The Mercy Seat. Minnie hadn't heard it mentioned since the days when she was a Catholic and lived in Chicago – the golden covering of the Ark of the Covenant where God was meant to rest. Now here it was again in this little stone church in England, built a thousand years ago – or part of it anyway, Arthur said, though about exactly which part of it he was rather vague. The Reverend Stacey was giving the sermon: Minnie liked him: he was young and eager, though some said he was too High Church for their liking and that he would have introduced a censer and incense had Isobel not put her foot down. Such were the dramas of Dilberne.

'Dear God,' Minnie prayed to herself, 'thank You for all You have done for me, but please help me now.' She realized she was miserable. She knelt in her usual pew this bright Sunday morning, second row of the three gated pews on either side of the aisle nearest to the altar, a small son, future Viscount and Earl, kneeling by her side, the Lord and Lady of the manor according to tradition in their allotted pew in front; she was sorry for herself. It was an unusual feeling for her and she did not like it one bit.

Time for the hymn. That should cheer her up. No. 442 in *Hymns Ancient and Modern*, Sir Arthur Sullivan's splendid march. 'Onward, Christian Soldiers'. Her father-in-law sang lustily in front:

Hell's foundations quiver
At the shout of praise;
Brothers, lift your voices,
Loud your anthems raise–

The Countess too lifted hers, in a light, delicate, perfect voice. But Minnie's own had a sudden quaver in it. She missed her mother. She missed her home town, its grandeurs and eccentricities. She missed the constant rattle of cattle trucks, the squealing of piglets, the grunting of hogs. Here the nights were so quiet and black. She didn't miss the stench of the stockyards when the wind was from the west, as it so often was – even after they'd moved out to Jackson Park you'd get a whiff of hog every now and then.

What was the matter with her? Surely, she had everything a woman wanted – wealth, security, a place in society, two healthy male children, a husband who was rapidly becoming successful enough in the automobile industry to be mentioned in the business pages of *The Times* from time to time. It wasn't just that she was bored, she was actively unhappy, enough to call upon the Lord to come to her aid. The prayer had come to her lips almost before the realization of her need.

What she needed was Arthur by her other side, flanking her in the pew, and he was not there. He had been too busy to come to church. Isobel had raised her eyebrows. The Earl had made light of it ... Arthur had two of his new Jehus entered in the Isle of Man touring race in September: a fifty-five-mile circuit, fuel allowance one gallon for every twenty-two and a half miles – this competition being more about low fuel consumption than speed – and adjustments to the motor house and gear fittings had to be urgently made. Every change of gear meant fuel wasted. He would be in church in spirit, he said, just not in the flesh.

'God will forgive him,' the Earl had said. 'A man has to do what a man has to do.'

'A man has a duty to his family,' said the Countess. 'Let us just hope our Minnie forgives him.'

It was good of her mother-in-law to be so concerned, but it was a humiliation to be so closely observed.

We are not divided, all one body we,
One in hope and doctrine, one in family–

Now Minnie had tears in her eyes. She turned her face so that little Edgar couldn't see them but now Molly the nursemaid could. She was trapped by circumstance. She had believed that with marriage and children everything would be safe and settled. There would be unity, and peace, and everyone would love one another. It just wasn't so. *'One in family?'* Those weren't even the right words. She should have sung *'one in charity'*. She was trying to persuade herself of something that just wasn't so. The family one joined in marriage should be one in hope and doctrine but they were not. Edgar, who was so small, fought with Connor, who was even smaller. Rosina fought with her mother. Minnie did what she could to be a good daughter-in-law but it was getting more and more difficult. Her own likes and dislikes, her own selfishness, crept in and got in the way.

The fact was, she wanted her life back. She wanted to run her own household, choose her own menus, bring up her children her way and not have perpetual arguments about how it was best done.

'Oh please,' Minnie said lately to Isobel, when little Connor was running round making a noise and nuisance of himself, 'don't slap him. He's just being a little boy,' and Isobel had just gone ahead and slapped him.

'For Heaven's sake,' Isobel had said, 'how else

are you going to make a child behave? What do you want them to be? Little Red Indians?'

And her mother-in-law had been spending more and more time at Dilberne, seemingly intent on pulling the house to bits. Arthur and Minnie had to move their bedroom to the green room while Isobel had the plumbing done and the old tree-of-life wallpaper stripped and replaced by a new flock stripe in pink and white from Heal's. Minnie had demurred.

'It's fresh and modern, but pink and white? With the old beams?'

'Well, you weren't there to ask,' Isobel had all but snapped. 'Chasing off like that after Rosina. What a waste of time that was!'

Rosina had been to visit her mother in Belgrave Square, Minnie knew, but apparently it had ended badly. Isobel had not actually said, 'Never mention her name again in my presence,' but she might as well have. Minnie asked for Rosina's address so she could write but Isobel said:

'I have no idea of her whereabouts, Minnie. And since she has not left me her card I have no intention of chasing after her to find out. You could ask Inspector Strachan if you really want to know but I don't advise it.'

Inspector Strachan had been recommended by the King as the man to advise Isobel how best to secure the new up-to-date Dilberne Court against thieves, flood and fire. The household had already been woken in the night several times by the gong which now sounded whenever a trip wire powered an electrical solenoid, and once or twice by day when Connor discovered how it was done. The Inspector was quite a frequent visitor, with his Lordship's assent, and very pleasant and friendly, but Rosina's whereabouts were scarcely his concern.

Minnie asked Arthur, but Arthur put on his pompous, fatherly, closed face and said: 'Oh, forget Rosina, Minnie. Let sleeping dogs lie. She made an uneasy ally at the best of times.' One way and another Minnie herself felt reluctant to press too closely. And after all, she too had been hurt and disappointed when Rosina had failed to drive back with her to Belgrave Square. It had been all but rude of her to go back to London the way she had with her friends. If the family had now set their face against her – in the same way, she remembered, they had once set their face against the orphaned Princess Adela – she was in Rome and must do as the Romans did.

But Rosina was fun. Rosina in the East Wing would have been company for Minnie in the West. Rosina would have come to church and knelt in the same pew as Minnie and Arthur, and giggled with them when the priest betrayed his Papist sentiments, voiced her outrage to him as they filed out of the church as to why in 'Onward, Christian Soldiers' brothers were to lift their voices in song but no mention of sisters. No one at Dilberne was ever enraged, or showed themselves to be, and Minnie was forgetting that it was even possible.

She would quite like another child, a girl to be a

companion, but the way things were going with Arthur it was beginning to look unlikely. Tonight Arthur would get home after dinner, look in to say good-night to his sleeping children – Nanny Margaret never let him wake them – take cold meats and chutney in their rooms, talk a little about shaft transmission and wheel gearing, call for Thompson his valet to help him pull off his boots and pick up his scattered clothes and then climb into bed and fall promptly asleep. That would be that for the day. He would stretch out a companionable hand when she joined him and she had no sense that he didn't love her – just that he was exhausted. He never slept in his dressing room – she would have to be grateful for that, she supposed. Some women would be glad enough to be left alone and spared a baby but she was a different kind of woman.

When Isobel came down from Belgrave Square it would be with a bevy of architects and designers, but they seldom had much to say for themselves, or else, more likely, saw no advantage in making themselves pleasant to Minnie, she being married and a mother. If the Earl came it was mostly to see how the shoot was coming along for the Autumn – foxes were being quite a pest this year – or to talk about the Matumbi rebellion at Samanga, and he would think the less of her if she admitted that she had no idea what he was talking about.

She never seemed to meet anyone young and lively. Arthur had his cluster of workshops near the

Big Gates at the end of the oak drive and had moved the motor works offices into the Gatehouse itself – modernized by Norman Shaw in 1890 from the original Palladian for Robert's father; everything, everything, had a history and the past was always being used to justify the present – so Minnie seldom met his colleagues and if she did they talked only about transmission gears and exhaust valves. Since Minnie's ill-fated excursion to Tilbury Isobel had not invited Minnie to Belgrave Square at all. It seemed Isobel no longer wanted advice: she wanted the new, improved Dilberne Court to be hers and hers alone. Yet when the Earl died – God forbid – would not she, Minnie, be Countess and Isobel relegated to Dowager Countess and no longer be in charge? Should not she at least be consulted? Some things were owed to history, and this debt did not involve conceding to Mrs Keppel's taste in all things bamboo and bright. Plumbing and wiring was one thing, flock wallpaper and chintz another. She was amongst Philistines.

She thought about Diana and her brother Anthony: they were her kind of people, but they'd flashed before her eyes like a tantalizing mirage, only to be snatched away by fate. Anthony had curious eyes, dark fringed and almond shaped. She had taken Thoreau's *Walden* out of the Boots Library in Brighton as soon as she got home to Dilberne, and read it and loved it but there was no one to talk about it with. Arthur liked the way gears worked, not the way trees grew.

She hated the way she was finding fault with everything and everyone. And now they were singing the last verse of the Reverend Stacey's favourite hymn about the Mercy Seat.

Poor tempest-tossèd soul, be still;
My promised grace receive;
'Tis Jesus speaks – I must, I will,
I can, I do believe.

Well, like Mr John Newton the slave trader, she was certainly tempest-tossed. She remembered what her mother always said: 'God helps those who help themselves.'

She would have to help herself if she wanted this dark cloud of sorrow to pass, and she would. *I must, I will, I can...*

His Lordship Gets Away

20th August 1905, The House of Lords

Reginald was waiting in the trap when his Lordship left the church. He was to catch the train back to London. The Ngindo tribesmen in German East Africa were causing trouble again – it was primarily a German problem but unrest had a habit of spreading. Lansdowne of the Foreign Office had called him to the Cabinet table – along with Sunny Marlborough and Alfred Lyttleton – for a consultation; the last thing Lansdowne wanted was a premature showdown with the Kaiser, but the excesses of the German governor, Peters, must be challenged in some way if a rebellion was to be avoided. Peters' tendency was to slaughter not negotiate, finding the latter tedious. Better for him to ship water into drought areas and relieve famine, but cheaper and easier to slaughter enraged hordes of savages who believed that millet and castor-oil fetishes turned bullets to air. Stirring up hatred was no way to govern. Boundaries were lines on a map and tribal areas overlapped. The British Luo territories might be next to go. No doubt the white man had to take up his burden, as Kipling was so fond of telling the Americans they had to do, but did it really have to be on a Sunday morning, thus depriving a man of his Sunday lunch with the family? These days Robert looked back almost wistfully at his days in Fisheries: nothing was ever urgent about the mating habits of trout: salmon with machetes lined no river banks.

The train failed to stop at Dilberne Halt – the initial agreement with the Railway Company that any passing train must stop there when requested was now some sixty years old and these days was often honoured only in the breach. The Company had offered to buy the rights back. The Earl and Countess were willing enough – it was a bore forever having to call up the Portsmouth stationmaster when one wanted a train, and there were other stations not far away – but Arthur was determined that his father should hold on to the rights. Easy access to the Jehu works was essential, and was not the village itself growing to meet the needs of the new plant? Rather, Dilberne should become a regular stop on the Portsmouth to Waterloo line. So if the railway management failed to remember that the train had been asked to stop, and it simply steamed on through, that was not surprising. Reginald had to drive on to Petersfield, and his Lordship had to catch the next train. He was just in time for the four o'clock appointment, only to discover Lansdowne and Sunny had been called away to meet with the King and the meeting had been cancelled.

Ponsonby, who had broken the news, took Robert along to the bar and bought him a whisky.

'I hope the King has something of importance to say,' said Robert, 'other than whether the shooting at Bowood or Blenheim will be better this year.'

'The King is much exercised about Lansdowne's wisdom in backing France rather than Germany in the Moroccan matter,' said Ponsonby, a little stiffly. 'He has received a letter from his nephew the Kaiser and sees trouble ahead.'

'And so the fortunes of our East African protectorate fade into insignificance,' said Robert.

'Up to a point, yes,' said Ponsonby. 'Britain can cope with any number of little wars. A big war between the major powers is surely a different matter. The King is right to be concerned. He is wise when it comes to matters of war and peace: he sees the wider picture, and is as good a diplomat as he is a shot.'

Robert thought that was not saying much. He

had seen too many sportsmen put their birds the King's way, and the King simply not notice, preferring to believe the myth of his own making, that he was the keenest marksman in the land. He was good with a gun and a stag, fairly good with a gun and a sluggish pheasant, not very good with a gun and a lively partridge, and with a mouthful of a woodcock to destroy, downright bad, let the beaters do what they could.

'Little wars lead to greater wars,' Robert said. 'And what goes on in East Africa should not be a matter of indifference to His Majesty.'

'You are very censorious all of a sudden, Dilberne,' observed Ponsonby and smiled as he spoke. Well, thought Robert, times were changing. He was a charming fellow and it was possible to overlook what once would have seemed impertinence. No 'your Lordship', no 'my Lord', just 'Dilberne', fellow to fellow.

'No doubt if one his sisters had married some naked African war lord rather than the Kaiser,' Ponsonby went on, 'he would be interested enough. His Majesty's skill in diplomacy, I realized long ago, comes from family. He is big brother to the nations: he understands the foibles of rulers and the patterns of jealousy between them. He is dealing with his brothers and cousins by marriage. But he is coming down to see you at Christmas: you must tell him your concerns then.'

Robert refrained from saying that by then it would be too late – Luoland would either be in flames or it would not, and Lansdowne's problems with Germany would be insuperable or they would not. He had done what he could. He would take Ponsonby's lead and talk about lighter matters. He said he could only hope the shooting would be good enough for the King: the foxes had been very lively in the Spring and had wreaked havoc amongst the nesting birds.

Ponsonby said that was not a matter of great concern. The King would get his fill of good bags at Sandringham at the beginning of December when he and Alexandra celebrated their birthdays: he would not be in a competitive mood: His Majesty just hoped to spend some pleasant and relaxing hours with Mrs Keppel, before returning to the bosom of his family for Christmas. Robert was quite taken aback. It was one thing to be friends with a monarch, another to find that friendship used as a cover for clandestine arrangements. It would certainly not be prudent to repeat the remark to Isobel. She was so taken up with the matter of a weekend four months in the future that she seemed to have entirely lost her sense of humour.

'But I like Dilberne Court as it is,' he'd protested, 'shabby and old-fashioned. What you have done to Belgrave Square is the talk of London Society. Can't you leave it at that?'

She could not. He resented it. He was a busy man. He needed peace and familiarity not continuous novelty. Wherever he looked in Belgrave Square there seemed to be swatches of fabric or reams of wallpaper and strange etiolated young men discussing the advantages of one and the disadvantages of the other. Dilberne Court was even worse. Familiar walls would suddenly not be there at all: what had once been a dressing room was now a bathroom. She had already told him she meant to put the King in one wing and the Keppels in another.

'Dilberne is a family home,' she'd said. 'I simply do not want any of the creeping-down-corridors-in-the-middle-of-the-night behaviour that used to go on in the fast set. There was no way I might simply refuse the Keppels, of course, once you had seen fit to invite the King in the way that you did, but if they are here together, that's that.'

He said he hoped she might reconsider: he doubted that much 'went on' down the corridors these days other than conversation with old friends and relaxation: the King was not a young man, nor an agile one. But her Ladyship would not relent.

'I will not be party to it, and nor should you,' she said. 'To place them near together is to invite the staff to gossip.'

Isobel had been much unsettled, Robert surmised, by Rosina's sudden return from the Antipodes and her equally sudden departure from Belgrave Square. What exactly had gone on between his wife and their daughter she would not tell him in detail. Enough that Rosina had 'behaved quite dreadfully'. It had involved Rosina's ruddy parrot, that much was clear: dreadful bird – and a book Rosina had written while away on the habits of the Australian aboriginals. Robert thought Isobel worried unnecessarily: it was unlikely to find a publisher – who would be interested? He was sorry to have missed Rosina – but she was in good health and spirits enough to defy her mother, and to all accounts well provided for. She would turn up again when she saw fit. He had other things to worry about.

When he had been in Fisheries, he reflected, his family and their troubles had preoccupied him. Now he was in the Colonial Office and responsible for the fate of millions, he had less patience with their problems. Power was a mixed blessing. Great men were seldom sentimental men.

In the meanwhile Ponsonby was talking to him about protecting the Monarch. Now his Lordship had a minute or two to spare, due to the unexpected postponement of the meeting, perhaps his Lordship would have a word with Inspector Strachan. 'His Lordship' now came to Ponsonby's lips with ease, thought Robert. Perhaps his own slight raise of the eyebrows at the secretary's earlier familiarity had been noted. Ponsonby was an astute young man. When an instant or two later the Inspector came to the bar, it even occurred to Robert that the meeting with Lansdowne had been cancelled on Ponsonby's instructions simply to make possible this more important meeting.

The other drawback to becoming a man of power, reflected Robert, was that you saw conspiracies everywhere. He dismissed the suspicion as unworthy or at any rate irrelevant, and concentrated on what Strachan had to say; namely that the

Inspector would send a few of his men down a couple of weeks before the visit to stay in the village, frequent the pub, and report on any untoward activities. Strachan said he would like to come down himself in a day or so to make a further assessment of the doors, windows and locks.

'The place is in something of an uproar,' said Robert. 'Today's door is tomorrow's window and vice versa, but by all means come down and inspect. You have my permission, though, I must say, my good man, you do seem to be making a mountain out of a molehill. What can you be expecting on the soft chalk downs of Sussex? Anarchist gangs, crazed madmen, roaming socialists, white-slave traffickers?'

Strachan did not smile, but then policemen were well known for having no sense of humour. The Inspector was a new kind of man: neither a gentleman nor in trade, but a public servant, as so many these days seemed to be, from County Council officers to School Boards, laying down the law from everything as to where one might build one's house, educate one's children or the speed at which one might drive one's motor.

As such the Inspector was granted respect but not quite trust, and certainly not familiarity.

'We can be certain of nothing, my Lord,' he said. 'Today even the chalk downs are not safe from wastrels and destitute wanderers. They roam further and further afield. Your own farm labourers, I understand, have been conspiring to form a union of agricultural workers. There is unrest everywhere. One does not want the King to encounter any unpleasantness.'

'Indeed not,' said Robert. In the past Rosina had stirred up agitation amongst the estate workers, simply by asking them questions about their wages. They had compared notes and felt oppressed. The shift from gratitude to resentment could be swift and sudden. Some of his best beaters were beginning to ask for more money, on the grounds they could always apply for a job in Arthur's workshops, and all Arthur had to say when he remonstrated was: 'If they have the ability and talent, then they deserve what they get.'

And when he queried the number of pheasant eggs per nest this season as compared to last, Alan, now the head gamekeeper, had given him an average of seventeen – not last year's triumphant twenty – and blamed the frequent noisy blasts which accompanied the Jehu engines' test runs.

'When they hears it them birds takes to the air,' he said, 'instead of keeping their heads down and their eggs warm.'

Robert had said as much to his son, who responded by saying, well, Alan would say that, wouldn't he, being a countryman, hating all things mechanical and only too happy to excuse his own inefficiencies by blaming the Jehu. The test runs continued.

Even one's own children rose up against one, Robert lamented. Isobel was right. It would probably be wise if Rosina did not publish her book about savages, given her gift for stirring up trouble.

Strachan was warning the family against any mention of the King's visit to the press. 'Let a word slip, and they'll be down to set up their cameras. The yellow press is both ungovernable and unstoppable. I have even known them break into private rooms to prove their own distasteful theories. But we will take our precautions. I'll have a couple of my men stationed outside the King's door all night.'

'One of the servants can do that,' said his Lordship, and Ponsonby shuffled a little and coughed, and said, 'It might be wiser if the Inspector's men stood sentry.'

'I don't see why,' said his Lordship peevishly.

'So they know to whom it is wise to allow entry,' said Ponsonby.

'Mrs Keppel, you mean,' said Robert and Mr Ponsonby looked pained. Robert said he was sure her Ladyship would welcome Inspector Strachan's men at Dilberne Court sometime in the future.

Let them fight it out: he had other more serious matters to think about. To arm one native tribe against another seemed an obvious solution, and was often tried, except it usually ended badly.

Another Week, Another Sunday

Sunday 3rd September 1905, Dilberne

'Mother-in-law,' said Minnie. Isobel and she were walking home from church side by side. They went down the narrow back lane that led to Dilberne Court. Connor and Edgar followed with their nannies, Connor in his perambulator and Edgar sometimes in his stroller, sometimes walking. They made sluggish progress. Her father-in-law and Arthur, who had things to do, had gone ahead, rather than slow their pace to one determined by the existence of women and children. The hedgerows crowded in on them, a wild tangle of hawthorn, blackthorn, field maple, shiny hornbeam and holly, convolvulus entwining with pink dog rose flanked by purple-headed thistle and white cow-parsley, with the more solid elm, ash, beech and oak pushing up here and there – the English countryside was intolerably, almost painfully lovely and romantic but Minnie still found herself longing for the simplicity of the flat Illinois landscape.

'Mama,' she said. It had taken her weeks to find the courage and to get the words right. 'It had occurred to me that Arthur and me and the children could perfectly well move into the Dower House. We wouldn't be in the way of the builders, and they could get on with taking up the floors without having to worry about the servants carrying hot water for the nursery.'

'Arthur and I,' said Isobel, 'not Arthur and me. Nobody's worrying. Why are you worrying about the servants? The servants will go on carrying water from the kitchens, just as they have since the house was built.'

It was a hot day. Isobel was wearing a dress in grey and white shepherd's plaid voile trimmed with pink silk, a wide embroidered bertha and a little white wing collar: her hat had a modest brim, but such a mass of lacy foliage piled upon it, Minnie thought, that it quite echoed the tangle of hedgerows they walked between. She herself wore a serviceable lined tucked white shirt, a circular navy blue skirt in grosgrain and a straw boater, and was aware that Isobel must think her very plain. Poor little Edgar had been dressed in a tweed suit – a miniature of the one his grandfather wore to church when he had time enough from affairs of State to attend – with a wing collar and the black Oxford lace-ups which Nanny Margaret insisted he wore – 'His little feet need the support' – and were so stiff and uncomfortable that he preferred his stroller than to run around as he normally did. Surely nature knew best: children were not born with leather boots on their feet, but that was not a concept familiar to Nanny. 'Few people know how to take a walk. The qualifications are endurance, plain clothes, old shoes, an eye for nature, good humour, vast curiosity, good speech, good silence and nothing too much.' No use quoting Emerson to Nanny, or any of the Dilbernes, come to that.

'And the Dower House? But it's perfectly horrid,' said Isobel. 'You can't possibly live there. Tiny windows, tall rooms, the staircase is crumbling; it's dreadfully damp and swallows and bats are nesting in the attics. I went inside the other day and the architect, old George Bodley – I think I introduced you – was quite horrified.'

'So you'll be doing it up?' asked Minnie, hopefully.

'Oh no,' said Isobel. 'No one "does" dower houses "up". I suppose that's American usage. Doing dower houses up is unlucky.' And, as lately upon so many other subjects, she refused to be drawn. But of course, thought Minnie; dower is short for dowager. It's the house where a deposed lady of rank is sent to live when her husband dies and the inheritance passes on. To do it up would be to invite that day: Minnie was hardly in a position to bring the subject up again.

But it was a pretty house, though indeed dilapidated; quite small and cosy – only one or two degrees up from a farmhouse – a whole quarter of a mile away from Dilberne Court. The staircase could be mended, the windows enlarged, the damp got rid of, there was a barn at the back that could be used as a studio – oh, the old dreams of doing something other than wearing clothes and being polite – the swallows could be seen as company, and she would live happily ever after with Arthur, as mistress of her own domain, her children her own, not Nanny's. Dreams, dreams.

One day in the far, far distant future, if it hadn't been allowed to crumble away altogether, the Dower House, or one like it, would be her own destiny. Well, as had Rosina, she had made her bed and must lie on it. All women had to.

But Isobel was talking.

'Besides, Minnie, the children's proper place is in the family nursery, where their own father was brought up and their grandfather before that. And change is the last thing Arthur wants; do you really want to upset him just when he's so busy and the business is going so well? I am his mother; I do know what's going on in his head.'

No mention of Rosina. Rosina was seldom mentioned. No one knew what went on in Rosina's head, which was presumably the trouble. And Minnie herself had been outflanked so simply. Her request had been anticipated, she suspected, and her routes of escape barred.

When they got back to the Court, Edgar and Connor went up to Nanny for their flaked cod and white sauce lunch with mashed potatoes and a slice of decorative tomato, and with any luck for Edgar to change out of his church clothes into a sailor suit and different shoes. Nanny thought going barefoot would make his arches fall.

The Earl was there for lunch. He had fallen asleep in church, he said, and asked Minnie what the readings had been. Minnie – who had been so busy brooding she couldn't remember a thing – shook her head mutely, and Isobel quickly stepped in. 'John, six, twenty-four to thirty-five,' said Isobel, *'Jesus said unto them I am the bread of life. Whoever comes to me will never be hungry and whoever believes in me will never be thirsty.'*

'Which is why you allow us a proper luncheon after church, I daresay,' said his Lordship to his wife, 'instead of the frenchified lunches you're so keen on nowadays.'

'Praise the Lord,' said Arthur, 'as they say back home in Chicago, do they not, Minnie?'

Minnie smiled sweetly as ever, though she felt like crying. They were not unkind, but they would never allow her to be one of them, not even Arthur.

Lunch was *potage aux petits pois, filet de sole à la sauce aurore, chaud-froid de volaille, gigot d'agneau, gelée de fraises* and *bouchées d'abricots*. Arthur left for his workshops after the gigot, pecking Minnie goodbye and saying he was sorry he couldn't be there when the children were brought down for Sunday tea, but their grandmother would be, wouldn't she, and Isobel said, 'Of course.' His Lordship commented that the Dilberne table was exceptionally good these days, frenchified or not, so presumably Isobel must be very near to God. Isobel remarked that considering the manna that descended to the servants' hall on a daily basis it was certainly the case. His Lordship suggested that the Rev. Stacey read the staff Exodus sixteen, verses one to thirteen at Evensong and that thus reassured they stopped their grumbling. The servants should be grateful for what they got.

'Exodus chapter sixteen, verses one to thirteen,' Isobel explained to Minnie, 'is when the Israelites grumble against the Lord because they're hungry, and he promises them meat in the evening and all the bread they want in the morning, and they end up getting manna. They now think we're *in loco dei* and grumble because they don't get manna all the time.'

At least, his Lordship put in, Rosina hadn't been near them lately stirring up trouble with her questionnaires. Isobel made a *'Don't mention that name'* face and Minnie thought: 'If my life is hardly worth living now, with these two as my allies, what would it be like if I had them as enemies?'

His Lordship asked her what she had been doing with her life and Minnie said she had had a letter from her mother. Her mother had suggested she go home to Chicago for the Christmas month. Tessa missed her grandchildren.

'A letter from your mother!' cried Isobel. 'Why didn't you tell me? How is the dear old soul?'

'She is very well,' said Minnie, 'and very busy. She is setting up an international arts and crafts exhibition at the Institute.' 'Dear old soul' did not seem to Minnie to be an adequate description of her mother, who though she was buxom and lacked sophistication in both life and dress, was amazingly good-natured and energetic. She rather suspected, judging from an indiscreet word or two in the letter, that Tessa had taken up with a young arts and crafts jeweller whose work was central to the exhibition.

She also thought it better not to say that Tessa had mentioned Grace. 'Grace sends her regards to her Ladyship,' was what Tessa had actually written. 'She and I mean to start a little art gallery and fabric shop in North Avenue. Grace turns out to have quite a business mind.' Grace had been Lily's predecessor as lady's maid.

'It's not sensible to take the little ones to God's Own Country, Minnie, and you know it, especially not to Chicago in Winter. They'd freeze to death. It's remarkably cold and windy, I believe, isn't it, Robert? You were once there for the World Fair.'

'I was there in May,' said his Lordship, 'and it was pleasantly warm. Warm and windy enough,' he added, 'for the stench of the stockyards to get to us. But they do say it's jolly cold in Winter.'

'I could go on my own, leave the children. Mother isn't too well, she has a bad leg or she'd come over to me.' Lies, lies. What was she saying? She had been pushed back into childhood.

'Chicago for Christmas is out of the question, anyway,' said the Countess. 'Robert's youngest brother Alfred is coming over from Bombay to see his children and to be with the family. Did not Arthur tell you?'

'Oh, of course,' said Minnie. Arthur hadn't. 'How silly of me. My brain is all to pieces, these days.'

'It's motherhood,' said Isobel cheerfully. 'Besides, the King is coming just before Christmas for the shooting. You are wife to a Viscount. You need to be beside your husband at such a time.'

The Earl grunted. 'Meanwhile the gamekeeper's worrying about his chicks and my son's bloody motors. Nasty, noisy, smelly things. Can't understand why the boy doesn't stick to horses.'

'The King will understand,' said Isobel. 'He so loves his Daimler.'

'Yes, but will the chicks understand?' and Robert laughed heartily at his own joke and took some more strawberry ice cream.

That afternoon Minnie lay on her bed in the green room and cried a little, which in itself was consoling. She would have gone up to the nursery floor but the children were having their afternoon nap and Nanny would be guarding them like a dragon, breathing fire on anyone who came near. It was very hot and very quiet. She would have gone down to the servants' hall for some gossip and conversation – she was sure it was livelier than any she got upstairs – but that was not the way one behaved. So she cried, brooded and half slept instead.

The builders were no longer in the room above, but dust motes from their labours the day before drifted down through the sunbeams. She thought there was a presence in the room, almost tangible, someone lurking in the brightness of the corner, a woman in a pale dress. She did not want to get up to see properly; simply closed her eyes to save the effort. She remembered that the servants said the green room was haunted. Servants were always saying that kind of thing; it gave them a good excuse not to carry coals or fetch water. The presence was not frightening. There just seemed to be some kind of pause in the continuum of things.

But she was glad when there was a tap on the

door and Lily came in with a pile of under-things fresh up from the laundry. She was a sweet and friendly girl and a favourite with Isobel, being quite a skilled little dressmaker; Minnie thought she made a pretty figure today, her fair hair looped under her frilly cap, her figure lissom in its maid's black dress – perhaps rather too tight a one. If she was in charge of her own house, she would think twice before employing a girl so pretty, and what's more so quick and clever.

'Is this room supposed to be haunted?' asked Minnie.

'Oh yes, ma'am,' said Lily cheerfully. 'Some kitchen maid hanged herself in here in 1723, put in the family way by the fourth Earl. But don't you worry about it. I've never noticed a thing, and you and Lord Arthur will be back in the West Wing in no time. Besides, it's not likely. What would a kitchen maid be doing up here? Now if it was the parlourmaid–'

'I thought you had Sunday afternoons off,' said Minnie, breaking off the anecdote, though she longed for more. If you gave staff an inch they took an ell, as Arthur would explain.

'You have to get the laundry out of the way by Monday when everything starts again,' said Lily, 'time off or not. You sound just like Miss Rosina, always tut-tutting about conditions of work while finding extra stuff for us to do, like her parrot. You're different. In fact, you're quite a favourite in the servants' hall.'

'I don't think I need to know that, Lily,' said Minnie, carefully. This was certainly too familiar. On the other hand, times were desperate.

'I don't see why not, Miss,' said Lily, pertly. 'I always tell her Ladyship things. She likes to know what goes on. I'm her trusted spy. I'm good friends with Mrs Keppel's lady's maid.'

'Tell me about Lady Rosina then,' said Minnie.

'What do you want to know?'

'Where is she? Has she gone back to Australia?'

'No, Miss. She's staying with friends of the family at No. 3 Fleet Street and publishing a rude book. Lady Isobel's brought in the lawyers to try and stop her. That's why everyone's acting so peculiar.' She hesitated. 'She gives me all her cast-offs.'

'Someone gave me three pairs of silk stockings which proved far too small for me,' said Minnie. 'Great big, galumphing American girl that I am. They're French with cherub lace inserts. Would they be of any use to you, Lily?'

'Thank you very much, m'Lady. They certainly would.'

'You can find them at the bottom of one of my stocking drawers.'

They were still neatly folded in tissue paper and a delicate oyster colour. Lily stroked the smooth, pale silk fondly. Minnie watched them go with some sorrow. They fitted well enough and she had looked forward to wearing them. But as Sir Francis Bacon said, knowledge was power, and she was sadly in lack of power and must do what she could to rectify the shortcoming. And perhaps God had taken notice and sent her Lily.

'What goes on at No. 3 Fleet Street?' asked Minnie.

'I couldn't say, m'Lady, though there was some talk about drink and drugs and goings-on. But that's probably just wishful thinking. Everyone loves a scandal. Same as they likes a ghost. What else is there to think about, stuck away at the ends of the Earth? What does galumphing mean?'

'Half-way between a horse galloping and a horse snorting, I guess.'

'If I may say, m'Lady, I think you're very elegant and gracious and not at all the galumphing kind. That's more Lady Rosina's style. She's a great disappointment to her Ladyship. Thank you for the stockings. They do say a Mr Anthony Robin and his sister Diana live at No. 3. He's in the book world, so I daresay our Miss Rosina has gone to live with them. Good riddance to a bad lot is what all the servants say, and thank God we don't have the parrot pooing to put up with any more.'

'That will be all, Lily,' said Minnie. But she had what she wanted.

Arthur Invites Temptation

September 1905, The Gatehouse

The gatehouse had been designed by James Wyatt in 1797 for a previous Earl. It was a vast and imposing – if rather less than graceful – stone arch which bridged the entrance to the long oak drive that led to Dilberne Court, substantial enough to serve as home to the gatekeeper but not much more. There was a door on the inner side of both piers leading to a windowed room, and a staircase up to a long room within the arch itself, long enough for a coach and four and a couple of out-riders to pass underneath. Old Tommy's duties had been to answer the bell and open and close the iron gates that linked the piers, deter unwelcome strangers, report unwanted predators, and keep the drives swept and the high beech hedges in good order.

During one of her sporadic attempts to persuade Arthur to live apart from his parents, Minnie had been down with him to inspect the Gatehouse. Arthur could see no need for change. The West Wing was very comfortable and convenient for his work: the children were happy and settled. His mother's enthusiasm for what her designer referred to as 'refurbishment' could not go on for ever – presumably when the royal shooting weekend had come and gone and Mrs Keppel been suitably impressed the hammerings and crashings and falling plaster would be a thing of the past. Minnie, Arthur concluded, was just a little homesick and suffering from one of the fits of restlessness which afflicted women every few weeks: what she really wanted, his father assured him, was another baby. He must see to it. Indeed, he meant to see to it, he just fell asleep so easily.

Fortunately, even Minnie had realized upon inspection that the Gatehouse was scarcely suitable for any family, certainly not for one with servants.

He knew what Minnie was up to – his mother had told him she had been asking about the Dower House. But she would soon forget and settle down when she had another baby.

'A gatehouse is such a peculiar building,' she'd said. 'An arch with rooms which does nothing but tell you how grand and important it is. This country is so full of the *unnecessary*.'

He did not like it when Minnie separated herself out from him by talking about 'this country' but he overlooked it. He loved her.

'It would be very useful to me as an office,' he'd said, and indeed, he realized, it would: just a few hundred yards from the workshops – now a cluster of six – at Isobel's insistence hidden from the drive by a curtain of trees.

He would at last have somewhere to put all the papers and blueprints, which as it was, flew about the oily floors and got neglected at best, and rendered unreadable at worst: an office where he could receive business associates properly dressed and with washed hands, where the telephone would be on the desk and not lost beneath a pile of metal on the floor. He would have a properly trained secretary to separate orders from invoices, probably even a female one. Plain, of course; he was a married man and a father and loved his wife, and had a business to run, and no time to waste for the emotional involvements which so preoccupied his friends, even the married ones, let alone energy for the sexual indulgences which made fools of them all.

'I thought perhaps you could have an office in London,' said Isobel. 'Surely you could run the business from there?'
'London is a place for gentlemen, not business men,' he said. 'And anyway it is too distracting.'

He meant it, too. He remembered Flora, the girl he had kept in Mayfair before he turned sensible and married Minnie, and what a fool Flora had managed to make of him. Sex was like a good meal, something you wanted most when you couldn't have it. But now he had Minnie. All the same he could see propinquity could be dangerous; female secretaries could be risky, they were said to be quick, adaptable and competent, but also had the reputation of making themselves most agreeable at first, but then turning out to be predatory blackmailers. Like Flora, of the ample bosom, pretty eyes, and soft, silky, entwining limbs.

Well, once bitten, twice shy. He would hire a Sussex girl, respectable and plain, even a married one, caught in the gap between marriage and motherhood. To have female staff was the mark of a forward-looking, modern, effective business, not afraid of risk taking.

Things moved fast after the decision had been made. Tommy was moved out, in spite of his grumblings about age, infirmity and so forth, to live with his nephew in one of the estate cottages, where he would doubtless be more comfortable. Traffic was now so heavy in and out of the Court it was tiresome to have to keep opening and shutting gates. Horses had quite liked stopping for a rest, but the motor traffic of today preferred to just carry on through.

Isobel had builders moved from the big house, and the Gatehouse was plumbed and wired in no time, the ground-floor room on the right pier was set up as a reception area, the one on the left pier as a little private room for Arthur. It was eccentric but it worked. The long upper room at the top was the office, complete with office desks and neat loudspeakers for quick communication between rooms, filing cabinets, two Hermes typewriters – the secretary might need an assistant – and high-backed office chairs.

Minnie was happy enough to help Arthur buy furniture for the reception and office areas. Indeed, they'd had a very happy outing to Liberty's, to buy some small, light, elegant pieces – William Morris, especially designed for small-scale living – and Minnie had chosen a carved Mackmurdo panel in pale elm to nail up over the office door – tree trunks and a recumbent female figure with a breast exposed; which he himself would not have dared put up, but he could see its charms. Minnie was no prude. But when over dinner with the family a couple of days later he asked Minnie to buy a bed for his private room, she burst into tears.

'But what's the matter?' he asked, taken aback.

'I know men,' she wailed, and ran from the room so the Earl and Countess raised their eyebrows.

Arthur was horrified by 'scenes'. He felt rather insulted. He trusted Minnie, surely she trusted him. It was a pity, he sometimes thought, he had married a girl with a past, who did indeed 'know men'.

He asked his mother later what the matter with Minnie was, and she said,

'She's American and sometimes it shows. She's homesick and broods rather a lot. Don't worry about it. I've found a dear little shop in Brighton – it's called Brewers – where I'm getting my wallpaper and paints and they have a little range of bamboo beds – I'll bring one back.'

'Bamboo? Is that strong enough?' he asked without thinking.

'What for?' she asked, and looked perplexed, and then quickly moved on, and a few days later the little bamboo bed was delivered. It was not so little and perfectly steady, and exactly fitted the alcove, but Minnie refused to admire it; and after that seldom walked up to see him at his office, or even his workshops, which he thought showed a lack of proper feeling – had he not delivered his own son with his own hands while finishing the prototype of a new Jehu? Did he not deserve a trusting wife?

He asked her one night as she got into bed if she would like to go home with the children to visit her mother in Chicago, but she just looked more hurt than ever and didn't even reply yes or no, just turned over and went to sleep. He concluded that women were simply an utter mystery and gave up all hope of trying to understand them. One simply lived with them.

Self-Inspection

30th September 1905, No. 3 Fleet Street

Anthony Robin looked into his mirror as he shaved and considered why he enjoyed the company of William Brown so much and why his sister Diana so enjoyed Rosina's. Perhaps something was 'wrong' with them both.

He had understood and come to terms with his own Uranian tendencies a year or so back. He had spent his twenties trying to prove his normality, both to himself and to the outside world, frequenting prostitutes, setting up mistresses. He'd given that up in his thirties, and, having no wish to go to prison, tried to live, at least in public, the life of a prudent single man about town, a bachelor with literary leanings. Perhaps Diana was his female equivalent? He had not heard that such a thing was possible, but he could see that it could well be. Why not? She and Rosina had persuaded him to go with them to the Royal Academy to see the latest John William Godward painting, *In the Days of Sappho*.

Sappho, sitting on a marble bench, every glint and fold of her chiton beautifully and carefully painted, had stared with cow-like eyes from out of an unadventurous classical background. He had not thought much of the painting, but had noticed how the two girls held hands as they had studied their heroine in apparent rapture. Girls were forever touching one another, as men were not, but it had seemed that Diana and Rosina, in taking him here, were trying to tell him something significant. Women were meant to have babies, not sexual pleasure, which was for the men; the fact that on occasion desire slipped over and happened between men and men was hardly surprising, though seeming horrific to ordinary men and women. It was not prudent to keep the company of one's own kind, and he had avoided associating with the greenery-yallery crowd as much as possible.

He was glad to have Rosina in residence, she was fun, and he could go round with her to Longman's and meet William and discuss the progress of the *The Sexual Manners and Traditions of Australian Aboriginals* – and no one find anything strange about it.

He admired the sharp unfleshy firmness of his chin as he stooped his head to splash the foaming cream away.

Earlier that morning his sister Diana had stared into the same mirror as she brushed her long hair the required one hundred times and wondered if she were right to do so. The one hundred times rule was meant to make your hair glossy and thick but so far as she could see it merely made it greasy, so that the once a month washing recommended in the interest of optimum hair health wasn't sufficiently frequent. And no combing it out until the hair was almost dry turned the combing into an act of attrition. Even though they now had a bathroom with hot running water at No. 3, a bath and a shower head, and liquid Palmolive soap to help with hair washing, doing so was still an ordeal. Even when all was done there'd still be a layer of white dried soap left on every tooth of the comb after use. She really resented having to pay her appearance so much attention. Anthony refused to let her bob her hair; it was, he said, in *The Modern Idler's* interests that she looked pretty, sweet and biddable, in other words normal, when writers came through the door. He had not minded when she had taken the scissors to Rosina's roughly cropped hair and tidied it up, taking the locks in one hand and simply cutting through at ear length.

'Cut away,' he'd said. 'Talent and eccentricity go together. They are encouraged in visiting writers but not in the editorial team.'

Being seen as part of the editorial team was flattering, even though it meant more washing coffee cups and clearing grates and making up spare beds than Diana had anticipated. Mrs O'Hennessy the charlady came in every morning, but she was as likely to smear every surface as clean it, so slimy were the cloths she used, and she breathed alcohol fumes over everyone when she came near. Anthony would not get out of bed before she had been and gone, for fear of running into her, but life at *The Modern Idler* seldom began before noon, so she supposed there was no cause for concern. Anthony still refused to let her write a piece on

Doric aspects in the excavated Roman buildings of Ancient Britain unless she (a) turned it into a ghost story, or (b) got married – or at least pretended to – so as to be taken seriously. But Diana was proud and would not. He would weaken in time, she thought. Now Rosina was staying everything seemed worth while.

Rosina had been welcome at No. 3 from the beginning. She paid a whole pound a week for her keep. Her bobbed hair, still bleached from the sun, now curved into her chin in a most fetching way. Her skin, in the comparative cool of the English climate, began to look less leathery and her face to soften: she began to look more, well – English, than the intrepid traveller who had stepped off the *Ortona*. Even her voice had become less strident. Anthony was happy enough to have Rosina as a guest: she would join Anthony and his friends as they sat late into the night drinking absinthe or on occasion smoking opium or nibbling slices of fresh fruit soaked in ether – no one ever seemed to settle as to exactly what substance best proved their bohemianism and talent. You could buy it all from Boots the Chemist across the road from the Law Courts in Fleet Street. Pappagallo entertained everyone with his 'Too right, mate, too right' interventions, and with the way his eyes would roll wildly if he smelt hashish.

Diana would excuse herself when the group grew somnolent, foolish or over-excited – she did not enjoy the changes of mental state that Anthony so craved – and would go up early to bed. Someone had to be around to keep sensible and clean up, and since it was generally assumed it was in her nature she had better accept it and just get on with it. She had been born boring, she supposed, a Martha to Rosina's Mary.

Rosina could be annoying, Diana conceded. Pappagallo had developed an infestation of mites, which kept the bird scratching and scattering feathers. Diana had wanted to use a solution of fly agaric from the Fleet Street chemist to treat it, but Rosina had become almost hysterical, saying Diana was trying to murder the bird with a deadly poison, and then had powdered him with arsenic instead, which Diana felt was far more dangerous. They had had their one and only major quarrel and had kissed and made up. After that Rosina would sometimes slip into Diana's bed when Diana had fallen asleep and embrace her and they would comfort one another – Rosina's wretched widowhood, Diana's orphaned state – and all was warm, soft and wordless. When sleep began to overtake them Rosina would slip back into her own bed in the spare room, and be there when Mrs O'Hennessy let herself in in the morning.

Rosina made no mention by day of these nocturnal activities and Diana did not like to bring the matter up. She thought perhaps she was in love with Rosina. Why else did she allow herself to behave in this peculiar way? Because, she decided, loving a man seemed impossible; they were so bristly and angular, all elbows and knees – while loving a woman seemed pure, gentle and sacred. Rosina had given her, wordlessly, a copy of Bliss Carman's translation of Sappho's poetry and then taken her and Anthony to the Royal Academy to see John William Godward's Sappho painting. Neither seemed particularly good as works of art, but Diana had taken the theme of the poems and the way Rosina had held hands with her at the Academy as amounting to a declaration of love. Women could love women, it seemed, in the same way women and men loved – not that she had ever been very clear as to exactly what that was either. Certainly she, Diana, would be dreadfully upset if Rosina decided to go back to Australia when the book was published. To miss her and their nights together would be unbearable. She supposed that amounted to love.

Rosina and Anthony, she knew, had long meetings with William Brown at Longman, discussing whether the book would come out under her own name or a pseudonym. Rosina was reluctant to publish under her own name for fear of unsettling her family. Robin guffawed at this and said that the Dilbernes getting unsettled might be the best thing that could happen to them. The days of the bloated aristocracy were coming to an end. There had been another clutch of articles in the press on her ridiculous brother and his Jehu motor car. Herbert Austin, a man of the people, was the one to watch when it came to automobile production.

'But Anthony,' Rosina had objected, 'you are as much a member of the bloated aristocracy as anyone. Like my poor brother Arthur, who is not very intellectual, it is true, but nevertheless a good

business man, you also are the son of an Earl.'
'But only a second son,' said Anthony. 'That makes all the difference. To be a penniless second son is to be cast back into the working classes.'

Rosina wanted Longman to publish under Anthony's name, but he refused and wanted her to serialize *Manners and Traditions* in instalments in *The Modern Idler*. William Brown would rather he didn't, so as not to steal thunder from Longman's publication. Book publishing was clearly not just a matter of getting a book into print, but of endless conversations. And Anthony vied with William as to who could dress most fashionably, and all the extra money Rosina brought in was soon gone.

Affairs of State and Matters of the Heart

30th September 1905, Belgrave Square

In Belgrave Square the Earl of Dilberne looked into his mirror and deplored the increasing greyness of his beard. He was annoyed in general. He had a meeting at the House at eleven, and then was free until five in the evening when Mr Balfour the P.M. 'wanted a word' about Curzon. It was an irritating gap in time, and not a 'word' Robert looked forward to. George Curzon – pushed rather than jumped – had resigned as Viceroy of India after endless and mostly pointless disagreements with Balfour. He had let it be known that he expected at least a further title for his pains. An earldom would suit him very well.

While Viceroy of India, George Curzon and his heiress wife Mary Leiter had enjoyed the greatest pomp and circumstance, while – as Mr Balfour was at pains to point out – 'millions of Indians starved to death and vast sums were spent restoring the Taj Mahal.' Curzon had caused the Foreign and Colonial endless trouble back home, forever nagging about the state of the Indian Army, interfering with accepted policies on Tibet, Afghanistan, Russia – insisting against all advice that the popular but quarrelsome Kitchener be put in charge of the Indian Army, and then doing his best to get rid of him. Balfour, irritated beyond endurance, had no intention at all of granting Curzon another title. Now if Balfour 'wanted a word' it would bc so that Robert could tell him that he was doing the right thing.

'Forgive my indulgence in using you as a sounding board, Robert,' Balfour had once explained. 'But you are a good man to have around me. I know you are not fat but you sleep sound a' nights, as Shakespeare recommended; and you are lucky, as Napoleon preferred his generals to be. If I am short of any quality it is the common touch. You have an instinct for the way a man should jump.'

'Sound away,' Robert had rashly replied. 'See me as the man on the Clapham omnibus.' But lately he had found his days much interrupted by Balfour's insecurities, as the Unionist government tottered towards collapse.

It seemed to Robert that Balfour was wrong about Lord Curzon. Balfour did rather tend to lack the milk of human kindness. The two great men had once been friends – now each was motivated by a personal animosity that Robert could see would do neither any good. Balfour regarded Curzon as a vain and self-serving simpleton; Curzon saw Balfour as a cold man of intellect who believed more in ghosts than in God and empire, and was unmoved by passion for anything at all. Both were partly right, partly wrong about the other and nothing could be gained by Balfour's act of meanness; this would be perceived by the public and press as a cruelty to poor Curzon, whose wife was ill and whose back was bad, and who was an honest man though lavish in his habits. The Indians themselves, not just Curzon, would be humiliated. But Balfour would be hard to persuade, and seldom, Robert was well aware, was anything gained by speaking truth to power. Besides, Balfour had a way of letting his cool contempt for anyone who disagreed with him shine through his courtesy. One way and another Robert did not look forward to the meeting.

This morning Robert found his normal fund of cheerful good sense depleted. He would have gone to inspect the new racecourse at Newbury but this new five o'clock meeting put paid to that. He needed Isobel. He did not like waking up alone. He liked to spring from the bed restored not just by sleep but by Isobel beside him as a perpetual reminder of what a lucky man he was. Had he not found her, this jewel amongst women, plucked her out of a *vie de bohème,* and been right? True, he had expected money to come with her from her natural father, the coal magnate Silas. It had not and he had not cared.

His Lordship looked into his mirror, and saw that he was growing old. And where was Isobel to assure him he was not? Down at Dilberne Court again, of course, and still thoroughly put out by the prospect of the royal shooting weekend, which once she would have taken in her stride, Mrs Keppel and all. A dreadful respectability seemed to be taking over the nation. It had been expected that with the Old Queen's death there would be a return to brighter, less censorious days. But no. Mrs Keppel, who once would have quite openly spent a private weekend with the King, must now dissimulate and bring her husband with her. It was too bad. And Isobel was down at the Court again, with her hovering Detective Inspector and her hordes of greenery-yallery young men, absurdly anxious that Alice Keppel should admire her taste.

'Greenery-yallery, Grosvenor Gallery, Foot in the grave, young man...' They had been to the first night of Gilbert and Sullivan's *Patience:* it must have been twenty-odd years ago; he remembered the children as being small. That was before his political career had taken off, when there had been time to spare, when the gay green and yellow shades of the Grosvenor Gallery aesthetes were viewed askance: all those lovers of Wilde and Beardsley and their like. Now it seemed they all

found sanctuary with Isobel. And Robert's younger brother Alfred was coming over from India for Christmas. Alfred was a man of tradition, a Brigadier in the Indian Army, a stickler for the proprieties even when a child. What would he make of it? His family had been against Isobel from the beginning – 'Fine stock, but all the same, the wrong side of the blanket, all that.' He could not bear Alfred to have been proved right. Though of the four brothers, only two were left.

Now Robert's valet Digby, young but morose, was putting out a suit in an apparently normal dark grey wool worsted. The cut, though, looked strange to the Earl; the legs bulged wide at the knees, and again at the cuffs. The jacket was more like that of a lounge suit cut away at the hips than conventional morning wear.

'They're called sponge-bag trousers, my Lord,' said Digby. 'They're all the thing.'

'Hardly for Ministers of the Crown,' said Robert. 'Take it away.'

'It is the modern style, sir,' Digby said. 'Her Ladyship had it especially tailored for you. She says it will be more in keeping with a new government. Young and forward looking.'

'Does she indeed,' said Robert. 'A new government? Then she knows more than I do. She can hardly be referring to Campbell-Bannerman. He's as old as the hills and never to be wrested from his drainpipes. Find me something less noticeable, Digby. It's not as if I were off to a golf course.'

'A pity, sir. Perhaps you could do with more relaxation. You work long hours.'

Robert looked at Digby sharply. The new race of servants made their presence felt. Valets were usually old and deferential. They shuffled around, foreseeing one's actions, attending to this and that. This young one, he remembered, had been passed on when old Ashenwold died. He had remarked to Isobel that his new valet looked rather young and Isobel had said he was quick, alert and careful and came well recommended. He had started out in Barnardo's orphanage – like Grace, who had been the best lady's maid she had ever had – become a telegraph boy, and then gone into service with Lord Ashenwold. Robert said no doubt that was interesting, but hardly relevant: servants needed to know one's own life by heart, he supposed, but why would one want to know theirs?

'My dear,' Isobel had said, 'there is such a thing as the servant problem. The bright and ambitious ones learn to type and get jobs in the offices; we are left with the slow and surly. Times change and it affects us all.' And she had quoted what young Churchill had said recently in the House, that 'there was a danger of some tremendous explosion of popular feeling, the result of passions long suppressed and pent up, and which when it came, not infrequently created evils almost as many as it cured.'

Robert had laughed and been obliged to point out to her that Mr Churchill was talking about the dangers of delaying the coming election, rather than domestic matters, and since servants did not get the vote her concern was misplaced. She had seemed to grow quite cross and walked out of the room: really he did not know what the matter was with her, these days. She was more like Rosina than had been apparent in her younger years; she'd developed some disregard for the normal procedure of things; a discontent with the way things happened to be. She might as well be a radical. She had banned Rosina from the house without consulting him, and so Rosina had vanished into the blue. It rankled.

Now he turned to the young man to whom Isobel attributed a soul and a life of his own, and attempted to involve him in easy conversation.

'I do indeed work hard,' he said, 'and, as Mr Churchill pointed out, it gets worse and worse, as this fag end of a parliament lingers on. Seven years is too long, Ministers get tired and muddled. There is a growth, an accumulation of bitterness and personal feud. Five years is more than long enough.'

'Oh indeed, sir,' said Digby, 'as the wonderful Oscar Wilde said, "cultivated leisure is the aim of man". Perhaps you could take up golf, like Mr Balfour. He believes it clears his head for decision.'

His Lordship could see that one was not wise to engage too closely with a Wilde-quoting valet, no matter what one's wife advised, and regretted he had spoken. One did not want to have to think while dressing. His Lordship contented himself with saying that no amount of fresh air and wind had managed to reconcile Mr Balfour with Lord Curzon, and the four short hours between meetings scarcely gave him time for a round, and thought that would be the end of that. But no.

'As it happens,' said Digby, 'my last gentleman

used to attend The Cardinal's Hat, a very pleasant and civilized retreat in Westminster, especially established to meet the needs of politicians.'

'Ashenwold? I don't believe it. Eighty-five if he was a day. I went to his funeral,' said his Lordship, so startled he spoke without reservation.

'Nevertheless, sir,' said Digby calmly. 'My Lord enjoyed the company of young boys, of course. Would you prefer the striped socks with garters, or the to-the-knee straight grey?'

'Straight grey,' said his Lordship.

'Of course the establishment also has many discreet and even fashionable young ladies on its staff. Some are very lovely indeed. The place was very popular with the Robin boys. Robin as in the Ashenwold family name, sir.'

'I know that,' said his Lordship shortly. It was outrageous. Digby had to be got rid of, and at once. Where was Isobel, to see to it? He was not yet in his suit and had yet to decide on his hat. He could not say, 'That will be all, Digby.'

'Just bring the normal pinstripe, Digby,' he said. 'I will spend the afternoon in the Lords' Library.'

The dressing continued to its end without conversation, and Digby did not presume further. And that was the end of the episode, except Digby left an embossed card on the dressing table: an address, *'The Cardinal's Hat'*, and underneath, *'Gentleman's leisure, Gentleman's pleasure. Utmost confidence, utmost discretion.'*

There could be little doubt about what the establishment was offering. Robert could see it might be wiser just to overlook the conversation altogether. It had been his own fault in starting it in the first place. Churchill was right, in this as in so many things; when you remove the blocks of oppression you must allow for a sudden uprising of anarchic fervour. He memorized the address – he knew where it was, above a very respectable gentleman's outfitters – before tearing the card to shreds and dropping it into the wastepaper basket. He left a five-pound note in its place. It seemed prudent. If one did not deserve respect, at least one had the money to pay for it. The meeting with Balfour would be tense. He needed to relax. What Isobel did not know her heart could not grieve over.

Through a Glass, Darkly

30th September 1905, Dilberne Court

Arthur too looked in their mirror that morning and gave what he saw rather half-hearted attention. He was preoccupied with the possibility of developing a battery-powered car in parallel with the petrol-driven Jehu Thunderer. He would advertise the range as: *Jehu Electric – For the Clean City,* the better to remind customers of the great advantage of the motor vehicle over horse drawn – horse dung mixed with rain turned to a filthy mud all Winter and to dust in Summer, to be spread unhealthily all the year round by the hordes of sparrows that now plagued the city streets. All responsible citizens, in Arthur's view, should abandon the horse and choose the engine – he had said as much in various interviews in the press.

Electric cars were no fun to drive or tinker with, but they were clean and quiet and useful for short journeys in town. Arthur envisaged the creation of a whole network of 'garages' in every city in the land, with forecourts extensive enough for the flocks of electric cars which would be parked in their cubby-holes overnight while serviced and charged ready for the next day. This business would be as valuable to their owners as providing petrol and oil. Why not? Perhaps he would write to Bertha Benz in Mannheim to see what she thought of the idea – she was a lively and influential woman in the auto trade, though he had heard she was over fifty. It would be wonderful to share his enthusiasms with someone. He could see in the mirror that Minnie was still asleep. Even if she was awake she would not be interested in the future of the electric car; she would be bored. He had thought when he married that all a man needed was love but he had been wrong. A man needed conversation too. He went downstairs to have a cup of coffee, then walked briskly down the drive to his workshops. There was an autumnal chill in the air. And so much to be done there was no need not to be cheerful.

Minnie heard the door close. She had woken earlier and pretended to be asleep while her husband dressed – or not exactly dressed – rather pulled on garments he grabbed at random to cover his nakedness, too impatient to wait for his valet. It seemed simplest to feign sleep. The fact of the matter was that she did not know what to say to him any more. She had disappointed him in some great way. She tried to be like an engine which ran smoothly but she wasn't. Her gears kept slipping. She made suspicious untoward noises, which maddened him because there was so little he could do about them: yet he listened out for them. The mysteries of human fine-tuning were beyond him; there was no proper system of calibration. In other words, he was a man and she was a woman. She missed Rosina: she could have discussed with her the notion of woman as a failed engine. But Rosina had gone to live in a better place, amongst her own kind.

She got out of bed instead of waiting for the maid to bring her a cup of tea, and found her silk wrap herself. She poked up the fire and sat by it for a little and found herself singing aloud, but softly:

Oh what care I for my goosefeather bed,
With the sheet turned down so bravely-oh,
Oh what care I for my new wedded lord,
I'm off with the raggle-taggle gypsies-oh!

Her mother had sung her that song. Who were the raggle-taggle gypsies-oh? The Robins in Fleet Street? Hardly. It was wicked to even think it.

It was late last night when my Lord came home,
Inquiring for his lady-O,

The servants said on every hand,
She's gone with the raggle-taggle gypsies-oh!

Oh what cares she for her house and her land?
What cares she for her money-oh?
What cares she for her new wedded Lord?
She's gone with the raggle-taggle gypsies-oh!

Oh, wicked indeed! The trouble was, these days she had to take her children with her. When she'd left Stanton she'd had none.

Minnie went to the mirror and studied her face to see if she could find signs of wickedness and corruption there, but she could not. It was still the innocent, cheerful face her husband had once loved with the corners of the mouth turning upwards as though it was more accustomed to smiling than to grief; still youthful, with its future before it: little white even teeth, bright eyes, bouncy hair. How gradually faces changed, she thought. Her own seemed the same as always, yet had turned from child to girl to grown-up woman.

'Oh m'Lady, you're up,' said Lily, startling Minnie as she set the silver tray on the dressing table. It was a surprise to see Lily, who usually attended to Isobel in the mornings, her Ladyship being once again in residence. 'Her Ladyship wants to sleep in late today and says she can do without me so I thought I'd come and see how you were getting along, and thank you once again for the stockings. What shall I put out for you today? There's quite a chill in the air. No more muslin sleeves, I fear, until next Spring. I was thinking of the blue and white spotted *moiré* for this morning. It's simple and easy and suits you so well.' Left to her own devices, she, Minnie, would choose the easiest and most serviceable costume around but it was pleasant to be relieved even of that responsibility. Lily always seemed to get it right.

'I daresay,' said Minnie. 'But if there's no one to notice it hardly matters.' She must be careful. Bitterness slipped out so easily.

'Oh m'Lady,' said Lily, 'you can't say that – there's three of her Ladyship's young designers coming in today to inspect progress – and the Inspector is back again. Mind you–' Lily stopped herself from finishing the sentence.

'Mind you,' Minnie could not resist finishing for her, 'the young men seem to have eyes only for one another.' Lily chortled.

'That will be all, Lily,' said Minnie. It was tempting to become over-familiar with Lily but it was not wise. 'I shan't go down to breakfast. Ask Nanny to bring the children up to my room. We will breakfast together.'

'Oh m'Lady,' said Lily, 'Nanny won't like that at all. They need their routine.'

'They need their mother,' said Minnie shortly. 'Tell Nanny to bring them up here and leave them.' Enough was enough.

Minnie went back to bed while she waited for the children. She reflected on the extraordinary weight of marriage, how it lay upon the senses like a dead thing, squashing the life out of you, immovable, there for ever. Once you were married your life changed completely. Your life became his life.

His friends' wives became your friends. His family became yours. Only death could part you. It was a monstrous decision to take, and taken when young. A wedding dress, a wedding ring dangled in front of you to lure you into what amounted to slavery. Women could get divorced, of course, but in this country only if their husbands were extremely cruel and violent as well as unfaithful and Arthur was not just faithful, but a good, kind, considerate man. His only cruelty was not to love her as she wanted to be loved. She should not be thinking like this.

The trouble was, she was. If she were unfaithful Arthur could divorce her and find someone more to his liking, someone more like a well-greased engine. It would have to be done through the English Crown Court and with a great deal of publicity, and there was no way she would keep the children. Husband and children, in the eyes of English law, went together. At home in Illinois if you divorced you could keep the children. Chicago might be windy and ripe with the smell of the stockyards but it was good to its children. Julia Lathrop, the great reformer, was a friend of her mother's and believed that the child's inalienable right was to the mother's, not the father's, care. Motherhood, Julia argued, was the most important calling in the world.

Forget nannies, forget her future as a Countess and mistress of Dilberne, forget the threat of Eton for her sons – those icy corridors, the harsh treatment which made men of boys – the kind of men who ran the world but who thought women were engines designed for procreation – just get the children back to Chicago. Forget Dilberne Court and its renovation, forget the chance to meet the King; just run away. She had run away from Stanton Turlock. That had worked.

There was only one real problem. She loved Arthur and did not want to leave him. He deserved to be left, but that was another matter. If he walked into the room and got into bed with her she would throw her arms around him and be the happiest woman in the world. Really, marriage was a terrible burden.

Edgar came running into the room and held out his feet for his mother to take his heavy shoes off. She did so. Connor tottered in on the nursemaid's arm. He was on his feet at last. There would be something to tell Arthur.

'Nanny says don't over-excite Master Connor. Nanny says his tummy's upset.'

'Thank you, Molly,' said Minnie. 'Or Maureen, as the case might be.'

'Molly,' said the girl, who looked rather spotty, heavy and plain, though perfectly amiable. Isobel had hired her without consulting Minnie. All the Dilberne nannies for centuries had been called Margaret and the nursemaids Molly or Maureen.

'The name goes with the job,' Isobel had explained to Minnie, when Minnie had said she'd prefer to call the nursery staff by their real names.

'But why?' asked Isobel.

'For fear of reprisals,' Minnie had replied, half

joking. Isobel had just looked baffled. Four years on, and the nursery staff were still Margaret, Molly and Maureen, and Minnie had little appetite for jokes.

'Why is his tummy upset?' Minnie now inquired of Molly.

'Yesterday he stole green apples from the tree. The wind got up in the night and one of the apple tree branches came down, it was that heavy with fruit.'

'Little boys of one and a half don't steal, Molly. They may take apples but they don't steal them.'

'That's what I said,' said Molly, 'but Nanny said he has to learn. It's a sin to take what isn't yours. She said she'd give Master Connor a good smacking only you might get to hear about it. So she put him in the corner for an hour and prayed for his wee soul instead. What a carry-on! I checked the pips and they were black, only thc skin was green, so what a kerfuffle about nothing.'

'What's your real name, Molly?' asked Minnie as she took Connor's little hand in hers. He looked like his Irish grandfather, wide face and blunt nose and bright-blue smiling eyes, bashing and rushing and stamping. He fell on his nose and laughed and got up. He enjoyed life. Edgar looked like his father the Viscount and his grandfather the Earl before him; the long patrician nose, the close-set eyes. Edgar seldom fell on his nose. The material world seemed to arrange itself around him. They might just possibly let Connor go; but never Edgar. He was one of them.

'I started out as Irene,' said the girl. 'My mother had ideas for me.'

'That will be all, Irene,' said Minnie. 'You may go.'

'Oh no,' said Irene. 'Molly will do. It's what I'm used to.' She went away and Minnie was left to roll about on the floor with her children.

Minnie thought that when the time came to run away she would take Molly with her. She seemed a calm, sensible and kind girl; Cook's food would give anyone spots.

Goings-on

30th September 1905, The Gatehouse

By the end of September Arthur still had no secretary, though the office was just about up and running. Lily had been making herself useful ferrying calendars, notebooks, orders, receipts and so forth from the workshops to the Gatehouse and sorting blueprints into the satinwood map chest Minnie had helped buy. Lily was neat, competent and literate and he thought she might possibly make a good secretary, but his mother said no, that was impossible; she was too good as a lady's maid. Besides, his mother said, Lily was needed up in London from time to time. She was a friend of Mrs Keppel's maid Agnes; the pair met on their days off in St James's Park and Lily was very good at eliciting all kinds of facts about the Keppel household in Portman Square.

'But Mother,' said Arthur, alarmed, 'you really can't get the servants to do your spying.'

'I don't see why not,' said Isobel, 'I need to know whether the odalisque's bathrooms are tiled or lined. How else can I find out? Tiling is practical but wall-papering is considered smart.'

'I am sure Pater would find it all very silly,' said Arthur.

'Perhaps your father should not have asked the King down in the first place,' said Isobel, in her gentlest, sweetest voice.

She had brought Inspector Strachan with her this particular morning. They had walked together up from the Court to look at Arthur's security arrangements. The King's visit to Dilberne was private and would be kept out of the newspapers: assassination attempts were highly unlikely: but the nation's borders were porous and maniacs and foreigners were cunning. The Court itself would be made secure enough: an empty gatehouse would be all too convenient as a base for evildoers.

'It's not empty,' said Arthur. 'There will be myself and others here during office hours. By night it may well be unoccupied. When the time comes, I will ask the night-watchmen to include the Gatehouse in their normal rounds.'

'Their rounds should be extended to include the Gatehouse from the beginning of December,' said Strachan, 'two weeks before the King is expected. Germans are the most efficient spies, and can make a very good show of pretending to be British. Extra security men need to be hired and a lookout kept for any suspicious comings and goings by day and night.'

'Oh I see,' said Arthur. 'A bevy of Teutons is expected to run in and assassinate our King while he is shooting birds and a World War will break out? Guarding against this eventuality will be very expensive in wages. Perhaps the King is paying?'

'Arthur!' remonstrated Isobel. 'You are too bad!'

'Entertaining monarchy is always an expensive business,' observed the Inspector.

'One certainly realizes that,' said Isobel.

'And no doubt alarmists may profit from it,' said Arthur.

'If not the Germans in their quest for Africa,' said the Inspector, without batting an eyelid, 'there are the Communists. Some very nasty things are going on in Russia. The place is in uproar. Strikes, riots, bombs. The wealthy are fleeing. The Tsar is about to do a foolish thing, to promise the Russian people a parliament with legislative powers – it is always dangerous to show weakness when under attack. It will make matters worse. It is when a tight lid lifts that the pressure blows. Now they will go on until they win.'

'That hardly means they want to assassinate Edward VII in his own back yard. And how can you possibly know what is in the Emperor of Russia's mind?'

'The Tsarina is His Majesty's niece,' said Strachan calmly. 'And this is not his back yard, it is yours. His is securely guarded night and day. Its doors are strong and the locks secure.'

Arthur fell quiet. Isobel tapped her foot. Strachan

expressed himself pleased to see that the grass and hedges round the Gatehouse were kept cut and trimmed. The best thing would have been a resident gatekeeper, but since there was none he advised Arthur to keep an automatic revolver in the top drawer of the office desk, with the bullets kept in the one below. At the first sign of danger he was to load the bullets. He hoped Arthur was acquainted with the use of weapons and Arthur said yes, he could load a gun and arm a grenade well enough – he had learned in the cadet corps at Eton – and added, in a last show of defiance, that no doubt he could use them effectively against any intruding pigs and chickens. Inspector Strachan sighed and said it was no laughing matter.

'Try to be serious, Arthur,' said his mother, as if he were eight, 'and be polite to Inspector Strachan. He was explaining to me on the way up just how very dangerous and different a place the modern world is. I only hope your father knows what he is doing.'

Arthur thought that his mother and Inspector Strachan seemed rather thick: she simpered and sulked as if she was a young girl. He hoped he imagined it. She was a Countess and the Inspector was at least twenty years younger; such things simply did not happen. Arthur said he had already fixed Yale combination locks on both doors and Strachan said he would suggest Chubb as stronger but first the doors needed to be strengthened.

'They look as if a couple of quick kicks would be an end to them. No point in having locks stronger than the wood they rest in.'

Arthur refrained from saying, *'Two of my quick kicks on your fat arse and there'd soon be an end to you'* as being perhaps too graphic for his mother. A series of small explosions told him that Reginald was on his way back from the station with his passenger, a journalist from the *Daily Mirror*. The newspaper had written ahead, asking for an interview with 'the man of the moment' – an English Viscount who knew his subject and was prepared to talk openly and freely about the future of the automobile industry. Arthur had allowed himself to be flattered, and the appointment with the motoring correspondent had been made.

'It's the yellow press,' he warned his mother. 'They're on their way. I have an interview.'

'I do wish you wouldn't,' said Isobel. 'It is so vulgar to be in the newspapers.'

'Bear in mind there must be no mention of the royal visit,' put in Strachan.

'Why on Earth would I mention it? I thought it wasn't until Christmas.'

'Christmas always comes faster than you think,' observed the Inspector.

'And I'll thump your fat face, too,' thought Arthur.

'It's one thing to have a piece in *The Times*, when one's amongst friends,' said Isobel. 'But hardly the rags! You shouldn't encourage them.'

'I am trying to start a company, Mother,' said Arthur, biting his oily nails. 'And as Phineas Barnum said, no such thing as bad publicity.'

'Phineas Barnum was an American,' said Isobel, as if this was dismissal enough. 'Please remember you are not in trade, Arthur. You are a peer of the Realm. Do you really want to be called "The Motoring Viscount"?'

Arthur bit back the retort that his maternal grandfather had been in the coal trade, his parents in gold mines, his wife in the hog business, his children half American, he himself in the motor trade, and what's more she was talking codswallop. It was out of character. Who was she trying to impress? A detective inspector? He feared it must be so. Could she possibly be in love with him? His own mother? *The Countess and the Policeman?* That would make a dreadful headline.

'I do remember, Mama,' said Arthur. 'You will not let me forget. And "The Motoring Viscount" certainly has its appeal. *The Jehu Automobile Company, brought to you by courtesy of The Motoring Viscount.* Pretty good.'

'Just keep the Dilberne name out of it,' said her Ladyship, and they walked off.

He looked after them as they went away. His mother was carrying a pretty little lace and gold parasol. He wished for once that she was more like other mothers, dull and plain. Alternatively he wished she was more like Alice Keppel, granddaughter of a Greek peasant girl, who yet consorted with kings, not commoners. The ground went gently uphill along the first stretch of the oak avenue and he saw the Inspector take the Countess's arm, as any gentleman would do. Except he was not a gentleman.

And then the Jehu was at the door.

'But you're female,' he exclaimed, opening it to a young woman who reminded him of someone –

the plentiful fair hair, pink cheeks and innocent mouth, the startled blue eyes and slightly raised eyebrows – as if she had just met a man who planned to take advantage of her and she was trying to make up her mind as to whether or not to let him. She did not look, in fact, at all like a lady. She looked like Flora, whom he would rather not remember: all having so nearly ended in disaster.

Once in his foolish youth when there was time for these things he had thought he was in love with Flora. But then he had met Minnie, the mother of his sons, and realized what love was truly about. Not sex, but family. When this girl stretched out her hand to shake his it was ungloved, and her wrist was bare – smooth, soft, silky and gently veined, a delicate blue tracery just underneath the whiteness of the skin. Her fingers were cool. Flora always had cool hands and a cool bottom. But what was he thinking about? This young person was one of a very new breed, a lady journalist, and a cunning one at that. She had given no warning, had let him assume that she was a man. No doubt she had adopted the name Evelyn to that very end. Another deceiving little minx. Women snared one. One must be careful. One thought one had no time for sex any more, but one could be deceiving oneself.

He glanced quickly at Reginald – Reginald must have encountered Flora once or twice when dropping him off at her Mayfair flat – to see whether he had noticed the similarity. He thought perhaps he had – he was staring into space with so set an expression on his face he was surely trying not to laugh. But perhaps that was merely Arthur's own guilty imagining. Enough that Reginald had gone to the station to pick up a man, found an unescorted young woman in his place, and one with obvious attractions, and delivered her unchaperoned into the clutches of a man. But either way Reginald was to be trusted: he did not gossip.

Indiscretion

30th September 1905, The Servants' Hall

Cook served an early tea. His Lordship was coming down for the rest of the weekend, so there would be an extra course of roast beef for dinner. He liked to eat as soon as he got in. Cook would have to fire up the stove and that took time. New gas ovens had been installed by the Southampton Gas, Light and Coke Company, and were well able to deal with a fancy eight-course dinner for thirty, but Cook did not trust them with a classic beef roast. The old iron range had been kept on, so she would use that. Beef needed a really fierce oven if it was to be properly sealed: the new namby-pamby steel ovens with their thermometers were all well and good, but nothing beat the back of the hand and experience. A good roast was burned on the outside with the fat well shrivelled up, brown on the inner layers and pinker and moister the further in you got.

Digby had telephoned to say his Lordship would be down by train as soon as he was free at the House. Lily had left the phone giggling.

'He told his Lordship about The Cardinal's Hat,' she told the assembled staff. 'Digby reckons he'll be going this afternoon. He's fed up with her Ladyship. I'm not surprised.'

'That's enough of that,' said Mr Neville.

'What with Mr Strachan and all,' said Lily.

'And even less of that,' said Mrs Neville. 'I dare-say they'll be keeping to their separate rooms.'

'I should hope so,' said Lily. 'I was going in with her cup of tea this morning, but she came out and told me not to bother. I reckon she had the Inspector in there.'

'God will curse you for telling such wicked lies,' said Elsie.

'So I took it to Lady Minnie instead and she was in a right state. All Master Arthur does is leave her alone. I reckon she'd be better off running away. She doesn't fit in and never will. And she knows it.'

'She made such a pretty bride,' said Elsie. 'She loves him. And those dear little children. They're just going through a bad patch, the way married couples do.'

'Not that you'd know much about that,' said Lily.

'You're just in a bad mood,' said Elsie, 'because you're having to go up to London to talk to Agnes, just as his Lordship is coming down here. I know you.'

'You're the one who ought to wash their mouth

out with soap and water,' said Lily, 'if you're implying what I think you're implying.'

Reginald came in from the Jehu and trumped them both. He helped himself to ham on the bone. He had missed his lunch.

'You'll never guess who turned up at the Gatehouse for Lord Arthur today,' said Reginald. 'Bold as brass and still overflowing, if you get my meaning. Putting herself forward as a gentleman. Fat chance. Miss Flora of Half Moon Street, not looking a day older.'

'Not that one? Not that Flora?' asked Mr Neville. 'The one he shared?'

'Well, I'm not quite certain,' admitted Reginald, 'but she's a dead ringer. I left them there together. And her Ladyship walked back to the house with Mr Strachan.'

'Oh dear, oh dear,' said Cook. 'What's the matter with everyone? One thing after another.'

'Royal visits are always unlucky,' said Mrs Neville. 'Everything was going so well until that was announced.'

'Never wise to throw out old furniture,' said Mr Neville. 'In my experience where things go, people follow after.'

Arthur Resists Temptation

30th September 1905, The Gatehouse

After Reginald had left in the Jehu, the lady journalist stepped inside the Gatehouse. She looked round appreciatively, and sat down in one of the Liberty chairs.

'Ah, Mackmurdo,' she said. She was evidently knowledgeable and cultured, and refrained from crossing her legs. She might even be a lady. She was wearing a nice crisp white shirt tucked firmly into a broad belt, so that her bosom appeared to advantage. It was quite plump. Women with tiny waists often had an unfortunately small bosom. She had no wedding ring, yet came unescorted. It was difficult these days to judge class or status. When she spoke it was with an educated, even refined voice, and quite melodious. Flora had tended to screech when excited. Miss Braintree would never screech. He put Flora from his mind.

Miss Braintree seemed quite pleased with what she saw.

'A strange place for an office, Lord Hedleigh, but most attractive and I daresay perfectly functional. It is so pleasant to get out of London for the day. The city has become so grimy and crowded.'

She spoke as if they were friends, when they were not. It was a very female strategy, thus to claim acquaintance when there was none. They were unchaperoned. He wondered if he should ask her to leave and send a male replacement but decided against it. Miss Braintree had the power of the press behind her and it was important that the Jehu Automobile Company was not represented in the *Mirror* as old-fashioned and stuffy. She took out the notebook journalists carried with them these days for their strange squiggles. Her fingers were long and neatly clipped. He imagined where the fingers would travel if they were in bed together and banished the thought as best he could. Perhaps he should ring up the house and get Minnie to come down at once and bring him back to his senses? But then he remembered how Minnie hated coming down to the Gatehouse, and he failed to lift the telephone. He would simply face the new world: Miss Braintree would listen and he would talk.

Miss Braintree warned him they had little more than an hour together and then she was catching the quarter-past-one train back to the station the better to meet her deadline. She had, she said, taken the liberty of asking his driver to call back for her at one o'clock. Careful not to be misconstrued, he refrained from saying a lot could be achieved in an hour.

'I thought lady journalists only wrote about fashion and how to look after babies,' he said, and if there was a hint of derision in his voice he did not care. Women who aped men must expect to be treated like a man.

'Many of them do,' she said, 'but I don't. I write about the beauty of automobiles.'

If only he could hear Minnie say such a thing.

Miss Braintree asked him for his views on Herbert Austin's new plant at Longbridge and his plan to mass-produce a new automobile, the Phaeton, to be on sale as early as next Spring. Was it feasible? Was it true?

'It sounds such a wonderful machine,' she enthused. 'A 30-horsepower, high-class, touring model, with magneto and coil ignition and a four-speed gear box, all for a mere £650.'

'I would be happier to talk about the colour of my shirt,' said Arthur, 'or whether I sing lullabies to my children, but automobiles? These are serious matters, Miss Braintree. It is a woman's place to sit in them and look pretty, not to understand them.'

'Then please be serious,' said Miss Braintree. 'I have a job to do, and not much time to do it in. It seems to me that young Mr Austin is a long way ahead of you in the race.'

'There is no race, only competition amongst enthusiasts,' he said. 'Let me give you some figures.'

Miss Braintree was doing her best to provoke him. He must play for time. Life was moving too fast. His mother and Mr Strachan? It was an absurdity even to imagine it. But now this: equally unbelievable that respectable women should behave in this way. Don't think about it. He needed Minnie.

He pretended to be looking up files: moved papers around. Women were so tricky. They smiled and smiled and then they traduced you. Flora had the same talent: she had so easily bamboozled him into paying her rent on the assumption that he,

Arthur, would be her sole visitor, only to find he was sharing her with another – who was it? – one's memories for these things was so vague. A bird of some kind? Of course, Anthony Robin; Redbreast, whose fag he had been at Eton. Some nonsense about the law and the technicalities of who paid the rent for what – the solicitor had sorted all that out. But he suddenly had a terrible vision of Miss Braintree, not Flora, velvet-handcuffed, naked and smiling up at him from the bed. The bamboo bed. These were not the visions meant to assail a man trying to run an engineering business in a competitive world. Where was Minnie? Keeping the company of her children, no doubt, neglecting her husband, scorning the love of his life: the automobile. Also, suddenly, gratifyingly, he recalled Redbreast's member: it was distinctly smaller than his own. He found himself laughing. He had soon got the better of Robin Redbreast.

Miss Braintree was looking at him strangely. He pulled himself together.

'Mr Austin rather overstates his claim,' said Arthur, summoning up the special smile that he knew well enough made women melt and envy Minnie. 'We have all heard of the Phaeton; Austin has a very good publicity team, perhaps even better than the one in charge of his engineering. But the Phaeton's horsepower will only be twenty-five or thirty at best. The Jehu's full four and three-quarter-inch bore and a five and a quarter-inch stroke yields a good thirty to thirty-five.'

'But the Phaeton's out next Spring and so cheap! And that adorable dark red! Our information is that the Jehu won't be coming out until Christmas of next year at £800 and no mention of colour. Have you not been rather trounced in the race by young Mr Herbert Austin?'

'Christmas always comes sooner than one thinks,' said Arthur and Evelyn wrote it down in her strange squiggles and underlined it.

'That makes a good headline,' she said.

'Also,' said Arthur, 'Mr Austin is not so very young. He has at least five years advantage over me.' He was rather beginning to enjoy this. Most journalists were either seedy, if they came from the yellow press, or unbearably pompous if they came from *The Times*.

'But he's a farmer's son,' said Miss Braintree, 'and went to a grammar school and you're a Viscount and went to Eton. Has he not done rather well?'

'Of course he has,' said Arthur, adding, 'but then I am a magnanimous fellow, you know.'

She asked him how to spell magnanimous and he told her.

'I trained at Pitman's Secretarial College,' she said. 'I can do a hundred words a minute shorthand,' she said, 'and I can type at sixty. But long words hold one up so. It's lovely and cool in here but so hot outside.' Miss Braintree dabbed at her brow with a little lace handkerchief and opened a button of her shirt. Now he could see the swell of the breasts. He wondered if the nipples were pink or brown – pink, he suspected. Minnie's tended towards brown.

'I am looking for a secretary,' he said, before he could help himself. 'Perhaps you know someone who would suit?'

Some plain girl, he thought, someone with bad teeth, no figure and a hairy chin, or else Heaven help me! I am a married man and have no time for frivolity. At the same time he was still a man.

'From the state of your papers you certainly need one,' she said. 'You need someone with knowledge of automobiles,' she said. 'And if you want a girl they will be thin on the ground and want paying at least as much as a man. And if they have an aptitude for publicity, so necessary in the modern age, they will want even more.'

'I can pay well,' he said faintly. The bamboo bed came into his mind for no apparent reason, just a few feet away, the solid smooth thick yellow-brown legs, the curly swirls at the head of the ornate bedstead: rather like Miss Braintree's curls. He shivered.

'Personally, I would be happy to work for you,' she said, tossing the curls. It was so hot some of them clung damply to her skin; others rioted and glittered around her skull. 'I so want to get out of London and write a novel. I need part-time employment. I'd work for you five hours a day: the rest of the time would be my own. The accommodation here would suit me very well – just right for one person. We'd get on, I imagine.'

'Yes, I do imagine, Miss Braintree,' he said, 'but I think it would be wiser not. Cheaper and more sensible to have an ordinary male secretary.'

'Ah, cold feet already?' she said, with another careless toss of those curls. 'And you so go-ahead! Anthony Robin said you were a stick-in-the-mud at heart and he was right. A pity. Let me know if you change your mind.'

'Anthony Robin?' Arthur was startled. 'What can you possibly know about Anthony Robin?'

'I take the odd glass of wine at El Vino's with him,' said Miss Braintree, coolly. 'He works in Fleet Street. He edits *The Modern Idler*. He seems very interested in your progress and not very fond of you. I wonder what you did to annoy him. He and I used to be thick as thieves, of course.'

Thick as thieves? Did that mean what he thought it meant? Quite extraordinary. And was the past never done? This was proving a most disconcerting day, one way and another. The sooner she was out of the place the better. But she hadn't finished.

'Nowadays of course he's as thick as thieves with your sister Rosina, but I can only imagine it's a meeting of souls, not bodies. She's one of his contributors, and these days I rather think he prefers the company of men, and now I come to think of it probably always did. And Rosina's written this startling book about Australia, hasn't she. I believe there's quite a split in your family. Your mother threw her out of the house. I won't write about that. I could, of course, but I won't. I'm much too nice. Are you sure you don't want to employ me?'

His mother had been right. *The Times* was one thing: the gutter press quite another.

'Quite sure, Miss Braintree,' he said, 'though I am sure it would be a delightful experience. As for the rest, the Dilberne view is Wellington's *publish and be damned.*'

'It is certainly your sister's, my Lord,' she said,

with a certain sardonic tone in her voice, as if the form of address was worth more mockery than respect: people split into two camps, he'd noticed: those who paid too little respect, and those – by far the greater number – who fawned.

She prepared to go. She asked him outright where the bathroom was and he told her. Most women of his acquaintance would have died rather than admit to so basic a need. But she showed no signs of mortification. Her backside stuck to her dress as she went upstairs. The fabric was thin. There was a cry of alarm from the bathroom, and she rushed out onto the landing. Her hair was dripping wet and her shirt was drenched. That too stuck to her body.

'But I turned on the bath tap and water came out of the shower,' she complained. 'Now look!' He went upstairs, pushing past her, and found a towel and handed it to her. One did not want to be written about as ungentlemanly.

He heard the Jehu clattering down the drive to collect her. He was glad that she was going but the clatter was something of a worry. The exhaust valve regulator might need more attention. And as the vehicle drew up there was a series of explosions, which made Miss Braintree giggle rather indelicately as she stood on the stair beside him. The sudden expansion of hot gases under high pressure made the unfortunate noise – suggesting that the silencer holes were still ragged and needed yet more smoothing. Anything which impeded the passage of escaping gases from an engine must be avoided, be that engine organic or inorganic. Back to the workshops.

The door opened and Minnie came in.

'Darling,' she cried. 'Little Connor took five steps on his own today. On his feet at last! Five whole steps. I thought you'd like to know.' Her voice drained away.

Arthur could see that the sight of Miss Braintree on the stair in her wet, all-but-transparent shirt, rubbing her curls with the towel Arthur handed her, might give Minnie the wrong impression. But surely not so great a one as to justify what his wife did next – which was to run off, get back into the Jehu and tell Reginald to drive her back to the house, leaving poor Miss Braintree to walk to the station.

'Oh dear, dear me,' she said, as she left, still giggling. 'That was most unfortunate. I can see I'll never be the secretary now.'

She could take nothing seriously. He claimed pressure of work and did not offer to accompany her. He locked up, mindful of Inspector Strachan's warnings, and went on up to the house to explain matters to Minnie.

Minnie Runs

30th September 1905, Dilberne Court

Minnie ran. She pushed through the great door, not waiting for anyone to let her in, and ran. She ran through the great hall where a team of embroiderers were restoring the wall tapestries, through the ante-room with its newly restored gold-leaf ceiling, and through the chandelier room with its glittering glass, where Mr Neville directed Elsie how to lovingly wash and polish each hanging prism and globe so as to be fit for a King – as if she didn't know. Minnie ran down a corridor which never got the sun, but builders were knocking in a new window, and another painted in three different colours to see which one was best; she ran up the steep back stairs which Isobel couldn't do much to but paint, and the fumes still lingered, into the East Wing where Mrs Keppel and her husband George were to sleep, and into her own and Arthur's quarters.

She ran away from her life and into her future. She ran blindly, all else blotted out by a vision sealed into her mind and she knew she would never get rid of: the sight of Arthur on the stairs handing a towel to a near-naked girl whose hair hung loose around her shoulders. It was as if she had always had it in her mind: there was a certain relief in being able to see it so sharp and clear at last. Abandonment, loss. She flung herself upon the bed and opened her mouth as if to howl.

But her feet were hurting, so she pushed off her little laced boots without bothering to undo the laces, using force – the right foot dealing with the left, the left the right – on to the floor where Isobel had taken away the old worn rug she loved and replaced it with a brassy one from Heal's which didn't suit the room one bit.

This was why Arthur wanted the Gatehouse. To frolic with a female secretary, some snippet of a girl: no, not some snippet, some blowsy trollop with creamy shoulders. Reginald had said to her as she crouched in the Jehu on the way back to the Court.

'Don't take on so, my Lady. It doesn't last long, with Master Arthur.'

Was that meant to be comfort? That it was a meaningless habit. And how dare he speak to her like that? He was a servant.

Now she was on her feet. She meant to escape, get away from this accursed place. Lily pushed the door open.

'Mr Neville told me to come up to see if you were all right, Miss?'

'I am leaving this house,' she said. 'Fetch me a suitcase.'

'How big a one, your Ladyship?'

Minnie said sharply, 'One I can carry myself, girl,' and Lily went off to fetch it, and no doubt to report back to Isobel first. She flung the things she needed on the bed. What did one want? A couple of skirts and dresses, some under-things, a toothbrush, soap and a towel. She wanted nothing that belonged to here. She wanted her life before Arthur back. She found her little drawstring purse – so pretty, antelope suede with a silver clasp, a present from Arthur when once they had loved each other (she would not cry, she would not) and in it two pound notes, three shillings, a sixpenny piece and two farthings. She found her cheque book, so long unused, at the bottom of a drawer where she kept her lace stockings and took it out. No. 3 Fleet Street. She was running to Rosina, of course, where else? One needed comfortable shoes if one was to run.

When Lily came back she did not wait for proper packing; one had to run or one began to think. If she gave herself a moment the sight came back, pulsing in and out of definition. Arthur stood upon the stair, looking up at the girl as she looked down. Longing, such longing. Her heart would break. She grabbed a coat, any coat; one needed a coat to keep out the cold. She was shivering. Her lips were salt; she'd been weeping, was weeping, and didn't know it. She ran; she ran from love and loss and the habit of endurance, she ran from the vision of Arthur and the girl upon the stair, she ran through rooms and down corridors and up stairs and past staring decorators and plumbers and servants and found herself at the nursery door. She pushed it open and Edgar and Connor were standing stiff and uncomfortable and ready to be brought down for tea. She held out her arms for them.

'You're coming with me,' she said. 'Nanny, get them ready.'

But they shrank from her and little Connor opened his mouth and started to wail. She realized she had frightened them; that she must look strange. Nanny put her arms round them and stood as if guarding them against an enemy.

'You leave these poor wee mites alone,' said Nanny. 'You wicked woman.'

Minnie looked towards Molly at the back of the room. Wasn't there an ally here? But Molly just shook her head. No hope.

'Go now,' said Isobel's voice behind her. She turned, and there was her mother-in-law, her face oddly soft. 'I know how terrible it is,' she said. 'Go now, come back when you can. I'll look after them.'

Edgar stuck out his little jaw as his father did when she had annoyed him, and little Connor hid his face in Nanny's skirts and Minnie brushed past Isobel and ran and ran from them all. Lily was beside her and Reginald driving – Isobel said the train was not advisable – with a picture of Arthur on the stair with the girl seemingly engraved into the very glass of the Jehu windows – she would never travel in a Jehu again – all the way to No. 3 Fleet Street where the door was opened by Rosina and Rosina let her in.

Reginald and Lily went off, presumably to Belgrave Square, where Minnie had been expected to go, but, just like Rosina, had not.

PART TWO

What Happened Next

...in Minnie's Life

Minnie marvelled at how quickly things could change. Three weeks after her flight from Dilberne Court, she stood in her stockinged feet in front of an easel and pasted up next month's edition of the *The Modern Idler.*

'I could spend my life doing this, and be happy,' she thought.

'Pasting-up' was a simple matter of working out in your mind's eye what the page would look like; making what was important bigger and what was less important smaller, cutting up typewritten columns into pieces and pasting them down with Mendine glue onto the large page sheets, getting the matching wood blocks in place, fitting it all together so it was aesthetically pleasing, and taking the finished sheets and a couple of white five-pound notes down to the *Daily Mirror* (where Anthony had a friend) and the typesetters could do 2,000 copies of *The Modern Idler* on good-quality paper in two hours using an old-fashioned flatbed. Minnie could do in three days what it took everyone else five. She just had a talent, rare in women she'd been told back at art school in Chicago, for spatial arrangement. The others waved scissors around and panicked and scattered the floor with bits of screwed-up paper and blobs of glue, and took days when Minnie took hours.

'You're a genius,' Anthony Robin said. It was a long time since anyone had said that to her. She thought she was probably in love with him. His face was all planes and angles.

They'd put her to work straight away, 'to stop her brooding'. She slept on the sofa the first night and after that she had a little back room of her own. She could see down to the Inner Temple church and gardens and even got a glimpse between roof-tops of the river. They'd been astonisinghly nice to her. Rosina had moved out of the spare room to make room for her when she'd turned up in the middle of the night, and now Rosina shared with Diana and said it was okay by her if it stayed like that.

People came and went all the time at No. 3: artists and writers. Conversation was lively, food came when people were hungry, not when meal-times dictated. Rabbit pie was a favourite and the Fleet Street butcher sold blocks of pastry to go on it. Diana did the cooking when she was not cleaning up after everyone, and now Minnie could help her keep up with the secretarial work. She worked and she was welcome.

Every now and then Anthony would emerge from his room and wander around, and if she was pasting up would stroke her head a little and turn her chin towards him and look into her eyes as if he saw her soul there, and then wander off.

Rosina slept in late and would then go round to Longman's in Paternoster Row to prepare her book for the printers: Minnie had begun engraving a couple of wood blocks for the illustrations: a group of thin, naked natives dancing round a fire – none of them seemed to have washed their hair, so the engraving of their tangled locks was fiddly and difficult. Minnie had not tried her hand at engraving before. Perhaps it was her true vocation. It was rather nice wielding a knife rather than a paintbrush. It made one feel more in control of one's life. Or perhaps she just wanted to kill? Only she wasn't like that, was she – or perhaps she was? She didn't know who she was, and didn't care. Here and now was good enough. Every night was a party of one kind or another, though she didn't use the same potions that seemed so to entrance the others.

So long as she didn't think of the children all was well. But when she did a terrible longing and anxiety seized her.

'It isn't rational,' Rosina assured her. 'Just because you feel anxious it doesn't mean there is anything to be anxious about. It's instinct working, it isn't *you*. They are perfectly safe where they are, more than safe. The only thing they're likely to die of is boredom.'

Minnie said she was desperate to take them home to Chicago and bring them up there and Rosina just laughed. They might let her take Connor out of the country as he was only a second son, but they'd never let her have Edgar the little heir.

'But a son belongs to the mother until he's seven; I thought that was the law.'

'Not if he's a peer of the land,' said Rosina. 'No English judge would allow it. How these old men close ranks against women! You'd have a better deal in the land of the aboriginal. Mind you, they just share the children there, hand them out amongst one another as if they were anyone's. You hardly have a name of your own. You're just someone's mother, or sister, or daughter.'

'Not so different from me,' said Minnie. 'I have no existence of my own. I am a future Viscount's mother, a Viscount's wife and an Earl's daughter-in-law. A long time since I was little Minnie O'Brien.'

It was a warm autumnal day. They were outside in the little overgrown garden. Rosina had rigged up an old fire grate on two stacks of bricks and had lit a charcoal fire under it. She had been down to the butcher and bought a pile of red rump steaks, and was preparing to cook them, using long handheld tongs to flip them over. Minnie thought she had never smelt anything so delicious. She hadn't been able to eat for weeks, she had been too upset; but now suddenly she was hungry and restless, she wanted something and she wasn't sure what. She wanted her children, but this was something different. She wanted Arthur: her body craved him, he was the architect of all her woes and yet she craved him. If he walked into the garden and said he was sorry and he loved her she would fall into his arms.

'You'll go back to him,' said Rosina, who seemed able to read minds. 'Women do. How will you live? Where? What on? If you leave home you have no rights. You can be divorced for desertion. I'll bet my brother has all your money tied up.'

Minnie had gone to the bank to take out money and found she had none. The bank also told her that though she owned shares in the Jehu Automobile Company, she had signed papers to the effect that she could not sell them. She had written to her mother asking her for funds and was waiting for a reply. She shivered: a cold wind eddied off the river. Rosina didn't seem to notice it.

'Arthur has done something unforgivable.'

'But Arthur can do as he likes,' said Rosina. 'Just as the King does as he likes. The Queen forgives the King, so you had better forgive Arthur. Sex means very little to men. Except they have to have it or they go mad. My poor husband was like that: he had to have sex, and got it, and still he went mad. It was not so dreadful a thing for me when he died. The aboriginals are just the same, except the women behave like the men. It's all in my book. It will make a great stir.'

'But I hurt so, Rosina. I don't understand it.'

Smoke and the smell of burning meat drifted towards them and Minnie began to cough, and then to cough and cry at the same time.

'Don't distress yourself so,' said Rosina, not unkindly. 'You are so soft, Minnie. It comes from being brought up in a heated nursery and never being beaten. We blue-blooded English toughen our young.'

Minnie thought of Connor and Edgar and wept some more. What was to be their fate? She had visited them twice at Belgrave Square. She had been allowed to see them for half an hour, in Nanny's and Isobel's presence. They had behaved towards her as when they were brought down for tea: looked at her curiously and showed her their toys and drawings with muted enthusiasm. Nanny had glared; Isobel had been amiable and sweet.

'Do visit again next Sunday, Minnie,' she had said. 'Just for the half-hour, so as not to disturb them. And come home when you feel ready.' And that was all. No reproaches, no questions. When she left and stumbled down the wide stone steps – the butler let her out as if she was a total stranger – Minnie had been the one to cry. The children had seemed unconcerned. Perhaps they thought Isobel was their mother.

'I did warn you before you got married,' said Rosina now, 'and I got into enough trouble with that. Arthur was furious. But you took no notice. Cried "love" like any simple dairy maid and went ahead.'

'Arthur loved me.'

'Really? We all thought it was for the money. He and Anthony shared a girl between them. They kept her in a flat in Half Moon Street. My brother nearly got Anthony in trouble with the law. Anthony's not the forgiving and forgetting kind. Don't trust him.'

'Anthony? Anthony Robin? Our Anthony?' She'd stopped crying. Her nursery might have been heated but she'd been brought up in the stockyards and had her father's blood.

'Our Anthony. Don't worry about it. He likes you, and you're good at pasting up. Just face it, Minnie. You're a married woman and a mother and you're soft. You're helpless. Go home to Arthur. Get over it.'

Minnie thought of her wood-carving knife. She would like to stick it into someone. Whether Arthur or Rosina or Anthony or the girl with the wet hair or her mother-in-law she was not sure, any one of them would do. Rosina was right: she was too soft. She'd thought somewhere in her head that Arthur would come after her, and kneel before her, and ask her forgiveness and she would grant it and they would be happy ever after. But he had not.

Diana came out to join them, pretty and girlish and nice. She put her arms round handsome, leathery Rosina and kissed her ear. Rosina turned her face and kissed Diana's mouth. They were like a man and a woman together.

'It's too smoky out here,' Rosina said, 'and the wind's getting up. We'll eat inside.'

And she took no further notice of Minnie and went indoors. Diana followed. Minnie was left outside to gather up the cooked steaks onto a serving dish and follow them in. Her fingers were greasy. She could see the advantage of living with servants. She felt abandoned, shut out. She'd thought she was Rosina's best friend but now Diana seemed to actually own her, by virtue of some other happenstance she didn't quite understand. It was all very puzzling, and none of it very nice, just somehow upsetting. She couldn't stay here for ever. She would have to steal the children. If only her mother would write.

What Happened Next

...in Arthur's Life

In the meanwhile Arthur was beginning to miss Minnie. In three weeks his mood had changed from anger to a vague feeling that perhaps he was in some way to blame, and that he might need to rectify the situation by looking her out.

By the time Arthur had composed himself after Miss Braintree's rather startling visit, had rearranged some vital papers and walked back up to the house, he had begun to feel quite angry with Minnie. The Gatehouse surely was his private place, the equivalent of any gentleman's den, and a wife did not enter unannounced. The privacy of both man and wife in a marriage was important. More, it was most un-English of Minnie – he could think of no truer way of putting it – to have reacted as she did, as though he, her husband, had something to hide, which he most certainly did not. Miss Evelyn Braintree had behaved in a deliberately provocative way, but he had not succumbed to her charms. On the contrary. He deserved consideration for this, not Minnie's frankly rather shop-girlish and immediate show of suspicion. His mother, in a similar situation, would have raised her eyebrows disdainfully and that would have been enough.

But Minnie had uttered a squeal and rushed back into the Jehu and Reginald had driven off, leaving Miss Braintree to walk to the station. And why, come to that, had Reginald taken Minnie down to the Gatehouse in the first place, knowing a young lady was visiting? It had been wrongheaded in the extreme, even delinquent. Had Reginald not been so good with the Jehu, understanding her inside out, this would have been a firing offence. As it was, Arthur put up with a lot. Reginald was a servant and one expected no better. But Minnie was meant to be a lady. This was the trouble, of course. She was just not. You could take the girl out of Chicago but you could not take Chicago out of the girl. His mother had done her best but it was not working.

Minnie's mother, from what small acquaintance he had of her, would no doubt in similar circumstances have launched herself like some banshee at her unfortunate husband. He supposed he should be grateful that Minnie had simply squealed and run off. Well, he would talk her round, and she would apologize. But when he'd got back to the Court Minnie was nowhere to be seen. It seemed his mother had sent her off to Belgrave Square.

'Minnie was upset,' his mother was saying. 'She

seemed to me to be in a state of shock. I thought she would go straight to Belgrave Square but she has chosen to take refuge with Rosina, who has lodgings, I hear, somewhere near St Paul's. At least it is perfectly respectable and she is safe. Arthur, you are too bad. What can you have been doing to upset her so? Everything seemed perfectly normal when we left the Gatehouse. What happened?'

He was a grown man, not a child. He did not want to be spoken to in this way.

'Nothing happened,' he said crossly. 'Minnie is being idiotic. More to the point' – and he spoke before he could stop himself – 'what were you and Mr Strachan doing together?'

Isobel looked at her son with incredulity, raised her elegant eyebrows and walked out of the room, flowered pink-and-white silk skirt swishing. She made a fine, haughty exit, he thought. She did grandeur well, unlike his wife.

He went up to the nursery where Nanny Margaret was putting the little ones to bed. He asked her what had happened, why wasn't Minnie with her? Minnie was usually to be found in the nursery at bath time.

'Lady Minnie has gone. She would have taken the children, Master Arthur, but I stopped her,' said Nanny.

'Gone? Gone where?' he asked.

'To her fancy man, of course,' said Nanny. Arthur dismissed the very idea as ludicrous. Nannies normally thought badly of mothers, everyone knew, but this was going too far. The old woman must be in her eighties: too old for the job. But

Isobel thought the world of her. And just because Nanny would have died in defence of her charges, as Isobel kept saying, and he had no doubt she would have, that did not mean she was a reliable, let alone truthful witness. He remembered an incident in which he and Rosina as children had walked with Nanny into a field where, unknown to them, an untethered bull had been left to graze. When it loped towards them as though to charge, Nanny had stood in its way and pummelled its head and shouted and the beast, rather surprisingly had given up, shaken its poor battered head and limped away. By which time the children had jumped the hedge. The tale had lost nothing in its telling.

But that did not mean Nanny was a dependable witness, just a rather stupid one. The sooner Edgar and Connor passed out of her care – why had Minnie insisted on this stupid Irish name? It would haunt the poor boy all his life – and into a school where the teachers were at least minimally intelligent, the better. That the thought of a 'fancy man' could even enter Nanny's head was what was so shocking. He blamed his mother for having led him into wedlock with a girl she well knew had a bad reputation. Minnie had a past – there was no denying it. She had once, in bed, even called him 'Stanton'. He had pretended he did not notice, but he had, and it had rather put him off her. One had hoped for a virgin for a wife.

Really he had no time for this absurdity. How could Minnie expect him to love her when she showed so little trust in him, suspected him of impropriety when there was none? Running off, leaving the children; what sort of mother was she turning out to be? He felt very angry – wasting good emotion on a wife when he had the Jehu III to think about? He had come second in the Isle of Man race, and it was not good enough. He had to get the vehicle-weight down somehow.

He kissed the children good-night, and it seemed to him they shuddered at his bristly moustache. The sooner they were away from the care of overwrought women the better. Until Minnie saw sense and came back his nights would be lonely. It was too bad. But he would not go after her: to do so would be an admission of guilt. And he was guilty of nothing.

What Happened Next

...for Isobel and Robert

The political parties had split over tariff reform; it was generally assumed that the Liberals would win the coming election; the King's relationship with his nephew the Kaiser worsened; in Russia the Emperor brought in his Duma, thus planting the seeds of further revolution. Forget the bolting of Minnie, all was tumult and change at home and abroad. A degree of governmental control over the level of gold production was beginning to seem inevitable and the row over the employment of Chinese miners in South Africa began to be a factor in the prospects of the Dilberne mine at Modder Kloof. Even the Earl had a brief spasm of worry as to his finances.

'My dear,' he said to Isobel, 'perhaps you have done enough to make a palace out of Dilberne Court; one must bear the expense in mind,' and to Arthur, 'Dear boy, one must hope the development of the Jehu III begins to see some kind of financial return,' but was met with such looks of pained bewilderment from both of them that he gave up any hope of economies, and wrote to Mr Baum for advice. Mr Baum came back with the observation that when times were hard it was always better to spend rather than save. 'Spend, spend, spend, while you can,' he wrote. 'By which I mean investing, not wasting.'

So his Lordship put in a bid for the house next door in Belgrave Square, now up for sale, so that Isobel could extend her empire sideways, and another £5,000 into the development of Jehu IV, and his family were satisfied. He sent Rosina £250 as a gesture, towards the publication of her book. Whatever Isobel thought, the family name would not be damaged by a dissertation on the habits of aborigines. Social progress depended upon knowledge: there was no such thing as too much information – another of Mr Baum's precepts. He and Mrs Baum wrote in a most friendly fashion from the Mount of Olives, where they were busily making the desert bloom. Mrs Baum had started her own Handel choral society, apparently involving Mr Balfour, by post, in the endeavour.

Rosina deserved to have her name shine; she was an intelligent girl and it was not her fault she was born a woman; his Lordship did suggest, however, at a brief meeting with his daughter at the House of Lords, that she did not let her mother know about the £250. She would regard it as disloyalty. He wanted to make it up to Isobel. He felt bad about his visits to The Cardinal's Hat, now a weekly occurrence. He promised himself he would cease after Christmas; it was a silly way for a grown man to behave. Carmen, as much a man as a woman, was a most sweet and exotic creature, but one could hardly believe her declarations of love, and one was exposed to blackmail. Digby had already asked for an increase in salary, and got it. Mind you, Digby was an excellent valet. His Lordship had taken his advice over the matter of the sponge-bag trousers, and Carmen had much admired them, saying in her delightful accent what a fine figure of a man he was, now looking like a man of forty not sixty. Isobel's taste in all things sartorial was always excellent.

Her Ladyship's changes to the Court were, thank Heaven, beginning to wind down. The loss of the heavy mahogany picture rails had been the last of the major changes. The old family portraits had been relegated to the staircases, and been replaced with a selection of French racing scenes by Edgar Degas, which she was convinced would please the King, if not Mrs Keppel, whose taste was not modern but lent itself to chinoiserie and chandeliers. Everything was finally to her Ladyship's taste. She was now busying herself with matters of security, which involved no end of locks, keys and the occasional man-trap in the grounds, which Strachan had recommended, but to which his Lordship had quickly put an end.

'One thing to trap a rabbit, or hare,' his Lordship observed, 'but a whole man seems excessive. No, and no spring guns either, Inspector Strachan.'

Strachan had sighed heavily, as was his rather annoying habit, but abandoned the idea. He seemed to have become one of the household, half adviser, half staff, putting Robert rather in mind of the Old Queen's Munshi, the Indian servant. But Strachan gave Isobel peace of mind: a man about the house, young and strong, and with Minnie away and Arthur spending so many nights at the Gatehouse, and he himself so often away at Belgrave Square, that was no bad thing. Neville the butler was the kind to become a gibbering mouse when faced with a night-time intruder; Isobel's designers and decorators would retreat under their bedclothes at the slightest alarm, the male staff would wait for instruction, and the females run around squawking like hens in a henhouse when the fox got in. Some farm workers might be just as likely to side with the intruder as with the gentry, times being what they were. Reginald was the only one strong and sensible enough to square up to danger. But he was as likely to be at Belgrave Square as at the Court. If Isobel felt the need to have the Inspector around, so be it. Arthur of course couldn't stand him, just as Bertie had hated the Indian waiter: failing himself in his filial duties, the son hated to think of another as taking his place.

Security apart, his Lordship decided, the improvement in Isobel's mood was probably because in Minnie's absence she now had full control of the grandchildren, those two fine little fellows.

What Happened Next

...at No. 3 Fleet Street

It was the evening of 31st October. *The Modern Idler* had been pasted up and put to bed. It was a most satisfactory edition, with an article by G. K. Chesterton about Friedrich Nietzsche, concerning the 'duty of praise', which Minnie strove to understand as a concept – and which the Reverend Stacey did sometimes refer to on Sunday mornings. Chesterton surprisingly described the duty of praise as being 'primeval', using the word as compliment not insult, and then accused Nietzsche of being a 'timid thinker' for defining the *übermensch* as if he were an acrobat or an alpine climber, instead of what he should have called him, a 'purer' or 'happier' man. It had seemed most interesting to Minnie and she had made headlines of the article, hoping to create what Anthony described as a journalistic hare. Both Rosina and Diana had seemed singularly uninterested when she tried to talk about this conflict of ideas.

'For Heaven's sake,' Rosina had said, 'none of it affects ordinary life. Just do the pasting up. No one expects you to actually read the stuff. Oh and by the way, Minnie, I have just found this letter in my pocket. I'm ever so sorry. I was meant to post it but I got distracted and forgot all about it...'

And she'd handed Minnie back the letter Minnie had written to her mother some weeks past. This was both vexing and something of a relief. It explained why Minnie had not heard back from Tessa. She had begun to worry that having heard her news, her mother had cast her off. But now she'd walked to Mount Pleasant and in person posted this second letter explaining everything, she could stop worrying. Well, she could, but she didn't. Perhaps there was an explanation as to why Arthur was upon the stair embracing a blonde woman? She shouldn't have run away as she had, without giving him a chance to explain. Perhaps he had been hurt by her lack of trust in him?

She ventured the explanation to Anthony and he just laughed and said he knew Evelyn Braintree, and it was hardly likely.

'Your husband and I shared a girl called Flora,' he said, 'in looks very like Miss Braintree, as it happens. But you knew all about that, I think. I'm not telling you anything new.'

'No, of course not,' said Minnie bravely, but it was hardly anything she wanted to remember. She had forgiven Arthur, Arthur had forgiven her. They had been equal; all forgotten, until this new terrible thing.

She felt a new surge of upset and jealousy so strong it even blotted out thoughts of her children. No, she would never forgive him. The rage receded slightly. And how were Edgar's little feet? Had Nanny relented and bought him new shoes for everyday? He'd had on his church shoes on Sunday, the ones that gave him blisters. But surely Isobel would notice; she loved the children; she would deal with Nanny Margaret. Isobel was being so kind; bringing the children with her all the way to Belgrave Square so Minnie didn't have to go all the way down to Sussex to see them. Though it meant she didn't get to see Arthur. She had the terrible feeling that if she did she would just melt into his arms and the horrible time would be over. But she couldn't; she shouldn't just let it go. If she did then it would happen again, and again, and it would kill her from grief. No, she must pay him a lesson.

Minnie was alone in the house. Anthony and the girls had gone to see *Lights Out* at the Waldorf Theatre, a new play starring Henry B. Irving, not *the* Henry Irving, of course; they were running an obituary on old Irving. He'd died on stage in a Bradford theatre a week before they'd gone to press. His ashes were now in Westminster Abbey, the first man ever to be buried as mere ash in that august building. Minnie had been there last at the time of the King's Coronation, in the Summer of 1902, walking beside Isobel behind a bevy of duchesses – past a box of royal mistresses – in a heavy velvet gown with an ermine trim, and wearing a diamond tiara which kept nearly falling off her bobbed hair. Was she really contemplating going into all that pomp and formality again? For love of a man?

She became conscious of how silent the house was. The front room gave directly onto the street. It was quiet outside; by day it was thronged, by this time of night almost deserted. Inside there was a brisk fire and a comfortable sofa and wine to drink and Rider Haggard's *She* to catch up with. She would take the evening off from worry and indecision.

Tonight was All Saints' Eve, October the thirty-first, the night the graves opened and the ghosts rode. There were certainly enough of them in this part of the city; Roman graveyards, Saxon graveyards, plague pits, gibbets, dungeons; remnants all of a gruesome past. Ghostly prelates were said to stalk St Paul's, as Anne Boleyn walked the Tower, the Woman in Black the Bank of England, the baker's boy Pudding Lane. It was all nonsense; ghosts were for servants, not intelligent, educated women.

Chicago had a terrible history too: phantoms abounded there as here, revenants from massacres, battles, great fires, Father Damien walked quite openly: even Tessa swore she'd seen the ghost of a ragged soldier casually limping around at Confederate Mound.

'And didn't I see the ghost of Mrs O'Leary's cow

in Jack Kennedy's tavern the other day?' Billy had retorted. Chicago's ghosts seemed less threatening, fit for a joke. Here in London they might drag you down with them into Hell. Though Anthony had reported that the Waldorf Theatre itself, newly opened, built on the site of an old flower market, was haunted by, of all things, the scent of flowers: hyacinths, lilies, roses. The smell wafted through the proscenium to the distraction of rehearsing actors. He'd laughed about it, and they'd laughed over the idea that perhaps it was the ghost of the great Sir Henry Irving, come to annoy his usurper son, Henry Broderick.

Minnie shivered and told herself she was being silly.

There was the sound of a key in the lock. The others weren't expected back until midnight – the theatre, grateful for a good review, was asking *The Modern Idler* staff for a late-night supper. It was either an earthly intruder or the shade of Jack the Ripper, often reported in the environs of El Vino's. She would not be frightened. She grabbed the poker, raised it above her head and stood facing the door.

And Anthony came in.

'My, aren't you brave,' he said.

'It's Halloween,' she said, and lowered the poker. She felt very foolish. He always made her feel foolish and inadequate. Why did she want his approval so much? When she bent over her work and heard his footsteps on the floor behind her and his breath on the nape of her neck she waited for a kiss which didn't come. It was absurd. She was a grown woman, not a silly girl. Back home she had had all the confidence in the world. Men liked her; she liked men. It was simple.

Here everyone had another agenda: something unspoken that was going on. You could never even trust servants to be on your side. She didn't quite trust Anthony. Rosina and Diana had shown themselves to be together in a way she didn't quite understand. She had thought on occasion Anthony showed special affection for William Brown, Rosina's publisher, who was an occasional visitor at No. 3, and for a boyish young novelist, Morgan Forster, who was trying his hand at literary criticism. But you couldn't be sure. She didn't herself mind in the least what went on, if men wanted to love each other why should they not: whatever it was they did was technically against the law, but here it madc cveryone so secretive and strange. It hadn't seemed to matter any which way in Chicago; if you lived near the Water Tower, as she and Stanton had, it was no great surprise to see men holding hands. Like William Blake's poem:

Never seek to tell thy love
Love that never told can be;
For the gentle wind does move
Silently, invisibly…

What did it mean? No one ever told one anything. Women whispered stuff in one another's ears. Her mother had lovers – she was quite open about that – but looked shocked and blushed if asked for information. Rosina had been quite informative about the aboriginals, though they were pagans and hardly an example; and Rosina's husband seemed to have behaved in a very bizarre way. But Minnie was beginning to think that in spite of all her facts and figures Rosina tended to record what she wanted to see, rather than what was there.

I told my love, I told my love,
I told her all my heart;
Trembling, cold, in ghastly fears;
Ah! she doth depart…

In the meanwhile, actual first-hand experience for a woman was barred. You married one man and that was supposed to be all you ever knew, and pleasure kept to a minimum in case you were tempted to run off to find more. At least she had had Stanton the artist, except he was crazy, and when he showed her his variety of the love that never could be told – which oddly seemed to involve throttling her and himself – that was when she left. She wanted to live.

Arthur was terribly polite and terribly affectionate and respectable. He made children rather than love. If she herself knew more, she could teach him and he wouldn't have to go hunting after women like Miss Braintree, or the earlier one called Flora. She hated sleeping in a lonely bed. She wanted to lie next to Arthur and change his respectful love-making so he wanted to do it not just to have babies. And now Anthony was throwing his arms round her, more like a big brother, it was true, than a lover.

'Oh you poor little thing,' he was saying. 'Poor little Minnie! Did you think I was Jack the Ripper? Out of the grave for his annual outing?'

'I didn't know who you were,' she said. 'You were meant to be at the theatre.'

'I was,' he said, 'but I walked out after the first act. The others stayed. Such a tiresome, grim play. As soon as there was talk of a court martial, one knew from that moment on it was going to end in tears: downhill all the way. Much lovelier to go home and keep poor little Minnie company.'

It occurred to Minnie that he had arranged the evening deliberately. Only three tickets had turned up, not the four he said he'd asked for. Of course Minnie would be the one to say, 'Oh, you lot go, I'll stay.' And Anthony had arranged the after-show supper so the others wouldn't be back until after midnight and here he was home at nine for three hours alone with Minnie by the fire. She'd been wrong about William Brown and Morgan Forster; Anthony didn't belong with the Water Tower crowd at all. It just proved how wrong you could be. Also how ignorant you were and how much you needed to learn.

She was sitting beside Anthony on the sofa. He had his arm round her shoulder, and it was creeping to the nape of her neck, and didn't seem brotherly at all. He was reading Haggard's *She* aloud to her. They were sipping wine.

'He was altogether too good-looking,' Anthony read. His voice was caressing and deep. It soothed her. *'And, what is more, he had none of that con-*

sciousness and conceit about him which usually afflicts handsome men, and makes them deservedly disliked by their fellows.' He broke off. 'Do you think I'm handsome?'

'Yes,' she said without thinking.

'I thought you did,' he said. 'Can I kiss the nape of your neck?'

'I don't think you had better,' she said.

'Time you did what you wanted, not what you ought.'

'I can't remember how.'

He kissed the nape of her neck, just two gentle lips, but it sent a shiver through her which he noticed and made him laugh. She didn't like him laughing that way, as though she were predictable. Well, perhaps she was. Perhaps all women were. That's why men despised them.

'You're a Viscountess, after all, you can do as you like. You just have to stop being afraid.'

'I never used to be afraid,' she said. 'I was ever so bold.'

'It's them,' he said, 'the Dilbernes. They've run you down like a clock. You need winding up.'

He took his arm from over her shoulder and she felt unprotected and abandoned, but he was only going to the cupboard to bring out the opium pipe and the paraphernalia that went with it. She had seen the others smoke but had never tried it herself. She was a mother, not a wayward girl. The opium came from the pharmacist across the way; it was good for the nerves. He set up the brass tray, the little lamp, the pipe, a spoon, the water on the table in front of the sofa. She was so tired of doing the right thing. He showed her how to lean over and breathe in. She took a very little puff.

'Coward,' he said. 'Cowardy, cowardy custard!' He took a deep puff, held it in his mouth, turned her face towards his and put his smoky open mouth against hers and blew the vapour down into her lungs. It was an invasion, uncalled for. But it was a great gift, and she was pleased. It was there to be taken so she took some more.

'It's winding me down, not up,' she said.

'Go where it takes you,' he said. 'Watch the clock. Watch the pendulum. Keep your eyes on it. This way, that way, this way.'

The clock was on the mantelpiece above the fire. She watched. It made quite small, quick movements, and needed concentration. The room was hazy with fumes. This way, that way.

'You feel really happy and sleepy,' he said.

'I do.' He gave her some more to drink. It wasn't wine.

'What is it?' she asked. 'The others will be back.'

'Not for ages,' he said. 'Hours and hours. Probably not tonight.'

'Why not?' she asked.

'They may have arranged to go off with friends in the cast. Drink up now.'

She drank. There seemed to be two people inside her. One which wanted to believe him and another part which knew perfectly well what was going on. If her father turned up Anthony Robin was in real trouble. She wasn't even married to him as she was to Arthur. Ah, Arthur. Arthur wouldn't like this at all.

'Close your eyes,' he said.

She did.

'You can't open them,' he said. She tried and couldn't. They were stuck fast.

'How strange,' she said. 'I can't open my eyes.'

'Yes you can now,' said the nice caressing voice. 'Open your eyes.' This time it was easy and she could see the clock. This way, that way.

'What a suggestible little thing you are,' he said. 'It's so very warm in here, don't you find? Perhaps you should take off some more clothes.'

'More clothes?' she asked. She didn't seem to have many left on. 'Can I have some more of the smoke?'

'It isn't smoke,' he said, 'it's a vapour. You have to be a bit careful of it, you can come to like it too much.'

'More,' she said. Her other self, the good wife and mother, kept waving at her from the other side of her being; a little stick insect, gesticulating. Isobel was there too, mouthing away, trying to remind her of something she ought to pay attention to. But here and now was so nice, and the sofa so soft, and Anthony was there on top of her, with no clothes on that she could see, all bare torso and muscle. Perhaps it was really Arthur? She wouldn't mind if it was, but how could one tell? And everything was so familiar and so inexorable. Inexorable was a nice word.

'Nice stuff, I know,' Anthony said. 'It makes a girl peaceful and pleased, and always very obliging. And a man can go on and on,' he said, 'and not be too fussy about where he goes.'

It was the wrong thing to say. It was so rude. 'Not too fussy' – what did he mean? Because she was a married woman? Because she was over thirty? She was a peeress of the Realm. She had a tiara. She had been married in St Martin-in-the-Fields. She had two little boys, one of whom needed new shoes. She had a husband whom she loved. He would be really upset and unhappy if he knew where she was. She was waiting for him to rescue her. She sat up abruptly and pushed Anthony off. He fell on the floor and the tray overtipped and he hurt his shoulder. His thing, which had been urgent and questing, turned flabby and weak. What had she been doing? She felt sick and dizzy and very irritable.

'Excuse me,' she said, 'I think I have made some mistake. I am going to bed now.'

She looked for some clothes so as not to have to walk naked to the stairs, but before she could find them Rosina and Diana came in, pink and rosy from a brisk walk home from the theatre on All Hallows' Eve.

'Oh, goodness me,' said Rosina. 'I told Diana we should come back and rescue you, but I see we're too late.'

'Oh Redbreast,' said Diana. 'It was a perfectly good play. It was very embarrassing when you walked out like that. And what *are* you doing with Minnie? I thought you were over all that.'

'I am,' said Anthony. 'Forget it. Everyone forget about it. I'm just a little drunk. Slate wiped clean, all right?'

'Slate wiped clean!' they all said. Minnie ran for the stairs.

What Happened Next

...at Belgrave Square

'Silly Minnie. High time she came back,' his Lordship was saying to Isobel the very next day. He had got used to having Minnie around. He had been right about her; she had made fine breeding stock – glossy-haired, bright-eyed, cool-nosed and spirited – interested in affairs of State while others yawned, and an asset to the household, if rather quiet in company. Minnie deserved respect and consideration. She had given the family what promised to be a worthy heir and another son to spare. True, she had bolted, as any spirited creature will. She'd left her young behind, which was a great pity; now she just needed to be brought back promptly to the stable. Say what his wife might, children needed their mother, needed that more than good feeding and a proper education.

He had lost his own mother when he was small and even thinking about it still made him sad.

'Leave her to come back in her own time,' said Isobel. 'She'll come to her senses soon enough. She's not much of a mother, or she would not have left them in the first place, no matter how badly Arthur behaved. If he did, of course, though I think it was mostly in her own imagination. And Arthur says not. But she is still enough of a mother to come back.'

He thought Isobel was looking exceptionally young and pretty and elegant, her pale skin slightly flushed and her eyes bright. She clearly enjoyed being a grandmother. Carmen was of the more luscious, fleshy kind: far nearer the animal than the spiritual; her skin a browny colour, her cheeks permanently red, her affections easy and her taste execrable; but her eyes were kind. No matter whom she married – as such creatures often did – she would never make a Countess, or even a Mrs Keppel. He remembered Flora, from a more distant past, and wondered if she had married: he remembered how the discovery of his liaison with her had upset Isobel, and reminded himself to be very, very careful indeed. Carmen would have to go, though probably not until after the New Year. One could keep such matters secret for a few months – after that, in his experience, they would probably surface. The King certainly knew that, so no longer bothered to hide his passing loves. But Isobel was not like the Queen Consort: she was not of a complacent turn of mind. Neither, it seemed, was Minnie.

'You are holding the children as hostages, then?' his Lordship asked.

'My dear,' said his wife, 'of course I am not, but put it how you wish. So far as I am concerned the longer Minnie stays away the better. She has such strange ideas about bringing up children. With any luck she will wander back to Chicago, keep her mother company and leave us alone.'

'But then Arthur will have no wife.'

'Arthur has no need of a wife,' said Isobel. 'He has his company, his toys, his automobiles. The boy takes after his grandfather. Silas had his coal business and any number of sons. He abandoned them, made do with the occasional company of my mother, and was perfectly happy. So was I.'

'Your father was not a landowner,' said his Lordship. 'I can only hope that when I am gone Arthur remembers that he is.'

'Of course he will,' said Isobel. 'He has been not just born but reared to the title. I have made sure of that, my dear. But in the meanwhile I have other things to think about. The King and his entourage will be here on Friday the fifteenth of December, only four weeks to the day.'

Isobel was punishing him, he was sure of that, for sins long past and forgotten by him. Men forgot easily: women did not. The excessive time, energy, money and emotion now being spent on Dilberne Court was no doubt her revenge for his past misdemeanours. Every new sin, such as inviting the King to stay without asking her first, brought to mind all the others. Women all did this kind of thing, but did not know they were doing it. He supposed she would have to be indulged. But it was becoming noticeably expensive.

She seemed surprisingly casual about Minnie's delinquency. It was all very well for Silas to have abandoned his sons but Silas was not a peer of the Realm. He had no social responsibilities other than to God, King, Country and his family. Arthur was a Viscount with a duty to an estate.

What went on between Arthur and Minnie was neither here nor there: she was his wife and that was that. Arthur must get her back.

Billy O'Brien's business had, thank God, survived the last fall in livestock prices, which as Baum had predicted were rising again. Minnie would have her inheritance. Besides, he was fond of the girl. When she smiled, she meant it. When she looked unhappy, that's what she was. She was rather like Carmen in this particular respect. His son, in Robert's opinion, was out of his bloody mind to have upset his wife, and then not gone after her at once to bring her back. Arthur, when it came to women, was deaf and blind to their needs. He seemed not to grasp that women, especially American women, took matters of romantic infidelity to heart. What to a man was over and done with and forgotten in an hour was to a woman a matter of untold significance. Infidelity in a man was of no importance, in a woman it certainly was. The law recognized that an energetic husband would always require interludes outside the marriage bed – men needed fulfilment or their health suffered. If a woman did the same it was reason to divorce her. Her very soul would be involved, her loyalty, and thus the paternity of her children forever doubted.

King Edward could do as he wanted, because his paramours didn't really count in the greater scheme of things. Bertie liked keeping the company of intelligent women but obviously he would never leave the Queen, any more than he,

Dilberne, would leave Isobel. Carmen was from a hot continent where passion ruled, not reason. In temperate Britain, as one educated the people so one extended the franchise. It was a great experiment. He himself was in favour of giving educated women the vote: the best of them were sensible enough. He gave up worrying about Arthur, prudently changed the subject, and asked Isobel what she thought of women's suffrage.

'Why do you ask?' she enquired. 'I hope you do not want simply to pick a quarrel. You are in a very strange mood. I know you are in favour and I am not. Your lot talked out the franchise bill and I am not at all sorry. Women have the municipal vote and should be happy with that; all they do anyway is vote as their husbands do, as has been proved time and time again. And if Rosina wants the parliamentary vote,' she went on, 'it is surely a very good reason for us to be against it. She is a born contrarian. She would vote against her own interests, her own class, just for the sake of it, the better to annoy. She prefers revolution to order, socialism to freedom.'

'So do many men,' said his Lordship, mildly. It was sadly true, he could see, as so many argued, that even clever women were inclined by their natures to use emotion and matters related to family in argument rather than reason.

'The only thing that does attract me to female suffrage,' she said, 'is that your friend the King is so against it.'

She was not at all herself; it was as he thought, she was still upset. Not just about the King and Mrs

Keppel descending upon them, but at Rosina's betrayal. She had expected Rosina to return within days, begging for forgiveness and asking to be let back into the family home, but Rosina had not. Now Minnie had done the same. Isobel would rather break than bend. He had a sudden longing for Carmen's company. It never occurred to Carmen to be spiteful or resentful, let alone wish or not wish for female suffrage. So he held his tongue, and refrained from saying that what worried the King was that women would tend to vote out of petty spite, or because they liked the looks of a candidate irrespective of his policies. Women bet on horses because of their colour. They were irrational, the King complained.

How strange that he and Isobel had bred such disparate children. Rosina, so 'difficult' yet full of concern for others; so long, as Isobel would have it, as they were not her nearest and dearest. Arthur so apparently amiable, yet so indifferent to the feelings of others. And Isobel, so ill at ease with both of her children, but seeing an opportunity to make a better go of things with her grandchildren.

Robert thought that as soon as he had seen to one or two important matters of State he would go in search of Arthur and give him some fatherly advice. In the meanwhile, to Hell with the female franchise; disunity in the party over Free Trade was splitting the government apart. The other Arthur – Balfour – was also in need of friendship and support. Balfour would probably stay on as leader of the party, but would lose the premiership to the amiable Campbell-Bannerman, mollifier to end all mollifiers. In this quality Robert felt himself out-ranked, and was therefore slightly put out.

What Happened Next

...at The Gatehouse

Arthur was busy in his Gatehouse office when his father called by. It was a busy day; he and his two new secretaries were going through potential mileages per gallon for the Jehu IV. Thanks to Robert's recent injection of funds, the Jehu IV was already on the drawing board: it was to be a heavy carriage to be used overland, not only for the transport of stock and goods, but for the convenience of the Guns – the ability to bring in an extra keeper and a dog or two at short notice would be much appreciated on any shoot, as would easy access to the duck pits and snipe marshes where horses found difficulty – and an extra ten minutes in bed on a frosty morning was always welcome.

Car transport meant no more worries about horses bolting and dogs barking, putting the golden plover and the wood pigeons to flight, and disturbing the nesting pheasants. So long as Arthur got the exhaust problem under control, so that the Jehu IVs moved quietly, the use of cars rather than horses would greatly improve the pleasure of the day. His father, in search of the finest shoot, was finally an enthusiastic convert to the automobile, though rather appalled by Arthur's suggestion of night shoots – you could drive hares and rabbits for anything up to a quarter of a mile in the glare of oxyacetylene lights before securing your quarry and blasting off without so much as leaving the car. Or even get them with your tyres.

'God forbid,' said the Earl. 'Then the poor creatures would be better fit for soup than a roast! Never!'

Now it seemed what Robert really wanted to talk about was Minnie, and made no bones about it. He was gratified to see that of Arthur's two secretaries one was a young man, Oliver Hawkley, a grammar-school lad with a head for statistics, and the other an extremely plain married woman, Effie Firbank, who had worked for the Daimler firm in Coventry, pleasant and competent enough but flat-chested. He suspected Arthur had inherited his own tastes for the voluptuous, and Effie was anything but. The receptionist, Marion Barnes, had been a parlourmaid at Dilberne Court until she'd married one of Arthur's engineers, and was already well trained in answering doors in a courteous yet distant way. There was no likelihood of trouble here. Perhaps Arthur had learned his lesson.

Arthur had indeed been thoroughly disconcerted by his encounter with Miss Braintree. She'd written an appreciative, even flattering piece in the

Mirror, two whole columns and a photograph of him by Tom Grant which even Isobel acknowledged made him look most dashing; and though she viewed askance the phrase 'The Motoring Viscount', she had shown the article to her friends. A letter had come from Miss Braintree repeating her request to be his secretary so she could finish her novel, to which he had firmly replied, 'No.' A dozen or so other letters, all in an ill-educated hand, had come from female members of the public asking to meet, or work for, him; he had consulted Inspector Strachan about these and Strachan had advised him to ignore them. 'Fans', as he called them, could be dangerous – it was no accident, he said, that the term derived from the word fanatic. The King was in as much danger from those who loved him for his splendour as from those who hated him for his privilege and wealth.

But in another respect Arthur's life seemed oddly empty. He missed Minnie. Sleeping in the Gatehouse was all very well. He was away from his mother's obsessive renovations, and he could concentrate on his work and not have to waste time in eating, female chatter, talk of children and fashion; but sleeping alone was chilly now that Autumn had arrived. Strachan had arranged for locks to be put on all possible windows at the Gatehouse, and the hired workmen had managed to break a few panes of glass in so doing and had not replaced them. He was reluctant to alert Isobel – it would probably end up with her deciding the Gatehouse had to be rebuilt altogether – it was the kind of thing Minnie could have organized without fuss or bother. And a man, he realized, needed domestic companionship; someone to sleep next to, to talk to about nothing in particular, to listen to him and admire, to join gentle forces with him against his mother's forays. Minnie was always tact itself. She had served so many purposes. Perhaps his anger with her had been misplaced. He had expected her to come running back with her tail between her legs, but she had not.

He went up to the Court twice a week to say goodnight to the children at bath time. It occurred to him that perhaps they were missing their mother, although they were well enough looked after by Nanny under his own mother's supervision, and Isobel had assured him they were perfectly happy. But in the past couple of weeks Edgar and Connor had seemed a little subdued; Connor had even asked him where his mummy was, and Edgar's little mouth had turned down in an unmanly way. Connor had blisters on his ankles. Arthur had queried whether the child's shoes were too tight and Nanny had said tight shoes were good for growing feet. They hardened the skin. He asked Isobel if this was the case.

'Don't interfere, Arthur, Nanny knows what she is doing. You're as bad as Minnie, worrying about this, that and the other,' she had replied.

Whatever was going on with Strachan was good for her complexion but not good for her mood. She seemed perpetually irritated. Minnie would just have got in the Jehu, gone down to Brighton, bought new shoes and thrown away the old ones. And surely Nanny was too old for the job? His mother saw only what she wanted to see. Minnie saw what was really going on. He missed her body and her hair and the shape of her, the curl of her foot against his when he woke. And then he'd leap out of bed, when he should have stayed with her, unable to resist the call of the Jehu. Sins of omission were as bad as sins of commission. He had resisted Miss Braintree but it was not enough.

'I am not going to last for ever,' said his father the Earl. They were in the long, top room of the Gatehouse. Arthur poured him a liberal glass of twenty-year-old Highland single malt. These days Arthur did not drink himself, claiming it clouded his brain, but his father took it as given that all discussions were lubricated by requisite amounts of good whisky or wine. 'These things must be talked about. I do not know what goes on between you and Minnie and I would prefer not to, but one day you will be an Earl, responsible for a large estate and all the people and properties that go with that inheritance. You in your turn will pass it on to Edgar and his children.'

'I am all too aware of this, Pater,' said Arthur. 'But need we talk about it now?'

'Yes, we must,' said his Lordship. 'You have brought it on yourself. You have let Minnie go, and the estate needs her.'

'Why?' asked Arthur. 'After you are gone Mama can take over.'

'Your mother is good at fashion and high society: she does not understand the needs of people or land.'

'But Pater, neither do I,' said Arthur. 'I understand the needs of the automobile, petrol and oil, water and air, but not, or so I am told by Minnie, of human beings. I find their emotions very trying, but why shouldn't I? I can produce heirs aplenty, it seems, but when it comes to wheat and forestry, it is quite true, I am at a loss.'

'Drollery aside, Arthur,' he said, 'when I am gone, Minnie, not your mother, must take over the estate. We chose wisely there. She has a good practical head on her shoulders and is not easily bullied. Your mother must retire gracefully as Dowager Countess to the Dower House – which she can renovate to her heart's content. You must go after Minnie and get her back, before she wanders off.'

'She won't wander off,' said Arthur. 'She loves me. She is safely with Rosina.'

'It is in the nature of women to wander off,' said the Earl. 'Even more than it is of men. They go in search of love; men go in search of sex.'

'But I didn't,' protested Arthur.

'The facts of the matter are neither here nor there,' said the Earl.

It seemed to Arthur very wrong that his own father should be talking to him about such things. It was embarrassing. Was his father referring to his mother and Inspector Strachan – or did he perhaps himself have some secret of his own? There had been a time when the Earl had been infatuated with Consuelo, Duchess of Marlborough, or so it had been rumoured.

'Even if any liaison had occurred,' said Arthur,

'Minnie should be man enough to accept it. The Queen does not worry about the King's infidelities. He had a whole loose box of mistresses at his own Coronation. And you and Mama are receiving Mrs Keppel in December for the shoot.'

'Very much against Isobel's wishes,' said Robert. 'The mood of the people has changed, and your mother is as ever sensitive to such things. Even Bertie no longer takes Mrs Keppel about in public. What matters is discretion. Women take romantic affairs to heart as men do not. The kindest thing is to keep them in ignorance of what goes on. There are a few highly passionate women about, true, but they, like intelligent women, are a minority and society both disapproves of, and pities them. Your sister Rosina, for one, is too intelligent for her own contentment and happiness.'

'You are not suggesting Rosina is highly passionate?' Arthur asked, shocked.

'Oh no,' said Robert, and then shocked his son even more, 'though I suspect she may be as interested in women as in men. You have no idea, it seems, of what company your wife may be keeping. She is your wife, for better or worse, mother of the future Earl of Dilberne, and Minnie is a great deal better than most. Go and get her back.'

So Arthur left Firbank and Hawkley in charge, and went to London in search of his wife to bring her back. He did so with joy, relief and anticipation in his heart.

PART THREE

Tessa Returns

7th November 1905

Minnie's mother Tessa sailed into Liverpool on the SS *Carpania,* the new Cunard liner. It was as luxurious and comfortable as the advertisements claimed, and with its two steam turbines and three propellers made a quick crossing if a rough one. It was, after all, Winter: the wind was wild and the waves tumultuous. Tessa too had come in search of Minnie, but with anxiety in her heart. This is the fate of parents everywhere. The birth of a child is a lifetime's sentence to anxiety.

Fathers are perhaps less sensitive to it than mothers. Tessa's husband Billy O'Brien had pointed out that no one took the trip in Winter if they could help it, but since his wife seemed helpless in the face of her own nature, he would have to put up with being without her for a couple of weeks. When the piglet squeals all must rush. It was the nature of the beast. He would come with her but unhappy marriages were female matters. He gave Tessa an open cheque book: if need be she must bring Minnie and the children back, but only if need be. He was an old man: he had bruised his knuckles once rescuing Minnie from the scoundrel of her choice: he did not want to have to do it again.

Grace was seasick nearly all the way over. They were on the passenger list as Mrs Tessa O'Brien and maid, for although Grace was now doing well in business and was quite the leading light in Cook County's juvenile charities, with her quiet voice, commanding air and perfect manners, she was still a British citizen and Tessa wanted no trouble with passports. There was no time to be wasted. Minnie's last letter had left Tessa perplexed. Her letters home – as letters home so often do – usually offered only good news: how kind the family were, how the children were thriving, how Arthur's business had taken off. But the last one had been strange, speaking of how she was missing the children, talking of Rosina (who so far as anyone knew had disappeared into Australia), and asking for money. Perhaps some earlier letter of hers had gone astray? And why could she possibly have no money – Billy had settled enough on her, God alone knew – and what could she need it for?

So Tessa worried and agitated on the first day at sea. Grace did what she could to soothe her. Her own opinion was that probably Minnie had fallen in love with some mad artist and run off: like mother, like daughter. The Irish enjoyed their sensuous pleasures and were romantics. On the other hand Minnie did not seem the hard kind of Irishwoman who would countenance leaving her own children in the name of love. So perhaps it was that her husband Arthur had been unfaithful – that too was most definitely in the blood – and Minnie, coming from God's Own Country and expecting more of life than an Englishwoman might, had taken offence.

On the first day of the voyage Grace did not say so: she did not want to upset Tessa further. After five years away from England she had forgotten what it was to be a skivvy, and had graduated to valued companion, even friend. Tessa still sought her advice on the art of cultivated and cultural living. Grace had developed her own little business selling art works and pottery, but she still lived in the O'Briens' household as one of the family and knew that alarming Tessa could be a noisy to-do. On the second day the *Carpania* hit bad weather and Grace was too ill to say very much at all.

'I wish I were dead,' was all Grace kept on saying, while Tessa, concerned, mopped her brow and held basins for her one-time lady's maid. The steward, since they were travelling first class, was attentive. He came quickly with fresh towels and bowls, and glasses of lemon and orange juice mixed, which Grace did her best to keep down. 'I wish I had never come.'

'May God forgive you, no you don't,' said Tessa. 'It's only the seasickness. Set foot on solid land and it passes over. And you'll be wanting to show yourself off to your old friends, won't you, and prove what a success you've made of yourself – the Barnardo's girl made good.'

Grace was unimpressed. She looked at Tessa with glazed eyes and vomited again.

The steward, a lanky Irish lad who when asked what his name was said, 'Finn – son of Erin', took Grace's forearm and pressed an inch or so above the wrist, saying it was a cure for seasickness he had learned from his father, a trawler man in Dublin Bay.

Grace recovered sufficiently to say to Tessa, 'What do you think I am? A cock to crow on a dung heap? All I want is to help your poor daughter out of a fix, same as you. It's all my fault anyway, that's all. I should have spoken up when I could, but I didn't.'

'What do you mean by that? Spoken up about what?' asked Tessa.

'About your Minnie marrying Master Arthur in the first place. I know what he's like and he's no gentleman for all he's a Viscount. He had his way with me and by the end of the school holidays couldn't so much as remember who I was.'

Tessa took time to take this on board and then said serenely: 'Well, he was a young man, wasn't he. What do they care for, but a notch on the bedpost? Many a man in my own lifetime has quite forgotten my face. Don't distress yourself, Grace. I was too busy selling the lace on my poor Minnie's petticoat to take any notice, and as for Minnie, she always did have an eye for a rotter. Let's face it, it's as likely to be her fault as his.'

Finn the steward, who had been doing his best to work out the relationship between the older lady and the younger, overheard this last and came to the conclusion they had switched cabins. Tessa, who was Irish, was the maid and Grace, who was English, was the mistress. He had no love of the English. He let the pressure on Grace's forearm go and she felt ill again at once and brought up the orange and lemon juice. Finn relented and went to fetch some Allen & Hanburys' morphine pastilles, and gave them to madam to suck and after that at least she slept a great deal more and vomited less.

Finn, considering himself in servitude to the English as he did, saw Mrs O'Brien as a true daughter of Ireland, and had a friendly exchange or so with her: he was jumping ship to join the Sons of Finn McCool when the ship docked at Queenstown. Tessa passed the time on the voyage purloining food from the groaning tables of the first-class lounge and giving it to Finn. He in his turn would smuggle the booty down to the third-class passengers. They were quartered in dormitories and dined on bread and cheese, stringy stew and watery potatoes. Tessa went down in person once, and found to her surprise that conditions below were not as bad as she had imagined, or certainly as Finn claimed, leaving the seasickness out of it. But then steerage was half empty – immigrant boats left for the United States full, returning only with those few who were disappointed with what they found, or single women who had been barred entry at Ellis Island, unable or unwilling to find someone to marry them on the way over. Their quarters were clean if Spartan; nurses tended to the sick, the food was plentiful if plain. Tessa's gifts were welcome enough: the oysters, filets mignons, whole roast duck, chocolate cream gâteaux, little bottles of whisky and brandy; anything Tessa managed to secrete without being seen, with the aid of napkins and pockets. Tessa's pleasures might now belong in first class but her heart belonged in third, as is so often the way with those who start poor and end rich.

On the third day the waves abated and Grace felt better. Finn had a word with the Purser to the effect that the ladies' cabins had been wrongly assigned, and Grace accepted an invitation to dine at the Captain's table, where she conducted herself with the manners and grace of a fine lady. Tessa dining without her companion was received with that excess of cool politeness which the English reserve for the Irish, a mixture of pity and a profound conviction of their own superiority. No wonder Finn resented them.

Tessa felt for her daughter – Ruth amid the alien corn: an American amongst the English, and Irish-American at that. Worse, Chicago Irish, not even lace-curtain Boston Irish, but stockyard Chicago, hog-baron Irish. What had she and Billy done to their daughter? Bartered her, sold her, used her lace petticoats to charm a Lord and boast about having a titled lady for a daughter.

By the time the *Carpania* docked at Liverpool – they had a different steward after Queenstown where Finn jumped ship and many of the steerage passengers disembarked – Tessa was thoroughly ashamed of herself and the more determined to bring her daughter and grandchildren home. As for Grace, she was the more secure in her right to be considered a lady. Anyone who could tell a kid glove from a suede glove, as could any lady's maid, but very few ladies, had, she decided, a right to consider well of herself.

They took the train to London and stayed at the Savoy on the Tuesday night. Tessa had thought Grace would prefer to stay at Brown's, where she had been so close to Eddie the concierge during her skivvy days. But Grace shuddered at the very idea, afraid of being sucked back into the humiliations of the past.

They took a fine breakfast in their suite; even Grace could find no fault. A team of three served it impeccably: the tablecloth was snowy and crisply starched, the silver salvers and coffee service polished to perfection, the Bircher Muesli (Lady Minnie's favourite) lavishly made with thick yellow cream, the sausages moist, the grilled tomatoes sweet and crisp, scrambled eggs from the freshest eggs and the apricot jam for the toast had been cooked French style, the apricots tiny but still whole, more compote than jam.

Later in the morning Grace wanted to take a taxi to No. 3 Fleet Street, where Minnie had last reported her whereabouts, but Tessa wanted to go on foot.

'Sure and it's a fine soft morning,' she said, 'and I need to walk, I'm bursting, fat as a stuffed pig.'

'It's a most pleasant morning,' corrected Grace, 'and never draw unnecessary attention to your physical state.'

'I'm done with all that malarkey,' declared Tessa, 'I speak as I find, I am what I am.'

And she led the way down the Strand, a round,

brave, squat, bright figure in a tightly-waisted, pink bombazine coat-dress, its skirt cut fashionably short to show the ankles, which was, Grace thought, unfortunate, since the ankles were rather fleshy and hung over the tops of her brown suede and very expensive lace-up boots. But *one-two, one-two, one-two* she went – to rescue her child, defiant in the face of fate and oblivious to others' opinion. Grace felt very fond of her, she herself being in a navy-blue coat with a fur muff and little felt cloche hat that kept her ears warm. She had a beau back in Chicago, a lawyer with the Board of Trade, who much admired her ears.

It was a fifteen-minute walk – it had looked shorter on the Baedeker map the concierge showed them – past the Aldwych corner with the new Waldorf Theatre, where Eleanora Duse was putting on *Lights Out* (with, so it said, Henry Irving acting: they must go when they had time), past pretty St Mary le Strand and St Clement's, into Fleet Street, and opposite St Dunstan's church there was No. 3. It was a small house, squeezed in between more august buildings, with a shop door and glass windows running across the frontage. It could have been a business or a home. It was certainly not likely to house a Viscountess, and Grace's immediate thought was that her 'run off with a mad artist' guess about the runaway daughter was perfectly possible.

And then Grace stopped short. Parked in front of No. 3 was a familiar-looking Jehu automobile, and who but Reginald sitting up in front waiting, well-scarved, but recognizable at once. Tessa had gone ahead and was banging upon the shop door. It did not open.

'Reginald, is that you?' It was a moment or so before Reginald recognized Grace, moments which, in spite of her protestations to Tessa, she did indeed savour. Why should she not?

'Grace,' said Reginald startled. 'You! What are you doing in London?'

'I am staying at the Savoy,' said Grace.

'Still the lady's maid?' asked Reginald.

'As a friend,' said Grace, haughtily.

'But still with the mother-in-law, I see,' said Reginald. 'Turned up like a bad penny. Young Arthur's come to claim his wife – so it'd be better she stays out of it. I don't think it's going too well.'

And indeed it seemed so. Grace could hear the sound of altercation and male shouts from within, over the noise of Tessa's knocking, now more like hitting. The little red hands were surprisingly strong; she was using the muff to protect the knuckles.

'You devils, you dirty skuds, you bastards, let me in! Minnie, are you in there? It's your ma!'

Scuffles, shuffles, and bangs came from inside, and little female moans of dismay and protest. Tessa shouted and hammered: passers-by stopped to stare.

'Do something,' begged Grace, but Reginald seemed to be enjoying himself.

'It's always been like this, Lord Arthur and Mr Robin after the same woman, as you know from of old, Grace.'

'But she's not just some woman,' protested

Grace. 'She's his wife!'

'She was never any better than she ought to be either,' said Reginald. 'What did anyone expect?'

At which point the door burst outward and the Viscount and the Hon. Mr Robin fell into the street, knocking Tessa onto the ground. Grace ran to help her up. Arthur and Mr Robin continued their scuffle too closely entwined to render the other completely helpless, until Mr Robin banged Arthur's head upon the pavement and he lay still for at least a moment. This allowed Mr Robin to extricate himself and lean against the doorpost, breathing heavily, laughing horribly, every now and then crowing, 'Too late! Too late!' A couple of street urchins cheered. A few more respectable passers-by stood and gawped – most hurried by. Minnie, barefoot, but at least fully clothed, came weeping to the door. Lady Rosina and another young woman whom Grace did not recognize peered out from behind her.

'It is not true, Anthony,' Minnie wept at Mr Robin. 'You know it isn't true! Why are you lying?' and to her husband, 'Arthur, my darling, he's lying. Please believe me!' And she tried to help her husband up, but he shook her off saying, 'Why should I believe you! Harlot!' so she shrank back. He might as well have hit her.

Grace was appalled. First a fight which reminded her of little boys in the school yard back at Barnardo's, now one of those melodramas you saw at the Selig five-cent moving picture theatre on a Saturday afternoon. Reginald was smirking. But Minnie was at least in Tessa's arms, her mother weeping and laughing all over her.

'My darling girl, my darling wee chick...' It was a hopeless task to make a lady of her; the Irish in her would always out. 'What have you been and gone and done now?'

'I've done nothing bad, Ma, nothing bad at all,' Minnie wailed. 'He's lying! I'm a good girl. He's making it up. It's because I wouldn't when he wanted–'

And this girl was a Viscountess. Grace didn't believe Minnie for one minute. She even felt sorry for Master Arthur, who even as she watched spat upon the ground, and Grace bent down and used her little lace handkerchief to pick up a bloody tooth from the gutter, and hand the small package back to him. When she was a girl of fifteen he had stood with golden-haired bare legs beside her iron bedstead in a sloping attic bedroom, and she had welcomed him in under the bedclothes, but he would hardly remember that now.

'A dentist may put it back, Master Arthur,' she said. 'I don't know about here but in Chicago they would. They're very ahead.'

Lord Arthur looked at her blankly but took the handkerchief. It meant a lot to Grace. She had bought it from haberdashery at Marshall Sears as a symbol of her new earning and spending life in the land of plenty. It was a lovely if tiny thing, ever so light and lacy, the body made of ecru net, embroidered with flower-of-life motifs, tambour style, enhanced with lace appliqué and cut work, and frilled with the most delicate coffee-coloured Belgian lace. She was glad Master Arthur had it. It had seemed something of a wicked waste at the time, two dollars, but now it was at least useful, if bloody.

Arthur moved past Grace and into the Jehu without looking back.

'Lincoln's Inn, Reginald,' he said, his voice hoarse and desperate. 'Courtney & Baum. To my lawyers.'

Reginald gunned the engine as once he had whipped up the horses, and the Jehu roared away to join the main throng of traffic, both horse and automobile, which now jammed the Strand as it narrowed into Fleet Street. Its progress was marred only by a series of rude bangs from the exhaust.

Lady Rosina and the other girl attended to Mr Robin, looking witheringly at Minnie the while.

'I never thought you would be so completely bloody silly,' Rosina said to Minnie and Minnie looked too shocked to retaliate.

'Oh Minnie, how could you!' sighed the other girl.

'But I didn't, I didn't! Nothing happened. Believe me!' begged Minnie.

'You leave my girl alone, you preening nancy boy,' said Tessa, pushing Rosina aside, and then to the other girl, 'and don't you lay hands on her or I'll be having to disinfect her.'

'Oh Ma, oh Ma,' wailed Minnie.

Not even Mum, thought Grace, let alone Mummy, let alone Mama. Just Ma. What kind of mother to an Earl would the girl make?

Then Tessa said to Mr Robin, pink bombazine quivering in rage, 'As for you, you nancy man, don't think I don't know one when I see one. I've no idea what you're playing at but I'll find out.'

Tessa bundled Minnie into a motor taxi that Grace had found, and they went off to the Savoy. Anthony Robin, Diana and Rosina went back inside No. 3 and they closed the door after them. The onlookers dispersed.

The Day After the Terrible Event

November 1905, Belgrave Square

Isobel, ignorant of these dramas, rose at ten the next morning and prepared for her day. Minnie would arrive at three for her Sunday visit to see the children, and her Ladyship rather dreaded the occasion. It was worse than any charity event where you had to dissemble, pretend to smile when you did not feel like it, and be friendly when you were not. The guests would pay their money and go away happy, and you'd sink back in relief that it was over, get on with your life, duty done, the evils of ignorance, poverty and illness duly battled. But it was a strain. You did not look forward to it.

This afternoon she would have to sympathize with Minnie about how badly Arthur had behaved when it was surely Minnie who had been at fault in her over-reaction. Her son said the occasion had been entirely innocent and Isobel believed him. Minnie was bored and loved a scene and had been looking for reasons to find fault, that was all.

'Minnie has everything she needs,' Arthur had said. 'She has a husband, a home, children, servants – for Heaven's sake, what more can she want? If you can put up with Pater's interest in politics I don't see why Minnie can't put up with my interest in the combustion engine. We both work for society as well as our families.'

He was quite right: women looked after the home, men looked after the progress of things, and women must put up with what went with having an energetic and handsome husband. Of course it was not pleasant to have a faithless one, as she herself well knew, but their infatuations quickly passed and meant little. If Minnie wanted her children back all she had to do was come home and live with them. No one was stopping her. As it was, it was she, Isobel, who was put to trouble, having to stop what she was doing just when there was so much to be done in Sussex, and haul the little ones all the way up to Belgrave Square for Sunday tea.

And Minnie going to stay with Rosina, at least it kept things respectable, and she was well and truly chaperoned by a married – well, widowed – family member, but it was an act of defiance and disrespect towards herself. If Rosina apologized all would be well – Isobel had made it easy for her by inviting Minnie to Sunday tea: simple for Rosina just to come along to hold Minnie's hand, but Rosina had chosen not to.

She wished Lily was here to do her lady's maiding, but she had left her back at the Court to help train the new agency staff, and so had to put up with Angela who was all fingers and thumbs and had run her bath far too hot – and now she was putting out a morning dress pretty enough but in a pale suede that would mark easily.

'Goodness me, Angela,' she said crossly. 'Do use your wits. I'm with the children. Little fingers get stuck in the lace, and little fingers smear suede. Take it away.'

Yes, your Ladyship, no, your Ladyship, I'm sorry, your Ladyship. Isobel could hear it before it was spoken. Servants so seldom thought for themselves, or said anything unexpected. Rosina had turned her back on the whole lot, determined to live an independent life free of men, servants, the world of maids and mistresses. But Rosina did not care about what she wore, or what people thought; she inherited that from her grandmother, Isobel's mother. Perhaps, thought Isobel, she herself would be a better person if she cared less about other people's opinions?

It was the kind of thing she would like to talk to Mr Strachan about. He would give the matter due consideration and come back with a proper reply, not something dismissive. Strachan was not highly educated, but he knew a great deal about human nature, how people behaved, about who was dangerous, who was not. He made her feel safe: he was good company; if only he was around she could take Minnie's visit in her stride. But apparently he must be at Windsor for the weekend; the King was away and there were new security measures to be organized – always simpler, quicker and certainly quieter in his absence. The King, like Robert, like Arthur, felt the need for precaution was much exaggerated.

Angela managed to bring out a more suitable dress, narrow-striped navy-and-white with puffed sleeves but which didn't make one look too formidable, so one could enter a room looking more like a woman than a ship in full sail. Mr Strachan would like it. She did not really want to think too much about Mr Strachan. She enjoyed his company and his conversation but obviously it could not go further than that. She was a Countess, he was, frankly, just a policeman, a figure of fun. She must put him out of her mind. The dress was formal enough to set an example for Minnie, and would easily enough withstand Connor's swarming without tearing. Edgar never swarmed: he had an inner dignity and formality as befitted his position in the family. She would not go to church today: it was necessary in the country, but in town one's absence was not so noticeable. Mr Strachan was an atheist, which was an untenable position, and Robert would throw him out of the house if he knew. Best, clearly, that Robert didn't get to know, since the Inspector was also of the opinion that the children would be better off with their grandmother than their mother, who was apparently unstable.

It was obvious that the children themselves barely noticed their mother's absence. When Nanny and the nursemaid brought them down to the drawing room for Sunday tea, Edgar actually turned his face away from his mother's kiss and Connor buried his head in Molly's skirts, which was hardly surprising. What little ones want to see their mother crying? Connor was a dreadful name. Minnie had insisted on it. Why anyone wanted to be reminded they were of Irish ancestry Isobel couldn't imagine, but the more one got to know Americans the more strange they seemed. Last Sunday Isobel had been courtesy itself and had kept the conversation light and ordinary. When their mother left, true, the little ones set up the most dreadful wailing, but as Nanny pointed out they were copying their mother's snivelling but at full volume. Tea time with Minnie and the children should not after all become a normal occurrence. It was too draining. This was the last time she was doing it.

She did her hair herself; Angela would pull so. She lunched lightly and at about one o'clock Arthur turned up at the front door. She had no idea Arthur was in town. Her heart lurched – had he come to see Minnie and the children? Did that mean there was some kind of reconciliation? She wished Robert had not interfered. The home and the family were her business, not his. She need not have worried.

'Arthur my dear boy,' she said, 'what a delight! Have you come to see dear Minnie? The children are upstairs with Nanny. They'll be so happy to see you. They see far too little of you.'

Her voice faded away. Arthur looked dreadful; he was distraught, wild-eyed and with a bruised mouth and speaking thickly. He had come home from Eton like this once when he was about sixteen, she remembered. Robert had taken him to boxing lessons on that occasion.

'Oh dear boy,' she said. 'Your father took you to the wrong boxing coach. But where on Earth have you been?'

'To the dentist,' he said, bitterly, and asked to see his father.

'I believe he's round at Downing Street,' said Isobel, 'helping poor Mr Balfour pack his books. I can have him fetched. Where on Earth did you find a dentist on a Sunday?'

She tried to straighten his tie and rearrange his collar but Arthur shook her off, which quite upset her. Common politeness seemed to have deserted him. She did not have to have Robert fetched. He arrived hot on his son's heels, back early, he said, from the House.

'I thought you were at Downing Street,' she said. 'I didn't know the House sat on Sundays.'

It was an innocent enough remark but Robert reacted angrily.

'You are very quick in accusation, my dear,' which quite shocked her. Nothing had been further from her thoughts. And now Arthur was looking at her, his own mother, with what seemed like acute dislike. Why?

'All women are the same, Pater, the pot calling the kettle black.'

'Perhaps one could say the same about men,' she said, sharply. But what was the matter with him? What could he be talking about? Did he think that she and Mr Strachan – she remembered the walk down from the Gatehouse to talk about locks and bars and pistols – surely he could not imagine – it was absurd. But he had already forgotten, lost in his own woes.

'I did what you told me, Pater,' he said. 'I wish to God I had not. I spent yesterday afternoon at the lawyers. I am divorcing Minnie. You married me off to a whore.'

Isobel could see that Minnie coming to tea was not the worst that this particular Sunday could throw at her. Arthur, a grown man, her son, wept as loudly and copiously as little Edgar had a week ago, and Robert scowled and paced. She called for lunch for the men: in her experience food often quietened them and restored their mood. Fortunately lunch was being served in the servants' hall – the kind of food they had so enjoyed in their school days. Brown Windsor soup, meat stew and mashed potatoes, roly-poly and custard. Some of that could be brought up for them.

Arthur told them all. Robert's fury at Minnie's treachery with Anthony Robin equalled that of his son's, and was unsoftened by the latter's distress which was so great that for a moment Isobel almost longed for Minnie's return to the fold. She pulled herself together quickly. Arthur would recover and marry again. Men always did. An empty marriage bed soon becomes an abhorrence. Divorce would be a scandal, but at least no court would permit Minnie to have custody of the boys. Visiting rights might be allowed but even that was doubtful. An affair made public was bad enough, but for a mother to leave her children to run off with a lover was beyond the pale. Society would shun her; no one of any consequence would receive her. Minnie would be obliged to live on the Continent, or go back to Chicago and her impossible family and be out of everyone's lives for ever. Arthur's new bride could be chosen at more leisure, and more wisely – and with any luck would be someone with more of a sense of style.

All was working out very well. But it seemed strange that Robert was so preoccupied by the name of Minnie's lover – Anthony Robin – which sounded familiar. She could not recollect quite who he was. Something to do with Rosina, who had so lamentably failed to chaperone Minnie? It was immaterial. Whoever he was, he was clearly a blackguard. But men *were* strange. Robert had been fond enough of Minnie in the past; his contempt for her was as sudden as it was absolute. She almost felt *poor Minnie* but not quite. One must be sensible.

She did not imagine that Minnie would have the face to come to tea; but at three o'clock precisely the front door bell rang. Robert went down to answer it himself, gesturing to the parlourmaid to stay back. Isobel followed behind him, while Arthur remained at the foot of the staircase. Minnie stood on the threshold, her face swollen, her hat awry, and her appearance unkempt. Worse, Mrs Tessa O'Brien stood there also, a red-faced Fury, a quivering jelly in pink. How little one could trust the ill-bred, Isobel thought, how quickly they reverted to type. This was the same Tessa O'Brien who had delighted everyone at Arthur's wedding with her naïve charm. But these were her true colours. The upper classes, when confronted with difficulty, were just the more restrained, the more courteous, as was her husband now.

His Lordship barred the door with casual ease.

'Let me in!' said Minnie.

'That is not possible. Not any more.'

'Arthur!' wailed Minnie, but in the background Arthur just shook his head.

'I've come to see my grandchildren,' said Mrs O'Brien, trying to elbow his Lordship out of the way. His Lordship stood fast, and smiled coldly.

'I am afraid this cannot come to pass, Mrs O'Brien,' said his Lordship. 'Your daughter has made her bed and now must lie upon it.'

'You stuck-up popinjay!' shrieked Mrs O'Brien. 'My girl's done nothing wrong. Let me through this door!'

Little Edgar and Connor appeared on the landing, flanking Nanny Margaret, who had brought them down from the nursery on hearing the front door bell. Stopped in her tracks, she stood aghast. Seeing their mother, the boys tumbled down the stairs towards her.

'Mama, Mama,' they cried and his Lordship had to use considerable strength to shut the door against the force of Mrs O'Brien's pounding fists. The children wailed some more as their mother was so rudely lost to their view, and Arthur, white-faced, bent to clasp them to him and comfort them, one on each side. They only wailed the louder and now Arthur wept too.

It was the worst Sunday Isobel could remember. She gave the pinstripe dress to charity. She would never wear it again. It was unlucky. A pity though that now Mr Strachan would not get to see it. She remembered how she herself had wept when Arthur, hardly higher than her waist, had been taken off to boarding school. Term after term it had happened until finally you got used to it and the tears dried up. Minnie would get used to it and see it was all for the best.

The Servants' Version

November 1905, Dilberne Court

'You'll never guess,' said Reginald. 'Grace is back in town. Looking like a lady, and so is Mrs Tessa O'Brien, looking less like one than ever. Straight off the boat to bring their girl back home, if you ask me, and who should they run into at the door of No. 3 but Lord Arthur on the same errand. Oh, but that Minnie does cause a lot of trouble, for all butter doesn't melt in her Ladyship's mouth. Butter melted a bit too fast, from what I can tell, and Lord Arthur was down to the Inner Temple to see his lawyer and take out divorce papers, in spite of all her denials.'

'But he can't do that,' said Mrs Neville. 'They're a married couple. Think of the scandal.'

'I don't think the Viscount was doing much thinking at all,' said Reginald. 'He spat out a tooth and our Grace, ever the lady's maid, handed him it back wrapped in a white hanky. The Jehu was backfiring like billy-o and he didn't even notice it. That exhaust's not half a problem. He went into that lawyer's office like thunder and came out blubbing like a baby.'

'Men have white hankies,' said Lily, 'to blow their noses on. Ladies have lace hankies just to dab. What was Grace doing with a white?'

'It was covered with blood,' said Reginald. 'I didn't notice the original colour.'

'Was it écru, perhaps?' asked Belinda. 'Écru lace is all the rage.'

Belinda was a pale thin girl in her twenties with elegant hands, hollow cheeks and large eyes, a lady's maid, one of the extra agency staff brought in for the royal visit. Mrs Keppel would probably bring her own maids but some guests liked to have extra staff in hand in case of emergencies. The ladies would have to change their clothes as many as eight times a day. She was a fussy eater, toying with her jam roly-poly and saying she was 'banting' which annoyed Cook. No one did that any more – no sugar, no flour, no salmon, no potatoes, and no pork? Senseless. Lily was delighted with her.

Belinda had seen service with the Duchess of Marlborough, and professed to find Dilberne Court something of a comedown, though there was now a W.C. wherever you looked, hot running water in every dressing room and bathroom, and electric lighting throughout. You could hardly find better at Blenheim Palace, though of course the scale was different. Nanny had been overruled and there were even radiators in the nursery. The young masters were spending quite a lot of the time in Belgrave Square. Lady Isobel liked to have them near her. As for the shoot, his Lordship had been lucky in the weather and the gamekeepers reported that the pheasants were in splendid form and the ground game was plentiful. New stands had been built and walkways for the ladies laid down.

Only the builders were behind schedule: they were meant to have finished a week ago but some chimneys needed re-lining – woodworm had been found in the attics, and dry rot in the back scullery where a tap had been dripping unnoticed for years. The source of the musty smell which had haunted the pantries for years was located – by the Inspector, as it happened, using his nose to sniff out trouble – and got worse before it got better as dusty, rotten beams were brought tumbling to the floors, and clouds of webby dust covered everything in sight. The fungus had reached as far as the third floor. All should be finished, but only just in time. The King was to arrive on Friday 15th December, straight from Sandringham, and return there on Wednesday the 20th.

'All this because the King has a mistress,' said Cook. 'It's beyond belief.'

'All this because his Lordship has one too,' said Reginald. 'Isn't that so, Digby?'

‘My lips are sealed,’ said Digby. He had come down from Belgrave Square with the Earl for a few days.

‘And now talk of a divorce. It quite makes you want to leave service,’ said Elsie. ‘If you can’t trust your betters who can you?’

Today there was beans and pork for lunch followed by strawberry jam roly-poly – perhaps Cook was trying to annoy Belinda, though it was a favourite with everyone; the suet crust made from best beef, rolled flat, spread thickly with strawberry jam from the home farm, rolled up, tied into a muslin bag and boiled for a good two hours.

‘Agnes told me last Sunday Mrs Keppel wouldn’t have a suet crust in the house,’ said Lily. ‘Mrs Keppel is on one long bant.’

‘Quite right too,’ said Belinda. ‘How else can she keep the King and her husband happy?’

‘Enough of that,’ said Mr Neville, but mostly because he wanted to return to the subject of Lord Arthur and his runaway wife. Even Mrs Keppel faded into insignificance.

Inspector Strachan was not at the table, for which all were glad. He put a blight on the conversation: it was hard to know which side he was on. Sometimes he ate with family: sometimes downstairs. Mr Neville wished he would make up his mind. He was a necessity, it seemed, with the royal visit pending, but who on Earth would want to assassinate the King?

‘You mean she didn’t go because of Master

Arthur and the lady journalist, all the time she'd just run off with a lover?'

'Not just any old lover,' said Reginald. 'She ran off with the Honourable Mr Anthony Robin of previous acquaintance, and note: there was a rare argy-bargy on the pavement, I can tell you, and in front of everybody: blood and gore everywhere. And after Master Arthur had gone all the way to London to bring his wife back home, full of remorse and the joys of Spring. He told me as much on his way up.'

'Stands to reason, a man needs his oats,' said Horace, the new agency footman, tall and handsome as footmen are meant to be. He was in his new livery: brown cord with velvet lapels, silver buttons and the narrowest of scarlet corded braids. *('Good heavens,' his Lordship had said, 'are you trying to bankrupt me, Isobel?' 'Mrs Keppel has her servants in grey and gold,' said his wife. 'Hardly more expensive. What do you want of me, Robert? To be outdone by the royal fancy-woman?)*

'That's enough of that,' said Mr Neville. 'We'll have none of that London talk round this table.'

'I don't see how a mother could do it,' said Smithers, the assistant parlourmaid. She had a hairy upper lip and a mole on her chin: she would have to take care to keep out of sight when the royal party arrived. 'Leaving her wee tots like that. She's little better than a hussy.'

'Like mother, like daughter,' said Reginald, 'and Mother Irish was there all right, bringing the tone of the place down, a sight in bright pink. But then they're Americans, we mustn't forget that. At least Grace was still looking like herself, just filled out, lost ten years, and quite the lady.'

'Too grand to visit us, I daresay,' said Mrs Neville. 'She always did have her nose in the air.'

'She's done well,' said Mr Neville, magnanimously. 'I'll give her that.'

'Fair's fair about Lady Minnie,' said Elsie. 'The engagement was far too short. They didn't give her time to think. Rushed her to the altar in a matter of weeks. We all thought she was in the family way, but no.'

'You're a fine one to talk,' said Lily, meanly. Elsie had been engaged to Alan Barker, one of the estate gamekeepers, for some seven years. The more she saved, the more Alan gambled and drank and spent the money. Soon it would be too late for babies, if it wasn't already. It was an ongoing joke. Elsie's lip quivered.

'Enough of that, Lily,' said Mrs Neville, and Lily actually nudged Elsie and muttered 'Sorry'. With so many extra staff employed to do the work of the household there was time and energy for such niceties.

'If you ask me,' said Digby, 'and I'm new to the family, but if this Mr Anthony Robin's the same Mr Robin as I know, then everyone's barking up the wrong tree. He's seeing a Mr Brown from Lady Rosina's publisher.'

'What's that got to do with the price of fish?' asked Smithers.

'Nothing you should know about, Smithers,' said Mrs Neville, 'and as for you, Digby, wash your mouth out with soap and water.'

'I speak as I find,' said Digby, darkly, and fell silent. So did they all, the soapy taste of childhood in their mouths.

Cook was the first to speak. She rang for Maria the agency under-parlourmaid to clear the plates. She turned to Belinda, whose plate was still sticky with cold syrup and suet crust, though she'd not been able to resist the jam, and said–

'As for you, Belinda, if you think you can come running to me for a piece of cheese before tea you've got another think coming.' Belinda tossed her head and Lily giggled.

'Talking of cheese,' said Mr Neville, speaking for them all: they wanted more from Digby, 'perhaps we could do with a little of that nice Cheddar we were eating yesterday, Cook, before we all get on with our work, while thanking God for his many mercies. Not to mention you, Cook, for the good table you make of what He provides.'

Cook beamed. Oat and wheat biscuits were brought in, with a large slab of golden butter and a whole half-pound of cheese. Belinda ate, while choosing the oatcakes rather than the wheat in accordance with her mother's instructions passed on from Mr Banting.

'Why would Mr Robin lie about a thing like that?' asked Lily.

'Stands to reason,' said Digby. 'Nothing would suit Mr Robin better than being named in a divorce case as a co-respondent. Turns the finger of suspicion away. No one wants to languish in prison like Mr Wilde.'

'That's daft,' said Reginald, 'I'll never forget waiting in Half Moon Street while he and Lord Arthur had their way with that Flora.'

'Please!' begged Mrs Neville.

'Because a man's one way inclined,' said Digby with authority, 'doesn't mean he can't be the other way too.'

There was another silence, while they took this in.

'What d'you mean?' said Elsie. 'Lady Minnie was caught bang to rights. All very well for Lord Arthur and the lady journalist but not for Lady Minnie. One law for the men and another one for us.'

'And why not?' asked Mrs Neville. 'A man can't help what he does, a woman can.'

'I'm not so sure,' said Lily.

'That's enough of that,' said Mr Neville. Nanny came in to find the cabbage cake she would slice for the children's tea. Minnie had insisted the children ate fresh vegetables though it always made them cry. Nanny would put on cabbage early in the morning, boil it for three hours, changing the water three times to get rid of impurities, squeezing the moisture out with the terrine press. By the time it was finished Nanny could cut it like a cake.

'Why are you still doing that, Nanny?' asked Cook. 'Giving that stuff to the children? It's only fit for horses.

Nanny thought about it and then dropped the slices and the whole cabbage cake into the pig-swill bucket.

'You're right,' said Nanny. 'There's no need for it any more. *Auntiescorbuticks,* my foot!'

'So you'll back me up then, Nanny,' said Reginald.

'My lips are sealed,' said Nanny. 'But yesterday the nasty truth came out, and Lady Minnie was barred the door.'

'What did I tell you,' said Reginald. 'A divorce is in the air.'

'Poor wee mites,' said Nanny. 'But at least they're out of that Jezebel's care and back here where they're safe. For nursery supper we'd like steamed cod and white sauce, Cook, with a sprinkling of nice dried parsley; Master Connor is partial to golden syrup pudding, if there's any over.'

The Snatching in Church Lane

Sunday 3rd December 1905

The lane was held fast in Winter's grip; the hedgerows were bleak, the path a horrid mixture of mud and ice. Nanny, the nursemaid Molly, and the two children were walking back from church to Dilberne Lane. Nanny held Edgar's hand. He dawdled and limped and said his feet were hurting.

'Stuff and nonsense,' said Nanny. 'The faster you walk the faster you'll get there. I thought you were a brave boy.'

Progress was not fast. Molly was wheeling little Connor in his stroller, but he kept wanting to get out and walk and cried if he wasn't allowed to.

The young masters had done nothing but whimper and whine since their mother left. Nanny denied it and said they'd never been happier. You could understand it in Nanny, thought Molly, she was old and daft, but Lady Isobel was much the same. They both only saw what they wanted to see. She'd even offered to go into Clarks' new shop in Brighton on her afternoon off and buy some nice soft sealskin button shoes for Mr Edgar's poor little feet – Mrs Neville said she could have the money – but Nanny said it would be doing the child no favours, the foot must learn to fit the shoe, not the shoe the foot. Which Molly knew to be nonsense, because her grandmother had trained with Nanny Margaret and said exactly the opposite.

Irene Barnes, Molly to everyone, was fifteen; a local girl who thought she was a disappointment to her mother, being not apparently interested in furthering herself. To be a nanny was the height of Molly's ambition; she liked children and she liked being told what to do. It was a relief; you could get on with your own thoughts. She hoped one day to be married, but as her mother kept telling her, that was the good fortune of only one girl in every three, and without more oomph she wouldn't make it. Molly could see she did not have oomph. Her mother had; her father had. Both had started out in service; both had got out. A pretty girl had opportunities; a plain girl without oomph was wise to stay where she was and make the most of what God had given her, which was what she was doing. What God had given her was a big house up the road where you got paid for what you most liked doing, where the mistress kept a good table, where you got £24 a year to spend on your afternoons off – and the little sealskin button shoes at Clarks in Brighton were darling, even if the child who needed them was someone else's, not your own. You were never likely to have any of your own anyway. She should have been allowed to buy the shoes. Master Edgar was a future Earl and deserved the best.

If she'd been pretty she would have dreamed of marrying an Earl and giving birth to a little Lord herself: as it was, she dreamed of Nanny dying or at least being retired for being so stupid and old, and herself, Molly, stepping into Nanny's shoes. If kitchen maids stepped over cooks when they died and just got on with finishing the dinner, so nursery maids could step over nannies and take over. Molly thought of how she had shaken her head at Lady Minnie the day she'd run away and wondered if she'd done the right thing. If only she'd had more oomph she'd have tucked the little ones under her arms and run with her. She'd liked Lady Minnie more than anyone. Nanny said Lady Minnie had odd ideas but Molly thought Nanny's were even odder. You thought people who were older than you automatically knew more than you but it wasn't so.

Thus, half day-dreaming, half attending to little Connor, Molly walked home with Nanny after church. It was rare for both the Earl and Lord Arthur to put in an appearance together, as they had today. Lady Isobel sometimes missed, but

Lady Minnie almost never. Now she had been gone for five weeks in a row. It was noticed and commented upon. Something was going on. There were rumours about the King's visit, which was supposed to happen in December, but nobody knew the exact dates. The reason for the secrecy was assumed to be because Mrs Keppel was coming with the King and the Queen wasn't meant to find out. For whatever reason, the locksmith was working overtime on new locks for doors, and the blacksmith on the bolts, and bars for basements. The Viscount was known to keep a pistol in the Gatehouse. What was going on?

After the service, Lady Isobel had talked with the Reverend Stacey about flowers for Mattins on the 17th December, so at least it could be safely assumed that the King would visit on the Sunday morning, and most of his staff would no doubt turn up for Evensong. The royal visit was bringing quite an income into the village. The trains were asked to stop more and more frequently at Dilberne Halt, to the despair of the Brighton and Portsmouth Railway Company.

Though the flowers for the church would be sent down by Frascati of Oxford Street, ladies from the Mothers' Union would arrange them. The white carpets may have come from Harrods of London but were fitted by Dilberne workmen, and the six white Angora cats that matched the carpets had been bred in an East Sussex cattery. Molly marvelled when she'd overheard Lily telling Nanny about the cats. Lily had got it from Agnes that Mrs Keppel had white Angora cats, it seemed, and white carpets. Molly thought it was rather obvious to do the same: if it was her she'd have got black cats and gone for the contrast. Everyone agreed The Change had turned her Ladyship a little strange. Though Molly acknowledged she was sweet with the children and was a frequent visitor to the nursery. It was more tempting for her to turn up, of course, now that radiators had been installed. Nanny kept all the windows open, which seemed to Molly a wicked waste.

The rest of the party had taken the carriage home – the Countess was complaining of the cold. Nanny and Molly went on foot so the boys' little lungs would get the benefit of the country air. The countryside was so peaceful and dank, not a soul to be seen. Damp foliage crowded in on them; there were still a few leaves on the trees and hedges. It looked as if it might snow: the clouds were low and heavy. If it did snow it wouldn't lie; just be wet slush. They were about half way home, had just passed the Drovers' Lane crossing at the top of the hill – after which you had to cling to the stroller to stop it speeding down, which was even worse than using all your strength to push it uphill – and had just rounded the bend where the path narrowed so she had to walk in front of Nanny and Edgar, when in front of them, out of nowhere, she saw that three women were walking determinedly towards them.

One she recognized, Lady Minnie, but looking rather odd and wild-eyed. Two she did not recognize: a tall and elegant woman in rather severe navy blue and a cloche hat, and a plump older woman wearing a pastel-blue outfit which was too tight. What happened was strange and very sudden. Lady Minnie walked past and plucked Connor out of the stroller, tucked him under her arm and walked briskly on. The tall one reached Nanny and simply released Edgar's hand and picked him up and joined Lady Minnie. Both then began to run, turning into Drovers' Lane and out of view. Nanny was left open-mouthed and staring. Then Molly herself was seized by the arm by the woman in pastel blue and hurried along.

'Nanny! Help!' she managed to cry out, but she wasn't sure she wanted help. She felt a decided surge of oomph. Anything was better than walking through mud on a day when it couldn't decide whether or not it was going to snow, with a little boy who couldn't decide likewise whether he was going to walk or not. As soon as they were round the corner – she was struggling mildly but not too hard: if she was being kidnapped it was obviously not by white slavers, and it might even turn out to her advantage – there was a motor car waiting for them. It was one of the new Austin Phaetons, she was sure of it, and driven by a man called Eddie, who seemed to be one of the tall woman's friends. She was called Grace. Perhaps she was the one they talked about sometimes in the servants' hall.

Lady Minnie sat in the front with Master Edgar on her knee; he had been too startled to say a word but seemed happy enough because Lady Minnie was already taking off his shoes and was fitting them with a new pair of Clarks' little sealskin boots just like the ones Molly had seen in

Brighton. It was all going to be all right. Molly was squeezed in the back next to Grace and the plump woman in pale blue, who turned out to be Lady Minnie's mother for all you couldn't understand half what she said. They plonked little Connor on her knee and he seemed to feel much the same as she did, that anywhere was better than Church Lane on a damp Sunday morning in December. Anyway, he started kicking away at the seat in front of him and annoying the driver so she knew he was not much damaged.

'We thought it was best to take you too, Molly. You're a familiar face to the boys.'

'Supposing I tell? Won't you get in trouble?'

'You're a good girl, Molly, you won't. And we'll keep an eye on you so you can't. It's only till tomorrow. We're in an hotel tonight and then we take the train to Liverpool and on to New York. The children are going home.'

'What about my things? My hairbrush? My nightie?'

'Grace has brought you some really nice things, Molly. And here's something for your pains.'

Grace leaned over and handed her two bank notes. They were large, white and silky. *I promise to pay the bearer the sum of five pounds* was written across it in a fine elegant script. It was printed on one side of the paper only. It was so beautiful and two of them were twice as beautiful as one. Everything the rich take in their hands is beautiful, thought Molly. Nothing scratched, nothing smelt, nothing hurt or made you shudder. She'd never seen anything with more than ten shillings written on a note before, though she knew such notes existed. Connor tried to snatch them so she stuffed them in her pocket. They were bribing her. Well, that was all right. She had everything to gain, and nothing to lose. And Master Edgar was sitting on his mother's knee, his hands locked round her neck, twisting round to stare at her face. He was so solemn and serious. Molly had done the right thing.

The Phaeton roared on to London as if nothing could stop it, Eddie driving intent and concentrated. It seemed that the woman in navy blue called Grace was a servant too. Molly looked behind, half expecting the police to be chasing them, but there was nothing: nothing on the road could keep up, let alone overtake. The roads were almost empty anyway. It would take Nanny ages to get home and call the alarm. You had to admire the ladies: ordinary criminals were stupid, but these three had everything so well organized. But Lady Isobel would be furious and Lord Arthur would not let his sons go easily. Edgar was the heir. The whole country would be in uproar.

The Phaeton they were in was a limousine; it could only be a prototype. Lord Arthur was trying to rush his own, Jehu, limousine into production. Molly had seen photographs of the new Phaeton down at his Lordship's workshop where her mother and father worked. In the flesh – or rather in the strong metal frame and brass-lined bonnet that seemed to smile, and with its two strong headlights like watchful eyes – it was rather glorious. The Jehu was all right but didn't have the Phaeton's glamour. Lord Arthur would be the more furious: not just his children kidnapped but in a rival's car, of all things an Austin Phaeton. The papers would love to get hold of the story. And Molly was the centre of the story. Whatever happened next, she would be famous. The two five-pound notes were only the start.

Doubt set in; shock at the suddenness of it all. Nothing to lose, she thought, but what about her job? If there were no children to look after why would the Dilbernes need her? She'd be out on her ear. Nanny might stay on because she'd been in the family so long, the horrid old cow, but she, Molly, had only just begun. And supposing she got blamed, for all she was kidnapped? Her father and mother might lose their jobs.

Molly tried to work it out. And the children, she wondered about them. Was it better for Edgar to be brought up as an Irish person in America or as a Lord in his own country with everyone bowing and scraping? Connor was no problem, he'd be all right wherever he was, but Edgar was different. He so seldom smiled; perhaps if you were born to a title you had to have the instincts that went with it or you couldn't thrive? Now he'd fallen asleep on his mother's knee. She was cradling his head in her arms to stop it banging against the dashboard when the car cornered. She was a good mother. Everyone said Lord Arthur was a good father but to Molly's eyes he seemed embarrassed by his own children.

The four of them were talking. She listened to find out what she could: in the circumstances it didn't feel like eavesdropping, just doing her duty by her charges. The man called Eddie was a friend of Grace's. He worked as a concierge at an hotel called Brown's. The Phaeton had been 'borrowed' by Eddie from the hotel mews, where it had been stabled by a Mr Herbert Austin, a guest at Brown's, but away in Birmingham for a couple of days. The worry was that Mr Austin would return early and find his vehicle gone. Grace had been booked in for the night at Brown's as Lady Stephenson from Dorchester; Minnie and her mother were Mrs O'Corcoran and maid from Chicago; and the children and Molly were the Masters O'Corcoran and nanny from Brighton.

'Meaning no harm, Mrs O'Brien,' apologized Mr Eddie, 'turning you into the servant, but we don't want to attract attention. In my experience the best lies are the ones that are nearest to the truth.'

'You're a cheeky blighter,' said Mrs O'Brien. 'So I'm the maid and Grace is the lady? I'm the one who pays the bills, remember that, and paying well over the odds into the bargain. Keep that straight.'

'And aren't I risking my job and worse for the sake of Grace's blue eyes?' asked Eddie, hurt to the quick.

'My eyes are brown,' said Grace. 'And don't think I'll be doing you any favours tonight, Mr Eddie, because I won't be.'

'Oh just let's get on back to London,' said Minnie. 'Bicker, bicker, bicker, I'm so tired. Who cares who's the maid and who's the lady? Isn't that so, Molly?'

'Yes, your Ladyship,' said Molly, 'but the baby needs changing. And there aren't any nappies.'

But Grace, who was obviously the one who thought of everything, had some baby things packed away in her hamper. Eddie drew the Phaeton to a gentle halt where the road to Hindhead met the Devil's Punchbowl and it was safe to park. Molly saw to the nappy and cleaned the old one off as well as she could with a couple of dock leaves before folding it back into the spare bag. She had been tempted just to throw it in the bushes but refrained. She had never stayed in an hotel before but presumably there would be somewhere to wash things out. A supply of nappies was less easy to determine.

'You're a good girl, Molly,' said Grace approvingly. 'Lady Minnie was right about you.' Molly glowed.

Molly had almost decided that when they'd got to the hotel she'd somehow slip out to Belgrave Square and let the world and the newspapers know that the Dilberne heir was being kidnapped, but now she thought perhaps she wouldn't. A word of praise made all the difference.

'Oh, do please hurry,' said Minnie, as they set off again. 'I feel so exposed on the open road. I won't feel really safe until I'm on the boat.'

'You won't be safe even then,' said Eddie. 'The *Carpania* carries a wireless telegraph. A day out at most and the police will alert the captain and the crew will start searching the boat high and low.'

'Oh dear,' said Minnie and she began to cry.

'But they won't find you. I've booked us all in third class,' said Grace. 'Nobody will be looking for a Viscountess and the heir to the Dilberne name and fortune in third class, rest assured. I'll go on board as a visitor, Molly can have my passport which calls me a maid, and if there's trouble I'll just leave.'

'That's not why I'm crying,' said Minnie. 'This is where I fell in love with Arthur. On this very road. In this very place. It was a steam car and we ran out of water.'

'Oh for Heaven's sake,' said Tessa, 'you daft eejit. Pull yourself together. If you loved him you shouldn't have run out on him in the first place. You think every man is like your father and you can do what you like and he'll still love you. Well, they're not and they don't. They take offence.'

'But I didn't *do* anything,' Minnie wailed.

'That's as may be,' said Grace sagely, 'but I daresay you might have wanted to. You know what the Bible says. Those who commit adultery in their hearts–'

Minnie wailed again.

'That's a horrible word. It wasn't like that!'

'Pure in thought, word and deed, that's what they want their wives to be,' said Mr Eddie, 'just not other men's wives.'

Minnie began to sob dreadfully.

'I love him so!'

Edgar began to cry and held out his little arms to Molly.

'Oh please, everyone,' said Molly, before she could stop herself, 'do be quiet. You're upsetting the little ones.'

They stared at her; shocked, she thought, that the dumb should speak. She straightened her blue and white nursemaid's uniform and tried to look as undaunted as Nanny. It worked. They quietened: even Minnie stopped her sobbing and pulled herself together.

Edgar went back to sleep.

'What will you do the other end?' said Eddie. 'You'll have three passports between four people.'

'We'll cross that bridge when we come to it,' said Grace. 'Molly can pass as another child.'

Eddie drove determinedly and skilfully towards London. There was no pursuit.

Connor stirred; Mrs O'Brien put him on her knee and let him swarm joyously all over her plump shiny pastel blueness, little heels digging into grandmotherly flesh, little teeth searching for her shiny nose, little fingers picking at her valuable pearls.

'The sweet darling!' said Tessa. 'A real O'Brien, this one. Just look at him. And a dead ringer for me, wouldn't you say, Grace? I'm not so sure about Edgar. He takes after the Dilberne side. Ever so grand!' It was true enough. Three-year-old Edgar was now sat upright on his mother's knee, quiet and composed, staring into space, with a slightly pained expression, looking down a patrician nose, as if well aware that he was a Dilberne to the manner born and that these others were probably not. He was, Molly thought, his grandfather Robert reborn, but without his Lordship's joviality.

By the time they arrived at Brown's in Dover Street, after a successful day's kidnapping, they gave all the appearance of a perfectly normal family party. Tessa, after Connor's manhandling, was perhaps a little more dishevelled than when she had started out from the Savoy that morning, Minnie not so much so – and Grace as self-possessed as ever. Molly was pleased to find there was a laundry service available and that her uniform could be boiled, starched and ironed overnight and returned to her first thing.

The Inspector Takes Charge

3rd and 4th December 1905

Better to be too active than too idle, Inspector Strachan thought. When the kidnapping crisis blew up so suddenly and dramatically he had found himself almost pleased. Frankly he had been marking time at Dilberne Court and could well have gone back to his Special Branch duties at Windsor. The likelihood of an assassination attempt on the King during a shooting weekend was low, though not impossible: he had men in the area and no report of any unusual activity had come to their ears, no sinister Irishmen, no wild-eyed Russians. If there was reason for alarm something would have surfaced by now: he could reasonably have gone home a week ago. But home, after the death of his wife Helen and little son in childbirth three years back, was lodgings in Camden Town with a landlady whose meals were meagre and grudging, where the hot water geyser in the shared bathroom erupted every few minutes and sprayed the naked bather with soot. Better far to spend as much time as he could in Dilberne Court.

Andrew Strachan was the only son of a widowed innkeeper in Leicester. He had won a scholarship to grammar school, gone on to University College London to study electrical engineering, then entered the Metropolitan Police. He had risen rapidly through the ranks, been seconded to the Special Irish Branch, then to Mr Akers-Douglas's newly formed Royal Protection Command, of which he was now Acting Commander: which he suspected meant 'not quite gentleman enough to be Commander, but someone has to do the work'. Mildly put out by the slight, he continued to refer to himself as 'Inspector'. That was what he did. He inspected; he sought out error; he looked out for danger.

He enjoyed the comforts of Dilberne Court. The towels were thick and heavy, never shared, and warmed before use by heated porcelain rails. He had a telephone line by his bed (a new mattress) with priority access to the Dilberne telephone exchange and from thence emergency connections to the Metropolitan Police and various local policing agencies. Cook kept an excellent table. There were some difficulties and embarrassments, of course. His social standing was never made quite clear to anyone. He was not a gentleman, in that he was obliged to earn a living: he was a public employee of comparatively low status, who yet had the ear of the King. It confused everyone, including himself.

Her Ladyship would say, 'Oh, do join us for supper tonight,' mostly when she dined alone or with Lady Minnie, if seldom when Lord Robert was expected down from Belgrave Square or Lord Arthur prepared to spend time away from the workshops. Neither seemed quite at ease in his presence. If the invitation did not come he would make his way down to the servants' hall and eat there. But then the servants, in their turn, would let him know, in subtle or not so subtle ways, that he was endured rather than welcomed at their table. He could understand why he put a damper on their conversation, but it quite upset him. He liked a joke and a good laugh as much as anyone. What he wanted really, of course, was a family. He had thought after Helen's death that he could perhaps find one in the Police Force, but found that as promotion succeeded promotion, his own staff became wary of him. Being mostly spies, they were not over-genial at the best of times.

When Nanny, dishevelled and incoherent, had fallen through the front door to report that the young masters had been snatched, and their nursemaid with them, the Inspector had both a sense of failure – he had allowed errors to occur, a danger he'd anticipated to come to pass – and also of irritation: he had warned them and they had chosen to ignore his warnings. A surfeit of righteous indignation had blinded them to the fact that Minnie might fight back. They had been complacent. Things could go wrong, did go wrong, sometimes horribly wrong. The French Revolution had happened; kings and princes got assassinated, governments were overthrown; yet in spite of all evidence to the contrary the Dilbernes and their like felt they were inviolable by reason of their natural superiority. When he had warned her Ladyship that something like this might happen, she had laughed him off.

Mr Strachan was not without sympathy for Minnie. She had had two births within a year, by a husband who paid far more attention to his cars than his wife. When he first met her she'd been an artless, bright little thing, eager to please and be pleased: over the months she had become withdrawn and depressed. Arthur struck him as one of those men who fall in love with Mary Magdalene but once she has a baby see her as Mother Mary, holy, pure and not to be defiled. If she then disturbs the vision, there will be no end to his outrage. If Lady Minnie wanted a love life like other women had she was probably wise to go home to Chicago: but she must accept that she would have to do it without her children. To try to include them in her new life was irresponsible and unkind. Nursemaids could always take the mother's place, no one the father's.

Nevertheless, he had suggested to her Ladyship that she had been unwise in shutting the door in

Minnie's face. It was tactless and unnecessarily hurtful. Some kind of negotiation would have been a better course.

'Standing between any female and its young is never wise,' he had said. 'A normally placid cow will batter the barn door down and kill you if her calf is on the other side.'

'For Heaven's sake, Mr Strachan,' she had replied. 'Stick to your policing and leave me to deal with my family. Minnie, moral imbecile though she may be, knows well enough that as an adulterous wife she is not fit to bring up children. And to liken her to a cow is absurd. Humans have souls and reason; beasts of the fields have neither. Minnie is a lady not a cow.'

'She is also a woman,' he thought but did not say, contenting himself with:

'It is hardly a matter of reason, your Ladyship, but of passion!'

She'd looked mildly puzzled at this and he wondered if she'd herself ever sacrificed reason to passion. Probably not.

His Lordship was a genial enough cove but wouldn't encourage his wife to behave other than decorously. Like so many of his class he kept passion for himself and his harlots, reserving 'respect' for his wife. At this moment the Earl was visiting a tart called Carmen, so it was reported by his guardians: Ministers of the Crown were discreetly watched over, though the Home Secretary Akers-Douglas had advised that it was better if they did not get to hear of it – they would only object, preferring to put their privacy before their security. So the watchers moved silently and secretly. The Earl in particular could too easily fall victim to blackmail; the King was open about his liaisons – those who have nothing to hide have nothing to fear – but the Earl, no doubt out of respect for his wife, kept his secrets.

Carmen was watched too. She was a Brazilian; Brazil was a polyglot state awash with mad dictators, agents provocateurs and anarchists: Heaven alone knew what plot she might be part of, what pillow talk she heard or passed on. And Strachan was keeping an eye on his Lordship's valet Digby, the one who introduced his Lordship to The Cardinal's Hat. Strachan knew about the place: it was little more than a sophisticated brothel, its customers international diplomats, titled gentlemen and high-ranking Westminster officials, many with devious tastes. It prided itself on its discretion and was anything but discreet; as it happened, Special Branch already had three paid informers on the staff: one cloakroom girl, one cleaner and one barman, who reported back on the comings and goings of the clientèle.

Digby was a rather unsavoury character who had exotic proclivities; how he had ended up in Dilberne employ had yet to be ascertained. This was enough to attract Strachan's attention, the more so because Digby had been seen to call at the offices of a Mr William Brown, a publisher, who was a friend of a certain the Hon. Anthony Robin, an editor, with whose sister Diana, the Dilberne daughter Rosina, a radical writer and agitator, just happened to be staying on her return from Australia. It was unlikely that No. 3 Fleet Street was a nest of conspirators but it all certainly seemed rather too close for comfort to the heart of political power, especially since Dilberne was in the King's circle. One needed to be sure that everything was innocent and coincidental. In his experience coincidence was actually rather rare.

In her recent runaway mode Minnie had chosen to take refuge with Rosina, and who knew what unhealthy influences the latter had? Mother-love could indeed provoke a mother to kidnap her own children, but so could spite, politics, greed. Sex was the most innocent motivation of all, and it was something of a reassurance that Mr Robin was to be cited as a co-respondent in Lord Arthur's divorce case. If the Viscount had not yet served papers on his wife, it was certainly not because he had changed his mind but for the simple reason that she could not be found.

The Dilbernes were charming, affable and well-connected; to cancel the King's trip would be a pity, but might yet have to happen. Poor Isobel. Her trouble was that she would not be advised. He knew well enough that she trusted him and liked him, and he suspected that had he been better born she might even have fancied him, and his thoughts did stray sometimes in that direction – though he kept a stern check on them. Just every now and then he detected a look from her which suggested that were he to do something drastic, such as tell her of Carmen's existence, she might in shock and distress, and the desire for vengeance – never to be discounted in a woman – fall into his arms. But it was not going to happen.

And she was rash, thus quarrelling with a clever daughter, and now with a wealthy daughter-in-law. At least it was pretty evident that the kidnapping was a domestic matter. A terrorist or criminal, anyone who offered a threat to the King, would have snatched the children but left the maid. Only a woman, a mother, would think of taking the nursemaid as well.

Nanny had managed to provide an adequate description of the perpetrators, and there could be no doubt but that they were Minnie, her mother the Irishwoman Tessa O'Brien and a tall woman who was as likely as not to be Grace, the ex-employee who might or might not be described as disgruntled. It was a possibility that the nursemaid was an accomplice; the plot could have layer upon layer to it, starting with some anarchist in Odessa, and point back to the King, but Mr Strachan did not think so. Local girls of fifteen were more likely to run off than conspire. Those who bring the bad news are often involved, true, but it was not likely to be Nanny. Nanny was an old, confused woman who after the snatch had dragged the empty pram after her down muddy lanes and all the way to the front door, thus taking twice the time to bring the news as she need have. It had not occurred to her simply to abandon it. She was in the first stages of senility, and in Mr Strachan's opinion should not have been left in charge of the nursery. He might in time say as much to her Ladyship but since all she was likely to say was, *'Oh for Heaven's sake, Mr Strachan, stick to your policing,'* et cetera, etcetera, he felt disinclined so to do.

He had put all necessary procedures in place without delay. They were not exactly normal procedures since obviously steps must be taken to avoid public attention. A divorce was bad enough but for a Viscountess to kidnap her own children would reverberate through the centuries. Or so her Ladyship observed, and his Lordship agreed. The Dilbernes had received the news calmly. That is to say they did not shriek, wail or call upon their Maker. They seemed more outraged than anxious. His Lordship had started to put through a call to the Home Secretary but changed his mind and said:

'Do what you must, Strachan, at whatever cost. Just get them back safe and sound, soon, and above all quietly.'

'Oh what a little horror she is!' was all the Countess said. 'What a mother for poor little Edgar to have!' and she called for Mr Neville to fire the nursemaid in her absence for disloyalty. She was not to serve out her notice.

'It is wrong to wish anyone dead,' said Lord Arthur, 'but I certainly wish my wife had never been born,' and went away into a corner with the Earl, presumably to discuss whether Mr Strachan could be trusted with the task of bringing back the children. From the expression on his face and the tone of his voice it seemed that for

Arthur the answer was no, Strachan was far from trustworthy. It occurred then to the Inspector that the Viscount suffered from paranoia and imagined there was something 'going on' between himself and her Ladyship. The idea was absurd. They had walked up to the Gatehouse together once or twice discussing locks and keys and how the pheasant chicks were doing. Anything else was ludicrous.

Her Ladyship joined her husband and son and after a few more words were exchanged turned to him and said, 'Mr Strachan, we are so lucky you are with us. We trust you completely. Now just get on with it!'

Perhaps the idea was not so ludicrous, but now was not the time to think about it.

In the interests of discretion he did not use the usual channels to inform the Liverpool Police of the kidnapping but made sure a few key figures in the Special Branch were put in the picture. He used his own team – some at the Court, some billeted in various cottages around – to scour the immediate area and found nothing. They were not expected to. Nanny had taken a long time to raise the alarm; the birds were well flown. But it transpired very soon that the absconding party had left in one of the new Austin Phaetons – a motorist had seen it pass.

If Minnie had any sense, the Inspector realized, she would get her children back to the United States as soon as possible, and in his opinion Minnie was both sensible and efficient, if over-emotional. She would try. Tracing the absconding party would only be hard once they were outside the country. The wealthy are easily remembered: they are watched where they go with envy and wonder. But speed was of the essence. By mid-afternoon ten of his team were on the case; enquiries at shipping lines and grand hotels were made and soon revealed that Mrs O'Brien and Grace had landed from New York on the Tuesday, spent the night in the Savoy, where they had been joined the next day by a distraught Minnie. The party of three had stayed until the following Monday – presumably the day after Minnie's indiscretions had led to her being barred the door of her home, her life and her children – when they had checked out of the Savoy leaving no address. Presumably they had spent the days thereafter planning the abduction.

The snatch had been very well achieved – place, timing and logistics flawless. They might have placed too much reliance on the nursemaid's co-operation – but time would tell. And of course they had not bargained on the speed with which the Inspector was able to act. The party, of three adults and two children, had booked into a suite at Brown's Hotel in Dover Street for the one night under the name O'Corcoran. AUST 1 was back in the garage by 6.15 – they had made good speed – and a uniform, white and blue, probably a nanny's, had been handed in for overnight cleaning at the cost of seven-and-ninepence.

They had had supper in their rooms. Pork chops,

sauté potatoes, lamb cutlets, cheese omelette, green peas, scrambled eggs, jelly and custard, warm milk, two glasses of wine. They had refused the turn-down service. They had rung through to reception and made enquiries about trains to Liverpool Terminus. They had asked for an alarm call at 7.30 a.m., and a taxi ordered for nine. Mr Strachan deduced they would be travelling on the steam ship *Carpania,* which sailed at 2.30 bound for New York. There were no O'Corcorans, O'Briens or Hedleighs on the passenger lists, but the Inspector and his men would be there to waylay them. He doubted that these particular child snatchers had the criminal contacts necessary to get passports changed – though it was possible – even so, two small boys could not be rendered invisible. He had known of a kidnapped child drugged and rolled in a carpet in a getaway – but that was not going to happen with Edgar or his little brother.

He called up the Brighton and Portsmouth Railway Company at ten that night and ordered a special train from Dilberne Halt to be at Liverpool Terminus by noon the next day. It would comprise a locomotive and tender and one carriage only. The journey, it was calculated, over two hundred miles, could be done in four hours, travelling via Reading, Birmingham and Stoke-on-Trent. Trains in the way would be re-routed to speed its passage. The Inspector and his team would leave early enough to allow time for unforseen eventualities. One trained officer would carry a Webley revolver against the remote possibility that the situation was more complicated than it seemed and terrorists were involved.

By eight the next morning a party of nine was assembled on the up-line platform of Dilberne Halt as the special puffed in, the engine a magnificent hissing creature in iron and brass, rearing to go. It seemed only reasonable that other trains should allow it precedence and get out of its way. The tender was elegant and in the cream and chocolate uniform of the Great Western Railway, as was the single carriage it hauled. Brighton and Portsmouth Railways had hired it in from G.W.R. and there had been no time to change its livery, as would have happened had there been any to spare. But this was a police emergency, even though no one was quite sure what sort of police or what sort of emergency it was. It was generally assumed that it was to do with the secret visit of the King, now only two weeks away.

Boarding the train that morning were Mr Strachan and his six-strong team, one armed – surely well able to deal with two Irish ladies, one maid, one nursemaid, and two very small children. They had to wait five minutes or so before her Ladyship, Isobel, arrived in her carriage, accompanied by her maid Lily. She had wanted to bring Nanny but Mr Strachan advised against it, and for once she had listened.

Come to wave goodbye were his Lordship and the Viscount, but having dropped Isobel off they departed at once, Reginald whipping up the horses, not even waiting for the train to leave, his Lordship to attend to affairs of State – Balfour could no longer hold on to power, and was actually resigning – and Lord Arthur to try lining his exhaust pipes with horse hair: if you couldn't get rid of the sound, you could at least try muffling it. Isobel would not travel in the Jehu while it continued to make these absurd little noises.

Molly Makes a Decision

Tuesday 5th December 1905, The Servants' Hall, Dilberne Court

All longed to know what had gone on at Liverpool the previous day but the Inspector, who had arrived back late on the Sunday night, was tight-lipped, morose, and would divulge nothing other than that Lady Isobel had gone straight to Belgrave Square to be with his Lordship. The Inspector took a late breakfast, refused the sausages and bacon Cook offered him but accepted toast with marmalade, and then retreated to his room and presumably his telephone, which by-passed the normal telephone exchange, so there was no finding out information from that source. Mr and Mrs Barnes, Molly's parents, reported from the Gatehouse that there was no news of Molly other than that Lord Arthur, before himself taking the early train up to London, had said that everything was under control and they were not to worry –

worry enough in itself.

Lily was their only hope of news, but Lily was still in bed, having arrived back even later than the Inspector and was now refusing to get up, saying her Ladyship had told her to sleep in. Nanny had nothing more to report about the events of Sunday, remaining speechless, still shocked, sitting in the nursery staring into space without even the strength to tidy up. Mr Neville had had to delegate Belinda to put away the toys left out by the poor lost little masters before they set out for church that tragic morning. The Special Branch men were a dead loss when it came to providing information; their lips, they had been taught to say, and did, were sealed. So all had to contain themselves until Lily surfaced.

Cook sent Belinda up to let Lily know there was onion soup, haddock pie, and stewed apple for lunch – Lily having decided to join Belinda in her banting. Cook, as it happened, ever obliging, was also serving side dishes of croutons, chipped fried potatoes and individual bread and butter puddings for those who wanted to supplement their light and healthy meal. The plan worked. As Cook doled out the first servings of onion soup, Lily took her place at the table.

'You'll never guess,' she said, 'you'll never guess!'

'Don't play hard to get, Lily,' warned Reginald, 'or I'll make it hard for you.'

'Talk about turn-up for the books!' said Lily.

'I know what it is,' said Elsie. 'The King's called off. Him and his Mrs Keppel aren't coming, and after all that.'

'It's on the cards,' said Lily. 'You're a psychic, Elsie.'

There was a gasp of dismay all round.

'She's making it up,' said Reginald, 'as per usual. Don't fret yourself, Elsie.

'Not necessarily,' said Belinda, who had spent the morning closeted with Lily. Thanks to none of the family being in residence, and the domestic improvements – no coal having to be carried or ashes cleared, no water boiled and baths or wash bowls filled, no slops fetched and emptied – and this particular morning no meals in anyone's rooms, there was a blessed lull in work, and time to spare. 'Tell them about Lady Rosina's book, Lily. Her Ladyship said something to Mr Strachan about the Queen not liking it, what with it being so really rude, with lots of naked savages dancing around with no clothes on.'

'I told you that in confidence,' said Lily. 'You have no business passing it on, Belinda. Her Ladyship was going on about it to Mr Strachan on the way up to Liverpool. I like Mr Strachan. I hope he's not in too much trouble. He told her Ladyship he thought the King wouldn't object to the book because His Majesty liked to know everything about his subjects even if the Queen didn't. He was too honest for his own good and her Ladyship snorted and hardly said a word to him all the way.'

'And we all know she fancies him,' put in Belinda. Mr and Mrs Neville exchanged a look. Belinda went too far too fast, for someone new to the table. But Lily, seeing a danger that she might be upstaged, took up her story without further delay.

The Special Branch party got to Liverpool later than they had hoped; there'd been some irritating delays on the way – including a landslip on the line north of Reading which required a detour. Her Ladyship had not been at all happy; she was naturally anxious about the children.

'Yes,' said Belinda, piping up again, unquenched, 'and in a mood because his Lordship didn't come with her. Always some excuse. Off to the House, my left foot. Off to The Cardinal's Hat, more like.'

'My lips are sealed,' said Digby.

'They'd better be,' put in Reginald. 'There's been enough trouble in this house lately without you two adding to it. Isn't that so, Mr Neville?' He spoke with a new authority.

'That is the case, Mr Reginald,' said Mr Neville, adding the 'Mr' with a new deference. Perhaps one day when he calmed down Reginald would rise to be butler.

'Carry on, Lily,' said Reginald, and she did.

'I was so sorry for her Ladyship,' said Lily. 'She went on smiling, but as we got later and later she got quite agitated and kept looking at her wrist watch. Then Mr Strachan told her to take it off and put it in her reticule – we would be moving amongst crowds. It's so pretty; a Cartier, all gold and diamonds. His Lordship gave it to her. She only wore it in the first place because she thinks it brings her luck, so she argued with him some more about that. But she saw sense in the end and took it off.' Belinda opened her mouth to say something but Reginald quelled her with a look.

Lily went on further, to say that by the time they got to Liverpool it was half past one and the train from Kings Cross had already got in, but a porter said yes, a party of women and children without a man in sight had set off for the boat train, so they went off after them; but a party of six men in uniform, plus a smart woman and a lady's maid, is hard to move through crowds, and by the time they got to the bottom of the *Carpania's* gangway the fugitives were half way to the top. There were two officers at the bottom and two at the top checking papers. The third-class passengers now streaming on board were of an undistinguished nature, many of them foreigners speaking strange tongues; most in the first class were already on board, sipping their farewell drinks with friends and relatives until the *'All ashore that's going ashore'* shout was raised. Third class said their goodbyes on shore.

'These immigrant ships are awash with trouble makers – criminals, terrorists, radicals – hoping to slip the nets of justice,' so Terry the armed Special Branch man had warned Lily on the journey up, as they ate the chicken sandwiches which Cook had provided. Security would be shockingly lax, he said: the *Carpania* was a Cunard liner and crewed by Americans and Irish and none of them friendly to authority.

Not lax enough, it transpired, to suit the convenience of the Inspector and his contingent. Lady Isobel got through easily enough saying she was seeing friends off, but Lily was asked for her passport and not having one was stopped, and asked to stand aside on the deck. The Inspector was stopped for the same reason. He flashed the Special Branch badge from the inside of his lapel, but the inspecting officer was not impressed, said it was unknown to him, and all must step aside while he called a senior officer.

Lily watched as Minnie, seeing the approach of her mother-in-law, vanished with her flock into the crowds on deck, presumably to take refuge below. The crowd, quick to understand what was going on, parted willingly for the fugitives but stood deliberately in Isobel's way to prevent further pursuit so she had no option but to retreat to the Inspector's group, equally unpopular, it seemed. It was a sullen crowd of men who now gathered round the forces of authority and murmured insults. The senior officer took his time arriving, and when he did it was no relief: he found fault with the Inspector's letters of authority. The passengers in question were American, were they not? Nevertheless enquiries had been made and after some time Minnie, her mother, Grace, Molly and the two children were brought back up to the top of the gangway to have their passports re-examined. The officer now held three passports in his perfectly uniformed hand and flicked through them.

The *'All ashore that's going ashore'* cry went up. Sirens hooted alarmingly.

'Dear Grace,' said Minnie. 'You really must be going. Thank you so much for coming so far to say goodbye,' and Miss Grace kissed them all and departed serenely down the gangway.

'All these are in order,' said the officer, 'and all are American citizens except the maid, who is British. The children are on the mother's passport, I don't see where the problem arises. You have no jurisdiction.' He said he had put a call through to the Metropolitan Police in London and they had no knowledge of the Strachan party: he must ask them to leave at once.

Her Ladyship explained that the heir to the Dilberne title and lands was being kidnapped and the officer would come to rue the day, et cetera, et cetera, but the officer laughed in her face and said he doubted it; if she was talking about lords and ladies why was the party not travelling first class?

'Because they are so cunning!' snapped the Countess of Dilberne, but then called out imploringly, 'Oh, Minnie, you can't do this to the poor little boy. If you have any scruple left at all, let him be where he belongs. In his own place, in his own class.'

'His poor little feet–' said Mrs O'Brien. 'All blisters! Whine all you like, you're not fit to bring up a jackass let alone my grandchild.'

Her Ladyship looked both puzzled and bereft and then said in a very different tone of voice, enough to break your heart:

'Anything, anything. Minnie, I'm sorry. I had no idea it had got to blister stage. Nanny must go. Please, Minnie, please. Arthur's eldest son, I know he's difficult but even so – you love him, you know you do.'

Minnie looked undecided, and equally bereft, said Lily. Mr Strachan said he refused to leave and demanded to see the Captain.

'It's impossible,' said the officer. 'This is a Cunard liner. What do you want? An international incident? This ship is ready to leave, about to leave. The pilot's on board and his time is expensive. We're about to cast off.'

And indeed down on the jetty men were shouting, and the anchor chain began to rattle.

'My men are armed,' said the Inspector. It was quite the wrong thing to say. There was much rustling amongst the crowd. They were on the ship's officer's side.

'So are mine,' said the officer, calmly. 'Stay on board and be incarcerated and delivered to the police at the other end. Our cells are not so very comfortable, they say, and our crew not so fond of the police. It is up to you.'

The Strachan party stood humiliated and hesitant. And then Molly stepped forward with Edgar's hand in hers. 'You lot had best keep Master Edgar,' she said to Isobel. 'He's a sight more his father's child than his mother's.' She turned back to Minnie. 'And you lot keep Master Connor, who's his mother's, and a proper little Irishman. That's fair.'

And Molly walked down the gangway, Master Edgar beside her. Isobel, after a minute's hesitation, followed, and then Lily. The ship shuddered. Mr Strachan and his Special Branch men quickly fell in behind Lily. Minnie did not go after them, but stood as if fixed to the deck in surprise. The ship had come alive. Those for ashore had reached ashore. The gangway was raised abruptly and jerkily, as if to save further argument. There was another lurch as more hawsers were loosed. Sirens hooted in triumph as slowly but surely the *Carpania* slipped away from the dock to face a new world, start a new life. The crowds at the rails cheered. Master Edgar, under Molly's instruction, waved up at his mother as the ship became more distant, smaller and smaller, and Minnie waved back. Little Connor waved too, vigorously and joyously, as the distance between him and his big brother grew.

And that was how it happened that Master Edgar was now at Belgrave Square with Isobel, and Molly, restored to favour to look after him; and Master Connor with his mother and grand-mother were on the good ship *Carpania* and on their way to New York. Mr Strachan was in disgrace and licking his wounds in his room, and his Lordship at this very moment was in a meeting with Mr Akers-Douglas the Home Secretary as they discussed the suitability of a royal visit, however private, so soon after certain unfortunate difficulties in the Dilberne family had so narrowly avoided being the cause of an international incident, and, worse, the publication of Lady Rosina's book had come to the attention of the Lord Chamberlain's Office.

A Disturbing Morning

8th December 1905, No. 3 Fleet Street

'It bodes no good,' said Anthony Robin. He was reading the morning mail. He had come down for breakfast in the kitchen looking exceptionally splendid in a purple silk dressing gown with mandarin collar, a lavish satin cravat and a grey velvet smoking jacket with corded lapels flung round his shoulders for warmth. Diana and Rosina, who as it happened were both wearing white shirts and grey woollen skirts, felt positively dull by comparison.

'What doesn't?' they asked.

'I refer to the theatrical censor in our new government,' he said. 'Sporty Eddie is out as Lord Chamberlain, Charlie Spencer is in. Strait-laced old fart.'

'But he's only a Mister,' said Diana. 'You have to be a Lord to be that.'

'They're making him a Lord for the occasion,' said Anthony. 'Viscount Althorp. The new age of decency and probity is here.'

'Oh Anthony,' said Diana. 'Calm down. We still have free speech. They won't dare touch the little presses.'

'I'm not so sure,' said Anthony darkly.

'At least Charlie's Harrow and Cambridge,' said Rosina. 'Makes a change from Eton and

Oxford. In with the Liberals, out with the Tories. Won't it be better, not worse?'

'The more they talk of freedom, the less they like it,' said Anthony. 'Say damn on stage and they'll close the theatre down. It's going to be all no, no, no, you bad boy from now on. We're going backwards not forwards. Who publishes Beardsley now?'

'At least my book's gone to press. The review copies have gone out. It's too late to stop it at this stage,' said Rosina. 'The die is cast. And nobody argued with Havelock's *Laughter as Demutescence* in the November Issue.'

'Only because no one bothered to read it,' said Anthony. He asked Diana to make more coffee and Rosina to stoke the fire; the room was cold and William Brown her publisher was coming down.

'Down?' asked Diana, surprised. 'Not round?'

'Down,' said Anthony and sure enough in a few minutes William came down the stairs into the kitchen, fully dressed for the office: double-breasted lounge suit, grey worsted, six buttons, high white collar, and the sharpest of pointed lapels.

'Oh Anthony,' said Diana, looking up as she ground the coffee. 'This is far too domestic, far too dangerous.'

'Anthony, are you out of your mind?' demanded Rosina, getting up from the grate. She wiped her cheek with the back of her hand, leaving a great smudge of ash and cinders on her cheek, but at least the room was warmer.

'I don't think so,' said Anthony. 'William and I

are just celebrating. I am the great Lothario, the breaker-up of marriages. I have it formally in black and white. I am cited as co-respondent in your brother's divorce case. Better a bounder, I always say, than a sodomite.'

'Oh dear, oh dear,' said Rosina. 'Poor Minnie, at least she got away with one of the children. But it's all rather a pity. She loves Arthur.'

'She'll mend,' said William. 'And yes, it looks as if we've got away with the book. The timing's right. To recall *Manners and Traditions* now would cause more of a scandal than letting it go. You're the daughter of the Earl of Dilberne, friend of royalty: next week the King is coming to stay, not to mention Mrs Keppel. No one will risk headlines.'

'But they may in future,' said Anthony, 'if we have the likes of timorous Spencer not Sporty Eddie to hold back the great tide of public outrage.'

'In the meantime, Rosina,' said William, 'I do think it would be wiser to heal the quarrel with your mother at your earliest convenience. We need friends in high places more than ever.'

'It's hardly a quarrel, William. It's a clash of values,' protested Rosina. 'The Philistines against the Aesthetics.'

'Too right, mate. Too right,' squawked Pappagallo from his perch.

'Oh, be quiet, be quiet,' said Rosina. Since she had found happiness with Diana she gave poor Pappagallo far less consideration than once she had. 'And I sincerely hope my book was published because of the value of its contents rather than because of my relatives.'

'But of course it was,' said William.

'And the speed of its publication, and the consequent failure to check various facts and figures, has nothing at all to do with the timing of the King's visit,' said Anthony, 'and even less to do with vulgar commerce. Or indeed that a daughter of a peer of the Realm has taken it into her little head to write of masturbation amongst the natives of Australia. Nothing at all.'

'Oh Anthony, do stop trying to make trouble,' pleaded Diana. 'Poor Rosina. One must be allowed to shake off the shackles of family.'

'Too right! Too right!' squawked Pappagallo.

'Oh do be quiet, bird,' said Rosina. 'This is serious.'

'That's not what Digby tells me,' remarked Anthony. 'Rosina is not interested in shaking off family shackles – she pops off to see her papa every now and then, when he can find time away from The Cardinal's Hat. Don't you, Rosina?'

'Digby?' asked Rosina, confused. '"The Cardinal's Hat"?'

'Anthony, you are too bad,' said William. 'Giving away our girlish secrets! There's no reason for disquiet, Rosina. Digby is your father's new valet and a Special Branch informer, but our informer too. You find yourself in print because I have the greatest faith in your literary ability and academic prowess, and an encomium from Seebohm Rowntree has helped greatly with this latter, if only because of his father's august name.'

'My left foot!' said Anthony. 'As the servants say.'

'Oh Anthony,' said Diana. 'Stop trying to upset everyone. As for you, William, I think it would be more prudent if you did not spend the night here.'

'You spend all your nights with Rosina,' said William.

'But nobody will think of closing us down because of it,' said Diana. 'We are women, not inverts or anarchists, and therefore above suspicion. Or at any rate, being women, not worthy of it. Though if Havelock goes on writing about female sexuality I don't know how long for.'

'What I would really like,' said William, 'is a poached egg – two, perhaps – on toast. Talk can be the death of appetite. How about you, Anthony? An egg or two to give us strength against the women?'

'That is a very good idea,' said Anthony. 'Poached, I think, with just a little vinegar in the water. But not too much or else the whites go brown and disgusting. Will you do the honours, Diana?'

'No I will not,' said his sister. 'I may be your dogsbody, but I will not be your slave.'

'Perhaps you would then, dear Rosina?' asked Anthony. 'Do stop brooding. I daresay your father only goes to The Cardinal's Hat to write his speeches. We fellows need nourishment. Do I not house you, advise you, shelter your runaway in-laws – is this not worth poaching an egg for?'

Rosina did not have the opportunity to consider her reply, which might well have taken some time. It was at this tense moment, at a quarter to nine in the morning, that there came a loud banging on the door, imperious and demanding immediate attention. The forces of authority were at the gate and would not be denied. Anthony moved slowly to the door; the others wiped crumbs from their mouths and hastily composed their faces to show no panic, merely a mild curiosity. Even before Anthony could get there the door burst open, the wood kicked in, any locks and bolts overcome by a splintering violence, and a uniformed Inspector Strachan and six of his Special Branch men crowded in, spread to the rooms at the back of the house, and made the upstairs safe. All had Webley revolvers at the ready. The four occupants were corralled at their single table.

'Oh dear,' said William, stage-whispering behind his hand. 'How very fierce! But what gorgeous young men!'

'Better you didn't say anything, sir,' said the Inspector, in a quite kindly manner. He must have had ears on the back of his head. He spoke with an accent that was almost educated but not quite. 'We are not in a frame of mind for joking. The national interest is at stake.'

'Not to mention my mother's peace of mind,' said Rosina.

'That is quite uncalled for, Rosina,' said Anthony. 'National security must be preserved at any cost. Please do what you must, Inspector. And as for you, William, please restrain your levity. I think you would be well advised not to aggravate our guests. You are one yourself, after all, having just dropped by for breakfast.'

'Mr Anthony Robin, I believe,' said the Inspector, with infinite courtesy, 'and your friend Mr William Brown of Longman's publishing house?'

Anthony agreed that this was so. The girls, shocked and surprised, stayed silent. The Inspector said he was not interested in friendships on this particular occasion, just the nature and source of various possibly obscene publications which were causing concern. To this end his men would be taking away such papers and records as appeared relevant to their investigations and would do as little damage as they could during the search. It was, as it happened, a thorough search: the sofa was ripped open and examined, various floor and ceiling boards levered open, and boxes of correspondence, manuscripts, both in handwriting and typed, bills, receipts and so on, loaded into cardboard boxes and carted off to a waiting police van which Rosina could see from the window. A blanket was roughly nailed in the door space to hide what was going on from the outside world. It did not keep the cold out. It was midday before they left.

'There goes January's edition,' said Anthony. 'I shall of course call my solicitor.'

'You are more than welcome,' said the Inspector. 'And I hope you realize there is nothing personal in our actions; that this is done in the national interest.'

'Oh, obviously,' said Anthony.

'As it happens, said the Inspector, 'I don't think you have very much to worry about.' He waited until the last of his men were gone. 'But just a word to the wise from me. It occurs to me that if

Lady Rosina and Mr Brown were to marry – both I believe are currently unmarried – it would save a great deal of unpleasantness all round. Much is allowed to the married that is not permitted to the unmarried. Many problems would be solved at a stroke. And do get your door fixed, Mr Robin – known as Redbreast, I believe? – Holloway Brothers in Belvedere Street are the people to go to. We use them all the time.'

He smiled, a rather charming and friendly smile, and left.

PART FOUR

The Guests Arrive

15th December 1905, Dilberne Court

To be loved by a king is a wonderful thing. Alice Keppel lived in a cloud of loveliness: her step light, her head held high, every wisp of her auburn hair the thicker, every glance of her great blue eyes the kinder and more generous, because of that love. Even the ropes of pearls which hung from her long, alabaster neck seemed to gleam the more lustrously, imbued as they were with so great a confidence, tranquillity and joy. She kept the pearls to a minimum that day, Friday 15th December 1905, when she arrived with her husband George at Dilberne Court. They were, after all, 'slumming it'. After the glories of Chatsworth, Blenheim, Hatfield, Sandringham and the rest, Dilberne was as nothing. But the King got on with the Earl, trusted him as a confidant, liked his company, looked forward to his weekend's sport and that was that.

So Mrs Keppel came in friendliness and kindness, eager to enjoy her weekend with the King, and wore only one rope of pearls on her arrival, the better to keep the Countess in countenance. Alice remembered Isobel as wearing a rather dull and rather thick navy *moiré* too hot for a summer's day when they had met at Newmarket, and did not want to outshine her. She brought only one lady's maid with her, though she still needed six trunks for the four days – and her own electric smoothing iron in case Dilberne Court could provide nothing but flat irons, though some swore they made a better job of starched blouses than did gas or electric. But Agnes her maid was able to assure Alice that the irons at Dilberne were modern, and well-padded, collapsible ironing boards were provided. That was better than Sandringham where the irons were flat, rusty and left marks on fine linen. George her husband brought a valet, his guns, his two Labradors and little else but his handsome, benign and affable self.

Mrs Keppel needn't have bothered to dress down. As she came out to greet her guests Lady Isobel Dilberne was prettily attired in a rose-coloured woollen suit with a suede appliqué collar in pink and even an aspiration to frivolity in a cluster of yet pinker ribbons on the jacket shoulders which, Alice thought, augured well. What Alice feared most was dullness. The men would be out shooting from early morning until dusk: the ladies would join them for lunch but otherwise would be in each other's company during daylight hours. At least Ripon's wife Constance was to be there: Constance knew any number of interesting people, artists and writers, though her husband, poor girl, was the most boring man in the world, interested only in shooting birds and known by the King, at his most jovial, as Ripon 29 p.m. – short for twenty-nine pheasants per minute, once upon a time his record bag at Sandringham.

Alice had brought her little girl Sonia with her, charming in her fur muff and tiny fur boots. Sonia was barely five, and so Alice, accompanied by Isobel, went up with her immediately to the nursery, which Alice was relieved to see was well-kept and warmed. One never knew with other people's nurseries what one would encounter. Some kept their children less comfortable than their horses. But here there was a splendid rocking horse, with a great quantity of toys and a small boy a year or so younger than Sonia playing happily amongst them. A pleasant nursemaid, Molly, young but competent, took them in charge after Isobel had introduced the little boy as 'Edgar, the son and heir'. This Alice thought slightly strange, as Isobel was obviously the grandmother.

'His mother has gone to visit her parents in Chicago,' Isobel explained, in her sweet, cool voice, 'I am fortunate enough to be *in loco parentis.*'

Alice had heard something rather different; that the Viscountess was being divorced from the Viscount for adultery and had been trying to kidnap her children and carry them off to Chicago, but the plot had been foiled by Mr Strachan of the King's security team. She had heard this from the King, who had been informed in person by Mr Strachan, so she assumed it to be true. But the world did not live by truth alone so she contented herself with saying: 'What a delightful child!' which was true enough, and Alice supposed that keeping his company would not in any way brush off on Sonia, though one did not normally seek out the company of the children of the divorced, or about to be divorced. Isobel preened and glowed at the compliment, and little Sonia made it clear that she approved of Master Edgar – the latter clearly had something of the legendary charm of his grandfather the Earl of Dilberne; the ladies fell instantly under his spell – so Alice Keppel and Isobel took their way back to the drawing room together.

'And I hear your son is doing so well in the world of motor cars,' said Mrs Keppel.

'Oh, indeed, he is,' said Isobel. 'Arthur is sorry not to be here for the weekend. He has to be in New York, discussing next year's Auto Cup with William Vanderbilt. There were no British cars entered this year. Such a pity.'

It had been the second permitted automobile race on Long Island, and was so noisy, dirty and dangerous an event, and caused such a row, there wasn't likely to be another. Poor Vanderbilt, thought Alice, who knew everything about everyone. Really, Isobel! Be more subtle about your lies. Certainly your son Arthur is not here, and when the King comes calling most family members bother to be around: but perhaps he is in Chicago trying to steal back his younger son, whom we know to have gone with his mother?

But – with a smile even sweeter than Isobel, and the more good-natured because she was loved by, and loved, the King, and had no reason to be catty or mean – all Alice said was:

'Ah, William Vanderbilt, dear Consuelo's father. Such an excellent man, putting so much effort into the automobile industry. And it's thanks to entrepreneurs like your son Arthur that soon our British cars will equal the German Daimlers and the French de Dions in speed and grace. And I suppose he'll be bringing back little Minnie with him? Such a sweet girl!'

'Of course,' said Isobel, 'such a sweet girl!' Neither pursued the matter.

It was nearly the shortest day of the year, and the dusk was closing in. Servants – there seemed to be any number of them – switched on electric lights as they came down the rather magnificent stairs. The banisters and floors gleamed with the softness of lovingly-polished old oak; though the new white stair carpets struck Alice as impractical – all very well in London but the country was so muddy it would need a full-time maid to keep them brushed and clean – and entirely out of keeping with the house, which was more Jacobean than Palladian, though as with all these old houses it was hard to tell where one style began and another ended. Alice caught her breath as she entered the drawing room.

'What a charming, charming room, Isobel,' said Alice Keppel, though in truth she thought it was perfectly dreadful. You could not, should not, try and teach these old houses to play new tricks. Better to leave them as they were, replace a worn rug or so, have a few old paintings cleaned, get rid of heavy Victoriana and leave the centuries to speak for themselves. But here were bare white walls, newly plastered, no central chandelier, the glare of modern lighting, family portraits replaced by strange modern ones, hideous yellow bamboo furniture, flower arrangements which turned out to be made of satin – vulgar, vulgar, vulgar – and more of the white carpets; nothing wooden, wormy or black with age, or faded, or worn thin. Nothing of the past, in fact, had been allowed to remain, and yet the Dilbernes derived nobility, standing and wealth from the past. How did the Earl stand it? He must love his wife very much – though the King said the Earl was currently entangled with a South American girl who was causing the Intelligence Service some anxiety. It had even looked for a time that his own visit to Sussex might be postponed.

They took tea in the drawing room and at least the cheese straws and the macaroons were good which meant the dinners probably would be, and within the half-hour they were joined by a bevy of amiable and lively ladies. Constance Ripon the shooting widow joined them – and surprised and alarmed all by reading from a list her husband had just given her: he had recently managed to kill sixty-five coots, thirty-nine pheasant, twenty-three mallard, sixteen rabbits, nine hares, seven teal, six partridge, six gadwall, four pochard duck, three swans, three snipe, two moorhens, two heron, one otter, one woodcock, one woodpigeon, one goldeneye, one rat, and a pike that was shot while it swam through shallow water: all in a single day. It was not surprising, Ettie Desborough whispered to Alice, that with a husband so busy and effective Constance had no children and collected art.

Most of the men were still down in the gunroom examining their weapons and talking to the shoot captain as to how the shoot was to go. It was expected to be a good day, even a record one. By five the King had not arrived: the message came that his knee was giving him trouble and he might have to attend in a Bath chair but 'nothing would keep him away.'

'He always does what he means to do,' Alice said to Ettie Desborough. 'He'll be happy to have got the Queen's and his joint birthday celebrations over and done with and escaped from Sandringham at last. They make a great thing there of birthdays but families can be so tedious and he has to be back up there for Christmas. On the whole we're a younger crowd, positively skittish – oh yes, he'll be here.'

'And what on Earth has Isobel done with this room?' said Ettie. 'It simply won't do. There used to be a perfectly good Rembrandt above the fireplace. Now there's a strange daub of a lot of swimmers about to jump into water which doesn't look in the least like water.'

'My dear,' said Alice. 'We're lucky there's a fireplace at all. People keep taking them out and replacing them with radiators. Personally I don't mind the bathers. I think it was little Minnie who chose it.'

'Ah,' said Ettie. 'Little Minnie. Least said, soonest mended.'

'Quite so,' said Alice. Ettie was having an affair with Balfour, everyone said. Constance Ripon had observed that since Balfour was the cleverest man in England it was only right that he should have Ettie Desborough as his mistress, since she was the cleverest woman in England.

'Unless we count you, of course, Alice,' Constance had been kind enough to add, thus spoiling a good line.

Not surprising, thought Alice, if Isobel seemed to be a little tense; overshadowed, as anyone would be, by the most vivacious and brilliant women in the land.

And then word came that the King had finally arrived. All moved to the doors. Bertie had arrived with Ponsonby in one of his Daimlers – he had bought seven in the year – and also with Detective Inspector Strachan, who seemed to be in high royal favour, though it had been rumoured he had messed up the Dilberne abduction, which no one was meant to know about but everyone did. The King's security cabal followed after – five strong young men who vanished into the servants' entrance. Strachan stayed with the King. Life became quite complicated these days. Who went where was no longer clearly defined.

To love a king was a wonderful thing. It was magic; a holy thing, like the love of a priestess for her God, a child for her father. You loved the greatest living being in the world; you encompassed the orb and the sceptre in your love: it was a great comforting blanket which had fallen on you, and him, protecting and inspiring, and kept you warm and safe for ever. The heart soared. I love the King. The King loves me. It had happened on the first day they met. He was only the Prince of Wales, then. It was on 27th February 1898. She was twenty-nine, and married to George. He was fifty-six, and married to the future Queen of England. He'd come to dinner. Their souls met. Both had mistaken it for something different. He came to her room at a house party at Cassel's place in Moulton Paddocks a few days later. She had been expecting it. The Prince of Wales! It was immensely exciting. He had parted from Daisy Warwick, whose politics and behaviour were increasingly strange. To sleep with the future King of England – to know how he cried out: that was the only way to understand a man – and the cachet was great. If the Prince wanted you, everyone wanted you. It had been base enough.

She had lain in bed waiting in her whore's underwear – for that was what it was, for all it had been designed by Worth and cost the Earth – and the Prince, this great burly magnificent creature, had stripped to his union suit, and simply lay on the bed beside her and said:

'This was the only way I could get to talk to you without other people interrupting. Do you mind?' and she had felt a great relief and said:

'Not at all, Your Majesty,' and he had said:

'Bertie.'

And that was that.

They had talked and talked and touch was pleasant, and there was a little childish rolling about and slipping of limbs between limbs to get comfortable but that was all they needed.

She was the youngest of nine children; he was the

eldest of nine. It seemed to be a connection. He understood the pattern of rivalries, the weight of expectation, the painful allocation of love in a large family: he understood what it was to be married to George, a mere Honourable in a world of my Lords and Sirs: she understood what it was to have been married off by a mother to a deaf Danish girl who was all charm and no brain. He talked about the Indian waiter, 'the Munshi', who seemed to have replaced him in his mother's eyes: that made him excitable and distressed. She realized how emotional he was, how easily tears sprang to his eyes, how his face lit up when he broke into a smile. How he would cry and smile at the same time.

It occurred to her to recite 'The Charge of the Light Brigade' to calm him down. Her father's favourite poem; he was an army man. She knew it by heart:

Half a league, half a league,
Half a league onward,
All in the valley of Death
Rode the six hundred.
'Forward, the Light Brigade!
'Charge for the guns!' he said:
Into the valley of Death
Rode the six hundred.

'Forward, the Light Brigade!'
Was there a man dismay'd?
Not tho' the soldier knew
Someone had blunder'd:
Theirs not to make reply,

Theirs not to reason why,
Theirs but to do and die:
Into the valley of Death
Rode the six hundred.

'That was better than sex. What a wonderful poem!' he said. After that they got together whenever they could. He healed her; she healed him. Everyone thought she was his mistress, but being the King's mistress was no bad thing. Anything, frankly, in Society was better than being a mere Mrs. Miss at least held the promise of future change but once a boring Mrs, always a boring Mrs. Mr Balfour could get away with not being Lord Balfour because obviously he would get to being that in the end, but George would never be Lord Keppel.

But Mrs Keppel, King's Mistress, was title enough; let peoplc think what they would; she would never disabuse them. Occasionally Alexandra raised her eyebrows and sniffed a little but it was Alice's opinion that she knew well enough what went on – that is to say, these days, precisely nothing – and if she was jealous of anything it was of time spent with her husband in intelligent conversation and Alice's understanding of politics and statesmanship – not the Queen's forte. And if she, Alexandra, wanted to present herself as wronged, she had grounds enough in Alice's existence.

The bedroom Alice and George Keppel shared that night at Dilberne was comfort itself. Alice was even quite impressed: one whole wall was taken up with a capacious wardrobe, beautifully finished and polished in burr walnut, with rank upon rank of drawers, compartments and brass rails and hooks, a real filing cabinet for garments – handkerchiefs, ties, gloves, spats, veils, scarves, hats – a paradise for Agnes. A soft new bed and mattress – no four-poster nonsense with dusty hangings and canopy – but one missed the feel of *country,* where you'd wake to ice flowers on the insides of windows and the floors were cold on one's bare toes. Here the heavy iron radiators gurgled, groaned and spluttered through the night. She missed the clatter of fire tongs, and the smell of apple wood burning in the fireplace, and flames that seemed to speak to you. The bathroom was well lit, so you could see yourself properly in the mirror, but the old latticed windows had been recently replaced by metal ones – practical for lunatic asylums where the inmates might escape – and she had some in her own basement area in London to guard against burglars – but really, deep in the country, in a Jacobean manor? She said as much to George, as they got undressed.

'It might be the police wallah's suggestion, of course,' George remarked. 'He's a great one for locking and barring. And of course it might all be in your honour, Alice. Where the King goes so do you, and long may it last.' Sometimes she would like her husband to be just a touch more jealous, if only for form's sake, but he never was.

'I don't think so,' said Alice. 'I think it just is that Isobel has no class. She tries too hard. Her father started life as a coal miner and the mother was some kind of courtesan. She's simply not born to it.'

'You were, of course,' said he. 'You've come down in the world. You should never have married me.'

It was true enough. She had been born impoverished in Duntreath Castle, home of her forebears since the fourteenth century, an entitlement older than any mere Dilberne. It was not in George's nature to make money. But she had enough for herself now, thanks to the King's and Sir Ernest Cassel's help and the sudden blossoming of the Congo rubber trade.

She laughed and said:

'Marrying you was the best thing I ever did. We have two lovely daughters and are happy.' It was true enough.

Later that night she crept along the corridor to Bertie's room, not taking too much trouble not to be seen. The corridors were warm and carpeted for which she was thankful. In Blenheim she had almost frozen to death on her way to him. She only stayed a short time: he was tired and his poor stiff knee was giving him trouble. He was sad, too, thinking of his sister Victoria who had died four years since, victim of her own son the Kaiser, who had refused her proper medical care. Sadness easily slipped over into anger, which he found easier to bear. He ranted against his nephew Wilhelm. She lay beside him and recited a soothing verse or two from Tennyson's *Maud.*

'Tis a morning pure and sweet,
And a dewy splendour falls

On the little flower that clings
To the turrets and the walls;
'Tis a morning pure and sweet,
And the light and shadow fleet;
She is walking in the meadow,
And the woodland echo rings;
In a moment we shall meet;
She is singing in the meadow,
And the rivulet at her feet
Ripples on in light and shadow
To the ballad that she sings.

He fell asleep, no longer angry, just sad. Poor Bertie.

A Day of Broken Records

16th December 1905, The Dilberne Estate

In the morning George was up and out before dawn, the gleam of killing in his eye. He was a good shot, just not so lavish with his pellets as the King, let alone Ripon – or so single-minded as either, but good-looking, well-behaved, a generous tipper and popular with the men. The whole village would come out on these occasions, wives and children to flank the beaters, control the dogs, and help with the picking up. If the shoot was good and the birds flew high their cooking pots and ovens would be full for weeks.

Alice breakfasted in her room, and took her scented bath – George liked a simple violet, the King *La Rose Jacqueminot* from Paris, and Agnes used the latter without asking. Alice had her hair washed and put up, and dressed in a new wonderfully low-cut Worth tea gown of purple velvet and silk which she knew would create comment, although almost within the hour she would have to change into a rather more cumbersome and *sportif* tweed suit for lunch. The ladies were to join the Guns in the marquee – Isobel had really outdone herself – walkways had been built through woodland and moor so the lunch would be brought to the Guns, not the Guns to the lunch. Daylight was short and precious. The ladies must be there, in their sporty tweeds and furs, to admire the splendour of the bags and the prowess of the hunters.

Should the day remain as fine as it promised to be Alice would stay on after lunch to keep the King company and assist his loader. She watched from the metal windows as the party gathered outside the front door. It was a frosty morning; horses whinnied and stamped. The Guns and their dogs piled into the assembling carriages; Strachan manned the King's wheeled chair. It would be tough going to the butts, Alice thought, once the walkways stopped and the rough ground began. The King was a heavy man, but then Strachan was not exactly frail. There had been some talk about Isobel and Strachan, but Alice dismissed it as servants' gossip. It was far too unlikely. The police cabal piled into one of the Daimlers: what possible likelihood could there be of an assassination attempt in such company? Balfour was far too imaginative. At least Campbell-Bannerman would just huff and puff and not fuss. Bertie had his brave face on: the one he put on for his subjects, benign and stoical. It would be better if he stayed at home in the warm and rested his poor stiff knee and admired the ladies – they would love that – but of course he would not. He wanted to outdo Ripon, Willy Desborough, George, and Dilberne too in the final bag count. It was an odd ambition for a man resolved to bring peace and concord to all Europe and so far doing well; surely he had nothing to prove.

She wondered if Ettie would join Willy at his peg after lunch but she thought probably not. She would be too sorry for the poor dead birds, and stay and flirt with Ponsonby. Of all the husbands, Isobel had probably done best. Robert shot birds *if* he had to, not *because* he had to – a *bon mot* she must remember. He had other things to occupy his mind, like the state of the colonies, the revolution in Russia, the entente cordiale, and by all accounts a girl from Brazil. She rather liked him herself.

Robert Dilberne, helped by Ponsonby, was now counting off vehicles, dog handlers, followers – and the Guns themselves: he was a good organizer, smooth and friendly. It was a jolly scene as the dawn broke, what with the barking of the dogs and the snorting horses, the cold crisp blast of the new day, the air of expectancy, a few brave ladies waving them off. Isobel was there, looking delightful in mink wrap and outsize muff.

A mannish young woman she hadn't seen before, booted and hatted, was going out to join Robert – Alice realized it must be the daughter, Rosina. The King had spoken of her: it seemed Strachan was quite the gossip and a source of entertainment to the King. Isobel had thrown the girl out over a parrot – an African grey: wonderful birds – and her publication of a rude book about the sexual habits of the Australian natives which Longman's had just published and which had made quite a splash. The King had read it – or at any rate opened and closed it: he'd met the daughter and liked her – but then he did like intelligent women. He was, Alice sometimes thought, a frustrated intellectual doomed to live amongst dolts. The Queen had flicked through the book and said it was disgusting, but then Alexandra would.

The King, in one of those acts of casual kindness which so endeared him to people, had reacted by congratulating Rosina in public on her fortitude and likening her to a female Joseph Banks whose subject was people not plants, which took the wind out of her critics' sails and neutralized all outrage. At any rate Rosina seemed cheerful enough to be back on speaking terms with her mother, even pecking her on the cheek goodbye and planning to go out with her father for the day's shooting. The parrot was on her shoulder, to the amusement of the guests, but to Alice's alarm. It was such a chilly morning.

Alice threw her ermine over her tea gown, thrust on slippers, clip-clopped down the stairs and out the doors and was in time to waylay Rosina.

'Rosina, isn't it?' she said to Rosina. 'Isn't it rather cold for the bird? It must be below freezing!'

'Too right, mate! Too right!' said the bird. 'Votes for women!'

Rosina said the day would warm up soon, and she would take Pappagallo to the marquee if the dear love seemed unhappy. But did Alice know about parrots?

'I have a pair,' said Alice, 'I adore them. They need to be kept at an even temperature.'

'He coped with Australia,' said Rosina, 'where it froze by night and boiled by day. But you may be right. Will you take him for the day?'

Alice said she would and if it warmed up by lunchtime she'd take him to the marquee.

'Too right, mate!' said the parrot and hopped onto Alice's shoulder.

'Just keep him out of Cook's way,' said Rosina. 'She'll make parrot pie. And that goes for Mama too.' She was a nice bright girl, thought Alice, if wary.

Lunch in the marquee was excellent: country cooking, none of this French-chef carry-on so many served these days, she heard Ripon say. Alice had ventured out with Pappagallo, for whom Cook had sent up a bowl of macadamia nuts, presumably as some kind of conciliatory gesture to the daughter of the house. The bird, seeing his owner, abandoned Alice and with another cry of

'Too right, mate!' fluttered over to Rosina's shoulder.

There were six courses only for lunch, but they were quickly and efficiently served, as a mere an hour and a half was allowed. Caviar, clear game soup, John Dory, prawns in aspic, roast ducks and iced pudding – the latter a triumph. The old icehouse had been restored and stocked. Isobel, on balance, forgetting the dreadful bamboo and the satin flowers, had done really quite well.

Valets were in attendance to remove and replace wet mackintoshes and leggings, though the ground had been quite hard and dry. The bag had been good, if not spectacular. But the King had outdone Ripon by twenty-eight birds and Desborough by thirteen, the rest lagging far, far behind, and was triumphant, and over champagne Alice regaled him and Strachan with news of the day – all having left too early for *The Times*. There was further political trouble in Russia, strikes and massacres – which sent Strachan prowling the outskirts in a nervous agitation.

'I told him,' Bertie said, 'I told the Tsar it would end in tears. Give them an inch and they take an ell.'

Alice reported that Alfred Walter Williams the painter had died and Miss Christabel Pankhurst was still in prison.

'Good,' said the King, and called out to the Inspector– 'And keep a good lookout for angry women in the undergrowth, Inspector. None of us are safe any more!'

Everyone laughed. The King was in fine good

fettle and when the King was happy everyone was happy.

'Thank you for coming out, my dear,' he said, patting Alice's hand. 'Stand by me on the peg and keep me company. So I feel all is right with the world, and that there are some proper women left in it.'

So at a quarter past two, when his Lordship called the return, and all trooped back to their pegs, Alice walked alongside the King's wheeled chair. Strachan was still inspecting the perimeter, so his loader, one of the estate gamekeepers, took over the task of royal wheeling. Bertie rose from his chair to shoot when the birds flew: sat again when he had finished, and Alan the gamekeeper would hand him the fresh gun. He only felt happy when there was a loaded shotgun in his hand – preferably one of his favourite double-barrelled 16-bores. Alan was a slow-moving, stoical countryman and noticeably red-faced to boot – either the outdoor life or too much drink, it was hard to tell. Bertie became impatient at even a second's delay, so Alice thought it wise to take over from Alan when the poor man fumbled – no doubt nervous in the royal presence. The pheasants flew; the King fired; the dogs ran; the birds rained down, glittering in red and gold, a magnificent sight. Surprising that so many seemed to come the King's way – but the beaters knew what they were up to and the dog handlers too. No wonder the King's bag filled so quickly, Alice thought.

And then it happened. Ripon, on the right cried

out, 'It's yours!' and a great cock bird flew overhead – rather too low for comfort, perhaps – but the King let off his blast and sank back in his chair even as the bird fell, when this time Robert Dilberne, on the left, cried out likewise, 'It's yours'; so the King was on his feet again, taking the gun that Alan handed him, but such an exquisite pain ran through the royal knee that he stumbled and the shotgun went off of its own volition. It was definitely in the King's hand when it went off.

There was a sudden cry to the left where Dilberne's head and shoulders could no longer be seen; then silence. Strachan appeared from nowhere to take the shotgun quickly from the King and hand it back to Alan, who stood transfixed. The King was back in his Bath chair, staring into space, clasping his knee.

'What happened? What happened?' he asked. 'Alice?'

There was a shriek and a shout and a 'My God!' from Dilberne's direction, and a woman's scream and then a dreadful silence; and then a Babel of dogs barking and people calling, and a confusion of cries and footfalls, and then Strachan's security fellows, young and strong and well fed, emerged through the tangles of leafless trees and wintry bushes to tower above the little people, the underfed, the leaderless, the gamekeepers, the beaters, the loaders, the flankers, the followers, to take charge. They seemed larger and taller than ever: they fed on emergency.

'Go and see!' implored the King, and Alice

went off to see, while Strachan handcuffed Alan and had him bundled off. He seemed too shocked and bewildered to object. Strachan tried to take the King's gun but His Majesty clung to it, and Strachan desisted and went instead with Alice, and found Lord Dilberne on the ground, and a fountain of blood squirting from a hole in his neck. Rosina was trying to quench the fountain with the scarf which had held her hat on, but it was already drenched and useless.

Strachan was at her side.

'Come away, Mrs Keppel,' he said. 'There is nothing to be done. The jugular vein is punctured. He will bleed out in two minutes. He is not conscious, he feels no pain. Come now. The King needs you. A dreadful accident. The loader was to blame. I think you witnessed that. A drinking man from the look of him.'

Alice could see there was no way that the King of England could have shot a close friend, even by accident. For all eternity it would be all a great King would be remembered for. Alfred burnt the cakes, Canute defied the tide, who was it drowned in a butt of Malmsey? Edward VII shot his best friend instead of a bird – no, Bertie deserved better than that.

'Yes, I witnessed that,' she said. 'The gun went off in his loader's hand. A drinking man.'

Strachan flickered a half-smile at her: he nodded almost imperceptibly. The ground beneath her feet was growing dark from blood. *'Who would have thought the old man to have had so much blood in him?'* She spoke under her breath.

'Macbeth, Act V,' he said, without a pause. The

Inspector was a man of surprises. Perhaps there was more to the Isobel-and-the-policeman rumour than she thought. Isobel was a widow now, the Dowager Countess. Arthur was the Earl: everything that his eye saw on a waking day belonged to him. The little boy playing with his toys on the nursery floor was now the Viscount; everything his eye could see when he looked out of the window would one day be his.

Pappagallo fluttered over to Alice's shoulder, and perched there. Alice could feel his thin, feathery body trembling against her ear. All day he had watched his own kind raining down as corpses from the sky. Now this. Or perhaps she was the one who was trembling. Strachan took her by the arm and led her back to the King, who sat with his face in his hands. He looked dreadfully old.

'It was Dilberne,' she said. 'Your friend, Bertie. I'm so sorry. Thc loader's gun went off. A dreadful fumbler. Your gun, but in his hands.'

He looked up and nodded. She loved the King and the King loved her.

They carried Robert Dilberne on a plank to the marquee, his white, white face staring up at the sky. Pheasants and partridges flew by above unheeded and unhindered, and the odd wild duck or two, and all lived to fly another day. The spaniels and Labradors were allowed to finish their work, nosing through the undergrowth, picking up the feathery corpses, filling up the bags: one of the keepers tallied the count. So many pheasant, so many partridge, so many duck; one lord of the manor. Will the new Earl go on with the shoots? It seems doubtful; all he cares about is cars. Nasty, noisy, smelly things.

The Captains and the Kings Depart

16th and 17th December 1905, The Dilberne Estate

First the death, then would come the funeral. A security man's nightmare. One was of course sorry for his Lordship, but it was no bad way to die. On a fine brisk winter's day, surrounded by friends, pleasurably engaged, and so suddenly. Unlucky in one way, that a single wayward piece of shot should strike the jugular at the exact spot it did, tearing through all protective tissue; lucky in another that the victim was spared the lingering embarrassments of the traditional deathbed scene; as the body collapses and the family gathers. This was the clean quick finish of a man still in his prime, and one could wish it for oneself. One had witnessed far more gruesome an end.

Sheer surprise neutralizes pain, Andrew Strachan was thinking. One loses consciousness within the minute, one bleeds out within two, and it is over. God's good earth sops up the blood: they kept the dogs well away, though no doubt they will be sniffing around for weeks. These rural people have their sense and skills, more than many a city dweller. They had his Lordship on a plank and out of there while my men, fine, young and trained though they are, were still searching for their notebooks and tapes to measure velocities, angles and so forth.

The one I respect greatly is Mrs Keppel. She kept her head in circumstances that would have most fine ladies screaming and distraught. Though in truth I have noticed a great stoicism and courage in the fine ladies I have met, from the Queen to the Countess of Dilberne – what I would call the straight-backedness of grandeur – in the way they face adversity. They are kind, they are beautiful, they are be-jewelled – but they take no prisoners.

'Poor man,' said Mrs Keppel, as she watched us take the wretched loader away, 'what a fumbler he was! But do make sure his family is looked after.'

And so they will be. He will lose two years of his life in prison on a manslaughter charge – and the prison will not be too uncomfortable – but will receive £5,000 in return for forgetting a few seconds of his life; a few seconds in which he handed the gun to the King. I do not think the King himself remembers those seconds; the pain in his knee was too acute, and the shock of such an event tends to block out memory. He is not a young man. And Mrs Keppel, fortunately for the nation, has chosen not to remember.

I was able to assure Mrs Keppel that the loader – Alan Barker, one of the gamekeepers, and engaged to Elsie the head parlourmaid at Dilberne Court – would be looked after. It was as well that both parties were so closely associated with the family: servants might bicker and gossip amongst themselves but, when it came to it, were fiercely loyal to their families. Alan would not argue, and Elsie would not encourage him to do so; they would get married and live happily ever after. Mrs Keppel was tact itself. I could not, of course, give her details, but she understood what I was saying; and I was amused by the implicit threat. If we didn't look after Alan Barker her story might have to change. She is a wonderful woman. Almost as wonderful as Isobel.

Her Ladyship behaved with such dignity and composure when the body was brought back it made an impression on me I cannot forget. The King returned in the Daimler together with the daughter Lady Rosina, Mrs Keppel and myself. The parrot, now back on Lady Rosina's shoulder, quite spoiled the solemnity of the occasion. It pecked away at its mistress's bloodstained jacket – a severed jugular creates quite a mess – and the poor girl seemed too distraught to shake the bird off or somehow distract its inquisitive beak. I could have wrung its neck.

The body was brought in and laid in the drawing room which Isobel had made so pretty, bright and light, and, under my instructions, so secure. Metal windows can be properly locked, ancient latticed ones, however attractive, cannot be made safe.

'How did it happen?' Isobel asked. She was in a daze. I quickly explained.

'I would have gladly given my life for him,' His Majesty said. 'A dear good man. A friend: they are so rare. Man proposes, God disposes. I have known so many die in my time. I will leave you to your grief, my dear Isobel. It will be hard to bear, I know only too well.' It was both eloquent and moving and Isobel, still dazed, nodded her appreciation of this tribute from the King.

'Too right, mate. Too right,' squawked the parrot, and for some reason on this occasion it seemed more like a tribute from the world of the beasts than any kind of offence. They were offering their sympathy.

My first concern of course was the welfare of His Majesty: I escorted him and Mrs Keppel back to his room. My priority now was to get him home to Sandringham and his normal security team. The grounds there at least are efficiently patrolled. There had been rumours in Dilberne that a disgruntled employee – the former Gatehouse keeper and one suspected of republican sympathies – had been seen scuttling about the woods in the past weeks, armed with a shotgun. He might well have been a poacher going about his normal business, but down at the Dilberne Arms the poaching fraternity swore he was none of theirs. We could take no chances: a resentful person is vulnerable to anarchist propaganda; reasonable protest can quickly turn to violence; an armed conspiracy could have been afoot. It was something of a relief to have His Majesty safely indoors once again, though the circumstances were deplorable.

I found her Ladyship looking down on the quiet, pale body of her lifeless husband. She ran her finger over the skin of his cheek. She made a picture I do not forget; graceful and slender in a lilac tea gown. It is engraved in my heart. Still her Ladyship did not cry. She swayed a little and I had to steady her. I will not say she leaned on me but I felt she needed my presence. It is true that through the past weeks I have been a great support to her. Then Lady Rosina emerged from her stunned state, noisily, like her parrot, and fell theatrically upon the body.

'Oh Mama, at least I was there,' sobbed Lady Rosina. 'It was an accident. I saw him die. It was so quick. Quicker than when poor Frank died. There was nothing I could do.'

I had quite forgotten that Lady Rosina too was a widow. Such was the company she kept it was easy to forget. Nor did she wear a wedding ring. Isobel was not the kind who would remove her ring: if she married again she would remove it perhaps to another finger. I would of course keep the matter of the Brazilian girl from her Ladyship, and indeed the nature of her daughter's relationships: what the eyes don't see the heart will not grieve over.

My masters had come to the conclusion that the household at No. 3 Fleet Street was not after all a cause for concern: the parties there were too involved with their personal situations to have much time for political conspiracy. Suspicions had been roused by the collaboration of Ford Madox Hueffer, of German origin, and Joseph Conrad, a

Pole, both of them using *The Modern Idler* as a mouthpiece. Conrad's essay 'Autocracy and War' had caused particular concern, but turned out to have been rejected by Mr Robin in favour of a piece of the Pole's rather gloomy fiction. I myself thought his essay was fairly perceptive and perhaps prophetic, but a nation has to keep its intellectuals under control. Mr Brown turns out to have protectors in high places: in a perfect world the Honourable Anthony Robin and his friend would be thrown in prison but thank God it is not a perfect world. In my opinion people must find their happiness where best they can.

By now other members of the shooting party were drifting back to the house, on foot, by carriage or cart. Those who had set out so bravely that morning returned so miserably that afternoon! All were stricken; the staff silent and dutiful. Most guests went to their rooms, others grouped in the great hall under the giant chandelier and stood around talking in hushed voices. Mr Neville, red-eyed, served brandy. I had had the chandelier's rusty iron chains replaced with steel – at least there was no danger, of further fatalities, as there had been when I first went to Dilberne Court. His Lordship had complained that the reddish-black of the old slender chains was more attractive than the shiny, solid steel of the sturdy new ones, but soon came round to my point of view. Safety must come before aesthetics. His Lordship was a reasonable man and will be sorely missed.

'Too right, mate!' barked the parrot into a room already disturbed by Lady Rosina's sobs. Isobel's grief emerged as anger.

'Oh, for Heaven's sake, Rosina,' she said. 'I can't hear myself think. Do go and get out of those horrible clothes and into something not so blood sodden. Just throw them away. Burn them. Let Lily choose for once. She has good taste. And get that evil bird out of my sight. I will not have it in this house again.'

Lady Rosina composed herself, I must say with some dignity, straightening her body and dashing away her tears. Women of breeding, even Rosina, command my great respect.

'Mother,' she said, 'this is not your house. It is now my brother's, and Minnie's. Minnie quite likes Pappagallo.'

Her Ladyship stared at her daughter, her face impassive. But in my mind's eye I saw a whole row of dominos falling, each one as it fell knocking its fellow over, inexorably, until all were down. The Ladies Desborough and Ripon came into the room to surround her Ladyship in a flurry of sympathy, concern and the pastel shades of the most expensive tea gowns imaginable. Their tweedy husbands followed to hum and haw. I went back to my room to organize the King's departure to Sandringham and check on Alan Barker's incarceration, and left them to it.

So far as the new Countess, Minnie, is concerned it occurs to me that her suspicions of her husband's infidelities are unfounded: equally that the new Earl's rejection of his wife is unreasonable: she is to be pitied and forgiven rather than condemned. Thank God the divorce is only talked about, not enacted. They could yet come together. Anthony Robin, who will no doubt go on spreading trouble like the green bay tree, rejecting what is good in favour of what is bad as in Mr Conrad's essay, is the villain of the piece; his sister Diana, so loved by Lady Rosina, is just an amiable idiot.

I, the Inspector, knowing what I do, find myself in a position of considerable power. But if I brought about a reunion, which is as I can see within my competence, husband, wife and two children would be reunited as God intended, and be as likely to live happily ever after as anyone else. They might even have daughters to carry on the blood line of beautiful and gracious women.

But what then will happen to her Ladyship, to Isobel? If I leave well alone, she will continue flitting between Belgrave Square and Dilberne Court, discarding this and choosing that, for the rest of her days. She might marry again: she is young enough and lovely enough. Though not, I fear, particularly rich: their mine at the Modder Kloof is not doing quite so well: the refurbishing of Dilberne Court has drained even deep pockets dry. Lloyd George is gaining power: he will probably be made President of the Board of Trade; his lot will end up taxing the landowning classes until they whimper. But she will cope, with her usual astuteness.

If I speak up, Minnie will be the new Countess. She will have Belgrave Square and Dilberne Court under her care; she will do what she wants with them. She will throw out the bamboo furniture and reinstate the old carved oak monstrosities: let Arthur turn the estate into one big racing track for his Jehus – which to my mind will never amount to much: he is far too indecisive. Unlike Mr Austin who makes up his mind and sticks with it: I have seen him in action. She will convert the billiard room into an artist's studio with proper north light. She may even disagree with him about sending the children to Eton. Arthur will argue back but Minnie could well win. They love each other, and they love their children: Master Edgar, whom Arthur brought into the world with his own bare (if oily) hands: sturdy freckled Master Connor: little lions, little lambs.

If I speak up, Isobel, as the Dowager Countess, will be relegated to the Dower House.

It is falling down; bats cluster inside it; swallows nest in the attics. Cesspits will have to be replaced with septic tanks. It has no proper heating, no electric lighting. But her Ladyship will enjoy that: something else to achieve, to improve, to make good. She might even come to terms with Minnie: they got on well in the beginning, and they might well again.

If I speak up, Isobel, widowed, may recreate the home of her childhood, simpler and happier, the laughing, loving demi-monde from which her husband snatched her, putting behind her a grandeur with which she was never wholly happy, but always made the best of, as is her nature. Alice, Ettie and Constance can come and stay and gossip about fashion, art, scandal and who's who in politics to their hearts' content, on holiday from their braying, sporting husbands. When Isobel is old, Minnie the young Countess will come down to the Dower House with her two strapping sons and bring her good soup and chicken pie, and perhaps a dainty shawl made of finest spun Angora wool from Liberty to put around her shoulders. And I might well be there as her husband, to grow old with her. Isobel has always needed someone to look after her and keep her safe.

I might well speak up.

Facing the Future

3rd and 4th January 1906, Westminster Abbey and Dilberne Church

The funeral service was held at Westminster Abbey as befitted the late Earl's rank and status. The interment was to be the next day, at the family vault at Dilberne, opened, swept and warmed for the occasion. One last task for the widowed Countess, Isobel. Hundreds attended the sombre Westminster ceremony. All were in black. Only the occasional diamond gleamed to relieve the gloom, the only other jewellery was jet. The deceased Earl, Robert, had been a great favourite, even tipped, so it seemed, to be a future prime minister, so meteoric had been his rise. Only a few short years from Fisheries to the Colonial

Office to the Cabinet. Now this.

Mr Balfour was there to pay his respects, as was Mr Campbell-Bannerman, and rather to Isobel's horror, David Lloyd George. Arthur the new Earl was there of course, and his sister – without her parrot: she had at least that sensitivity – but the absence of Melinda, the young Countess, was noted. She had been prevented by illness from travelling back from the United States.

All the former Earl's sporting friends, amongst them Desborough, Ripon and Keppel, turned up to pay their respects. There was a sprinkling of gambling friends and racing enthusiasts, someone who looked suspiciously like a bookmaker, and various political friends and allies. Robert had been a man of many parts, as the Bishop of Bath and Wells, who gave the funeral oration, recalled. His Majesty, alas, could not be present: the trouble with his knee had flared up.

Also there, weeping noisily and disturbing the congregation, was a rather torrid-looking dark beauty in a quite unsuitable red hat, who attempted to throw herself upon the coffin and had to be moved by the ever-vigilant Inspector Strachan. Fortunately the girl had been sitting at the back of the church, and the family, seated as they were in the front pews, did not see the incident.

It was a much humbler party who turned up for the entombment in the family vault a day later.

Such servants who could be spared from the running of the house and the preparation of the wake attended, and there was much weeping and lamentation. The coffin was closed not open, which disappointed some. As it was carried into the vault by six bearers, one of them the new Earl, Strachan saw two women and a child draw near. One he recognized as the new Countess, Melinda, charming if pale and wrapped in Russian black sable – not even her mother-in-law had a fur so grand. The other was the woman he had seen disembark so quickly from the *Carpania* at Liverpool on that shameful day, leaving her passport behind. Grace. She was in a sensible black rabbit fur, and had Master Connor on her hand. The little boy was also wearing fur. Nanny would never have stood for it: 'Nasty germy stuff – Lord knows what's lurking in there!'

Though Isobel did not notice Minnie, Arthur did. He faltered in his measured stride, and put his corner of the coffin down with a little more speed than perhaps he should have. He strode over to his wife. She shrank away from him as if expecting to be hit.

'I know you don't want to see me here,' she said, 'but I loved your father. I've travelled four thousand miles to say goodbye to him.' That said, she found her courage and looked her husband in the eye. 'I've come back if you'll have me back,' she said. 'I've brought you Connor. He misses Edgar. He misses you. So do I.'

Arthur was silent. The servants were all ears. She ignored them. She was a Countess now.

What did she care what the servants overheard?

'You can do what you like,' she said. 'Go where you like, be with whom you like.'

He was actually smiling.

'I say, that's a bit rash, Minnie,' he said. 'I won't have you doing that.'

Master Connor tottered over and put his hand in his father's hand.

The Inspector spoke up. 'If I may put in a word, sir–'

'You may not,' said Arthur with sudden, shocking and savage rage. 'You incompetent, you bungling lecherous meddler–'

Connor, frightened, began to cry. Grace led him away to where it was dark and quiet and peaceful, between the stone-covered rows of Hedleigh dead.

'Minnie!' said Isobel. 'What are you doing here? And Arthur, what can you be saying? Here in this place, with your father in his coffin!' But seeing Connor being led away she forgot Minnie, forgot Arthur, forgot Strachan, and ran after the little boy, knelt beside him and embraced him.

'Oh dear Connor, Grandmama's here!' she cried. Connor looked surprised, but gratified; and he stopped crying.

Grace waited until Isobel released Connor and then said coolly, 'Why hello, your Ladyship.'

'Good God,' said Isobel. 'Grace!' She sat down on a slab – the second Earl of Dilberne, as it happened, 1560–1613 – and began to cry, at last without restraint. She cried for lost hopes and aspirations, for her mother, her father and now her husband, all of whom had died, and left her more and more alone, until finally here she was, altogether lonely, with a son who was going to go back to his wife and who thought she was having an affair with a police inspector when she wasn't. She cried because her daughter Rosina was so peculiar and had fled back to her louche London life after the funeral and had not come down to the family vault to comfort her mother: she cried because no one really liked what she had done to Dilberne Court and everybody hated bamboo furniture, and now Minnie was back and Minnie was the Countess and she was not, and Minnie would hate her and drive her out to the Dower House which was falling down, and she didn't think she had the heart to do anything about anything any more. It all ended in death anyway.

'Oh, your Ladyship, don't take on so,' said Grace. 'I'm here. Your eyes will be so red! We all depend on you so!'

Connor buried his little blond head in Isobel's lap and she felt better.

'I can assure you, my Lord,' Strachan was saying, 'I hold your family in the greatest respect. My only desire is to keep them from harm.' He spoke so earnestly that Arthur seemed almost pacified. But Strachan could not leave it alone, as was in his nature. 'And in case you have any fears I can assure you that my relationship–'

'No, no,' said Arthur. 'For God's sake keep your feelings to yourself. I want to hear nothing more of them. I have no fears, I have my wife back.'

A glorious smile spread over Minnie's face. Strachan could see words were inappropriate and went to console Isobel. She took his hand and they sat on the tomb of the second Earl side by side, and contemplated their future.

'Redbreast – that rat,' the Earl said into his wife's ear. 'Why should I play into his hands by divorcing you, just to provide cover for him? The whole world knows what he is, the prancing ninny. Does he think I'm stupid?'

'It didn't happen anyway,' she said.

'Of course it didn't,' he said. 'Why would you want him when you have me?' He seemed most inordinately cheerful.

When they were back in the Court, Isobel said, by way of acceptance and indeed apology:

'Dear Minnie, the bamboo furniture never really worked. You were quite right. With your permission I shall take it with me to the Dower House.'

Bless You All

22nd June 1906, St Martin-in-the-Fields

The Times reported the wedding between Mr William Brown and Lady Rosina Overshaw at some length, as did the *Mirror* and the *Express*. It was not surprising; such a romantic story! Mr Brown was the senior editor at Longman of London, the publishers, and Miss Rosina Hedleigh (as she preferred to be called) was the author of the best-selling book *The Sexual Manners and Traditions of*

Australian Aboriginals, which Longman had published, and which after some initial controversy had done so well thanks to the *approbatur* of the Sovereign. A romance had quickly blossomed.

It was the wedding of the decade. Everyone who was anyone was there: the mother of the bride, of course, Isobel, Dowager Countess of Dilberne, rather shockingly out of mourning and in pastel silks, represented the older generation. Otherwise, it was noted, everyone was so *young*. Unfortunately she had to leave early due to indisposition. The bride's brother, Arthur, the Earl of Dilberne, and his wife Melinda, the Countess, and their two delightful little sons were in attendance. (The *Express,* being the *Express,* hinted that Minnie was in the family way: *The Times* would never be so indelicate.) Mr Herbert Austin the motor manufacturer was amongst the many who lined the aisles. It was rumoured in the *Mirror* that Lord Arthur was to sell his business concern to Austin's Longbridge firm, and devote himself to running the Dilberne estates. The recently promoted Superintendent Andrew Strachan of the Metropolitan Police sat on the bride's side. Writers from a variety of social strata were there, as the *Express* pointed out; from those in the aristocracy to Mr D. H. Lawrence, Mr H. H. Munro to Mr Siegfried Sassoon to Mr Rudyard Kipling. The *Express* observed that social niceties were a thing of the past, and welcomed the end of class petrification.

The airy and elegant church was bright with

smiles and fresh hope that day as the young couple were united. Mr Baum the financier turned pioneer farmer had sent orange trees all the way from Palestine to decorate the aisles, and the whole building smelt of orange blossom. Many had chosen to wear white, and hats gleamed with jewels as was the season's fashion with the younger set.

All in all it was an enchanted and enchanting occasion. The groom wore the latest thing in male fashion, a bleached sealskin suit with a white silk cravat worn high, a red tie and high spat-style boots with blue buttons. The Honourable Anthony Robin, the best man, wore a similar suit and cravat but with a blue tie, and shoes with red buttons. The bride amused everyone by wearing a tightly-bodiced, low-cut white satin dress but with the freeing and voluminous split skirt of the moment, which to some looked suspiciously like bloomers; an orange-blossom head-dress rather than a veil, and her parrot on her shoulder as an accessory. The only bridesmaid, the Honourable Anthony Robin's sister Diana, was dressed in a corseted satin white tuxedo silk shirt with satin ruff, and a skirt with vertical red and grey stripes, the shade of red matching Pappagallo's tail feathers.

Rosina's parrot had been trained to utter a new cry for the occasion which he squawked at appropriate intervals throughout the ceremony, only occasionally lapsing into 'Too right, mate! Too right!' or 'Votes for women!' The bird seemed to have an uncanny ear for the right line at the right moment. All declared that he understood perfectly well what was going on, and that he approved.

'Bless you all! Bless you all!' said Pappagallo.

The publishers hope that this book has given you enjoyable reading. Large Print Books are especially designed to be as easy to see and hold as possible. If you wish a complete list of our books please ask at your local library or write directly to:

Magna Large Print Books
Magna House, Long Preston,
Skipton, North Yorkshire.
BD23 4ND

This Large Print Book for the partially sighted, who cannot read normal print, is published under the auspices of

THE ULVERSCROFT FOUNDATION